tapestry

tapestry

Philip Terry

REALITY STREET

Published by
REALITY STREET
63 All Saints Street, Hastings, East Sussex TN34 3BN, UK
www.realitystreet.co.uk

First edition 2013
Copyright © Philip Terry. All rights reserved.

Reality Street Narrative Series No 14

A catalogue record for this book is available from the British Library

ISBN: 978-1-874400-62-2

ACKNOWLEDGEMENTS

Thanks to the AHRC, whose generous support helped get this
book started. Thanks also to Jenny Uglow, Sarah Kember,
Harry Mathews, Joseph O'Neill and Marina Warner, who
helped it on its way. And thanks to Ken Edwards, whose
inspired editorial advice helped its completion.
The drawings, based on the Bayeux Tapestry, were supplied by
The Hidden Dingbat.

For Ann and Lou

Heard melodies are sweet, but those unheard
Are sweeter; therefore, ye soft pipes, play on

JOHN KEATS "ODE ON A GRECIAN URN"

CONTENTS

Prolog

Contegnyng what the readr may, or may not, expect to fynd in it

WEEKS AND WEEKS OF INCESSANT dull regn,
which falls off the sky lyk cow piss. We haue
nefer seen the lyks of it. So heavy it es that
the watter-tracks boorst theyr banks spillyng ofer into
the fields and mice run vertically up the trunks of trees
to take refuge on the branches, where they hang in theyr
hundreds, lyk strange unsaisonable fruit. Stickleback and
perch swim out of theyr ponds and ofer the lan and
efen, at tymes, into the air. Som thing which has not
been seen since the greet drownyngs of 1014, when the
tide of the herring-way swept widely ofer this lan, sub-
mergyng many villages and a countless number of
pepill, may theyr souls rest in pais. Oure prayer-hus es
an islan refuge. Look out of the tour of St. Ethelfledas
and there es no thing but watter as far as the auga can
see. Only, here and there, the top of an isolated hillock
pokyng above the glassy surface, on which are gatherd
birds and bestes, men and woe men, childern and hungry hundrs. Now and then a petyte bot can be seen in
the gloom, ferryyng its watterloggd cargo from islan to
islan; the bloated carcass of a cow twists on the spume,
fought ofer by angersome buzzards.

The prayer-hus es engulfd in a deluge

Noahs drownyng es on everyoons lips; talk of divine
retribution; apocalypse. The tyme es at five-fingers,
whispers systir Gytha, pullyng on my sleeve, proddyng
me in the bras with her bony lead-colourd fingers in a
manner I do not lyk. For weeks on ende the sky, lyk
Gythas gloomy audlit – her raven-dark augabrows knit-
tyng ofer the pale and tremblyng upper lip – es black
with angry storm clouds. Doom fills the air, mayhap

doom es too strang a word, then, on the eleventh of Mars, the eve of St. Gregorys Dag 1071, we wake to the shock of bright sunlight and, gradually, the watters begin to subside.

A messenger of the kings arrives As the tide recedes around the precinct walls we dislodge the sandbags from the geatway and inspect the damage to the claustral buildyngs. The tithe barn, I discover, has sprung a leak which must be patchd at once before any more stocks are ruind and, worser still, untold damage has been causd by floodwatter in the book-hus where precious word-hoards – among them Nasos *Metamorphoses*, an enlumynd copy of Bedes *Ecclesiastical History* and a codex of Caedmons hymns – float about in a muddy soup. Armd with mops and buckets we set about clairyng up the mess before any more word-hoards are lost. It es disheartenyng work – many precious texts are ruind and the rolld scrolls of the prayer-hus chronicle, which the abbess has bidden me keep up to date in her absence, are badly soild, and must be hung out to dry in the wash-chambr. Yet soon, lyf returns to normal. The anxieties which come with tymes of drownyng are replaced with othir cares. When will the abbess return from St. Augustines at Canterbury? When will the promisd plans for the bishops tapestry materialise? When will the wool come – or es it true, as som haue whisperd followyng matins and lauds, that the bishops word amounts to no thing? For som dags these questions hang on the air lyk the prayer-huses soggy chronicle in the wash-chambr, then, on the Fridag, we haue news from a messenger of the kings that Bishop Odo will be comyng in person any dag, accompanied by his Flemish woolwright, Turold.

So it es true! Oure litell prayer-hus has been pickd above its rivals at Winchester and Canterbury and London to stitch a tapestry for Bishop Odo, half-brothir of King William, to hang on the nave of his newly consecrated cathedral at Bayeux. There isnt a moment to lose – for if what the messenger says es true, the work es to be ready in tyme for the Christmas celebrations at the ende of the year. At once, in a fluster, we set about preparations. As there es no suitable space in side – the parlour es too petyte, the fyr-chambr too busy, the book-hus too damp – and since the light in the cloister es mych brighter than anywhere else in the prayer-hus, this quiet quadrangle with its carvd capitals of dragons, birds, warriors, hundrs, lions, seints and arbers es quickly fixd upon for the task. There es a buzz of anticipation on the damp spring air. Soon, carpenters run to and fro, cuttyng and sawyng and plegnyng and notchyng the timber which, before lang, will be knockd together to make the frames and the trestles which will support the work. Sawdust and wood chippyngs are everywhere, as are the songrs and curses of the workmen who haue drownd oure precinct, in contravention of the Rules of the Hus. As the nuns go about theyr business in the cloister, the mens greedy augas follow theyr steps, they shout and whistle, as workmen do. Yet when they see me they are silenced – they cross themselves and, oon by oon, return to work, mutteryng to each othir words I do not care to record, there are som things best not repeated.

Around the hour of sext on Mondag – just as systir Ebba, the guest-mistress, puts the finishyng touches to the visitors chambrs, hastily throwyng linen sheets ofer the lits, jammyng fresh candles on prickets – Bishop Odo at last arrives, accompanied by his woolwright, the dwarf Turold. The abbess, alas, es not with them. Odo es a fat tonsurd man in middle age, clairly at ease in the saddle of his powerful black stallion. He es possessd of an unmistakable nebb: lang and hookd, lyk the beak of a haukr. At his side, hangs a heavy studded mace, a wapen which – held aloft – we will later broider into the scenes of the tapestry showyng the Batalle of Hastings. It es the only wapen which bishops may carry with impunity – for while it es swift and deadly, it es sayd that it does not spill the blod of its victims, though vou woud haue to be a fool to believe it.

Turold, the dwarf, in contrast, es visibly ill at ease on the dappld grey donkey he rides: he curses loudly in a shrill voice as it lurches out of his control, bangyng its flank, and Turolds heafod, agegnst the portico of the geathus, as he enters the courtyard. Wheelyng the beste round to get it under control, he gives it a sharp kick with pointed spurs, drawyng blod. Yet as a result the donkey starts brayyng loudly – *Heehaw! Heehaw!* – and then, kickyng its leggrs, catapults its unsteady rider into the air where he es at pegns to improvise a brief somersault before lanyng with a bump in the dirt. As he hauls himself up, dustyng down his worsted tunic, he stands only stirrup-high to his mount. He cuts a curious figure, and not only because of his diminutive size – after the Norman fashion, his har es shorn on the bak, yet he sports too a pointed money-lenders beard on the tip of his chin, which singles him out from his clean-shaven companions. His nebb es flat and broad, his augas bright, lyk those of a stoat, or a weasel.

The systirs practice theyr skills

In the parlour, guided by the experienced five-finger of Agnes, the sub-prioress, schoold from infancy at oure systir hus of St. Marys in Winchester, renownd throughout Christendom for its skill in the art of broidery, we practice the stitches which we will employ in oure work. It is important, says systir Agnes, stabbyng the air with her needle to emphasise her point, that you alle make your stitches in the right manner, for while the tapestry, because of its size, must needs be the undertakyng of many five-fingers, it shoud appear to the auga to be indistinguishable from the work of oon woolwright. Stitchyng down and up, through and ofer, down and up, through and ofer, we pull the woollen threads across the linen ground on oure laps, movyng from left to right, into the twisted lign of the STEM STITCH (\\\\\\). We call this the stem stitch, says systir Agnes, since it coils round itself as it grows, lyk the stems of certain plants, and lyk the gropyng tendrils which give them support. Yet to my unschoold mind, it bears more resemblance to two snakes entwind together on the gras, such as those Tiresias es sayd to haue stumbld upon in the clairyng of a forest, and which, because he attackd them with his stick, causd him to be changed into the shape of a woe man, so that he in turn coud come to know what it was lyk to be attackd with a stick. There es a certain voluptuousness about the stem stitch, a sensuality, a curvaceousness, as in the bone-hus of a woe man, which marks it off as the feminine stitch *par excellence*. It es as important to be aware of the bak of the stitch, systir Agnes megntegns, as it es of the front – though sche does not trouble herself to explegn whi. We practice too the OUT LIGN STITCH (----), or bak stitch as it es commonly calld, which creeps across the linen ground from right to left – bak and down, under and through, bak and down, under and through – the simplest of alle the stitches, which, seen from a distance, appears to run in a straight and uninterrupted lign, lyk the sturdy prow of a lang-bot cuttyng through the wavefroth, carryyng its cargo of proud heroes in theyr batalle-tackle towards theyr goal. This es the most masculine of alle the stitches, and lyk the men of oure own lan, who, if they are willyng, can turn theyr five-fingers to many diverse tasks when occasion requires it of them, its strength lies in its versatility.

Later in the dag, before an audience which includes Odo and Walkelin, Bishop of Winchester, and alle the systirs who will work on the tapestry – Aelfflaed (the cellaress), Anna and Hilda, Gunnrid the Grinder, Beatrice (the almonress), Geta the Geatkeeper, her gaze fixd east, Ethelguida the Mute, Ebba and me – Turold displays his designs. They are in lang ungegnly rolls of parchment which he lays out on the floor of the fyrroom in rows, weightyng them down round the edges with litell colourd pebbles which he has pickd up in the precinct. The figures are out lignd in black ink, there es no pigment, though Turold has indicated in his curly script which colour shoud be used where – the hross

The parchments are unfurld

which carries Harold Godwinson to the coast es to be chestnut, the tunic of William Duke of Normandy es to be golden-yellow, the stallion of Guy de Pontieu black. As he lays the stiff parchment out on the floor, Turold darts to and fro, lyk a wasp, it es no exaggeration, explegnyng his design scene by scene and elucidatyng too the complicated ways in which oon episode relates to the othirs which follow or precede it. Here, right at the start, es the aged Edward the Confessor, a tremblyng finger raisd as if to underlign the gravity of his request, sendyng Harold on a mission across the herring-road; then here a litell later on es Harold, seizd by two ruffians as he lans not, as intended, at the muthr of the river Seine in Williams territories, but at the muthr of the Canche near Beaurain in the lans of Guy de Pontieu; and here es William himself mounted on an imposyng war-hross, accompanied by three heavily-armourd knights, deliveryng the kings ransom which will secure Harold Godwinsons release. Here, once more, es Harold – vou can tell him by his ploughshare moustache – swearyng an oath of fealty to William on holy relics; and here, a litell further on, es the death of Edward the Confessor which, placed as it es beside the crownyng of Harold in the next scene, suggests a certain hastiness, an irreverence efen, in the new kings seizure of the throne (and it es true, I will record it here, that the meats which servd for the kings funeral on the Feast of the Epiphany 1066 were dishd up agen later the same dag for the guests at Harolds coronation). And perhaps this accounts for the appearance of the lang-haird star of ill-omen, a litell further on? Whatever the truth of it, across the channel – Turold es there at once with a douce step – William immediately sets about buildyng a huge invasion fleet. Look, says Turold, now pointyng out Williams own lang-ship carryyng the Popes banner with the tip of his toe, here es the sea-crossyng, and here, now in Englan, es Bishop Odo himself! We gather round his diminutive figure to get a closer look and there, sure enough, es the round audlit of Odo, presidyng ofer a banquet held in Williams honour, as the Norman army prepare to do batalle with the English.

The bold conception of the design, efen in this rough out lign, its sheer scope – for it tells the story of conquest right up until the moment of Williams own coronation at Westminster – inspires awe, if not respect, in alle who behold it. Odo es so overcome with emotion that, for a moment, he forgets himself entirely and, puttyng his five-fingers together as vou might at the ende of a mummers play or a dance, he begins to clap! At first, alle are taken completely by surprise, and audlits turn to look on him in astonishment. And yet, before he becomes aware that he es makyng a prize fool of himself, anothir five-finger – es it the Bishop of Winchester? – joins in, and then anothir and anothir, and now I too join in, and then we are alle clappyng furiously, and the room es filld with the din of oure clappyng five-fingers, which rises to a peak before Turold, enteryng into the spirit of the bishops enthusiasm, takes a lang and studied bow, then makes his exit.

Chapter 1

*In which the readr may discover the utility
of a barrel, and othir matters*

*Preparation
of
the
frame*

THREE DAGS LATER, straight after chapter, we gather on the cloister. It es cold, yet bright. Dew sits on the gras. We work swiftly, in silence, first twistyng lengths of spare fabric round the frame so that it does not mark the linen, then stretchyng the rolls of stiff flax-cloth ofer the timber skeleton, fixyng them in place with loops of strang thread which we secure with widows knutrs. Then Turold steps forward to make the first stitch. At once, he proves to be too short to be able to comfortably reach the stretchd linen, and systir Aelf-flaed (*Ale-flood*, we say, for sches the cellaress), lumbers off to fetch a barrel on which he can stand. Once this difficulty has been ofercome, however, he quickly hops onto the barrel, then plunges his needle of whale-bone into the virgin flax-cloth. Mostly, woolwrights are too mych in demand to devote mych tyme to any individual piece of work, efen oon of these dimensions, and yet, after Turold has made his first stitch or two he does not at once step down off his perch as we expect, but continues to work for som tyme, lips pursd, threadyng his needle in and out of the linen. Usyng a tightly-workd stem stitch – mych more close-knit than the practice-stitches we haue workd under the guidance of systir Agnes, which now seem crude and ofersizd by comparison – he manoeuvres the sharp bone-dart through the field-fresh linen, markyng with a firm five-finger a series of danglyng points in olive-green thread, which resemble no thing so mych as the poisond tentacles of the many-leggrd polypus, or octopus, take your pick, which can be seen illustrated in the Latin Bestiaries of oure book-hus. And yet, as he continues his work upwards, stitchyng in bold strokes, we come to see that the figure he broiders es not that of som horrible sea-beste, but that of a human audlit, for now alle at once oon sees clairly a beard, a quizzical lopsided muthr, a broad nebb, and – swiftly added with the FRANKISH KNUTR (•) – two bright determind-lookyng augas. And then, quickly changyng threads, he adds the roial contours of a gold-wrought crown. Were it not for this kingly heafod-gear, and for the many-pointed beard, oon woud say that this were a feminine audlit – though mayhap this es merely an accidental effect of the curvyng contours of the stem stitch – and yet, when he has finishd his work, and at last steps down off the hoopd barrel, there es no mis-takyng the figure: Edward the Confessor. The disem-bodied audlit of the seintly king looks down at the very fabric on which the tapestry will be stitchd – it es a look which, on Turolds absence, will be watchyng ofer us, augayng and judgyng every stitch that we make.

Turolds work done, Odo steps forward to make a speech. Systir Gunnrid, the pittance-mistress, grinds her teeth, the noise es horrible, take my word for it: *grruuun-nddr-gruuunnddr!* There are som who question the author-ity of my brothir Williams right to the throne, pro-nounces Odo, yet I was there, when in 1064, Harold made a vow of fealty to William ofer the holy relics of the English seints, Raven and Rasiphe! (*No thing but old bones from pigs and hundrs*, whispers Gunnrid, unable to hold her tongue.) The Norman invasion, Odo goes on, had *right* on its side – whi else did it receive the sacred blessyng of Pope Alexander? And yet, properly under-stood, it was less an invasion... – here, lyk a proud pea-cock fannyng out its tail-feathers, Odo puffs out his broad chest, raisyng up his bras and spreadyng wide the wings of his cope – ...than a *Crusade*, a *Holy War*, whose mission from the outset had been pious: to wrestle the throne of Englan from its usurpyng upstart commoner

Odo blesses the tapestry with pious words

king, and place it in the rightful roial five-fingers of William! (Systir Gunnrid grinds her teeth, from left to right: *grrruuunnddrr-grruuuunnnddr!*) Of course, Odo continues, while sinners to a man, the power-hungry Godwinsons remegn oon of the most renownd families in the lan, and there still are som... – here, nebb twitchyng, he looks sideways at systir Gunnrid – ...who do not see things in this light. But if the facts of the matter are seen truly as they haue been depicted in Turolds design – no-oon can contest Williams right!

Odo says he has every confidence that oure renownd skill in broidery, a gift which has been granted us by the grace of Dieu – agen, five-fingers are raisd to the heavens – can fynd no more fittyng subject. That we fully understand the privilege we haue been granted in beyng given the work, that he has finally been right in selectyng this oure prayer-hus ofer its rivals to carry out the task, that we will fulfil it to the very best of oure abilities – of these things, he adds, he has *no doubt*. And now, Odo crosses himself accordyng to the dictates of St. Samuel – nebb, navel, left nipple, right nipple – and blesses the work of the tapestry in pious words, before he turns to go, eager to return to Canterbury.

The systirs study the designs

Odos words are still ringyng in oure eyras. Yet before we can begin work in earnest, we must study Turolds designs. Only when we haue examind theyr every detail, committyng their forms and out ligns to memory as best we can, do we tentatively take up oure places round the now prepard linen on its frames. We sit for lang hours before the vast blankness, none of us daryng to broider the first stitch. Instead, we file the sharp bonepoints of the needles, or practice the stitches which we haue learnt from systir Agnes on scraps. Som sit threadyng theyr needles with the fine strands of colourd wool, lickyng the frayd endes with rounded lips; othirs twist and turn on theyr stools, adjustyng the height with cushions and frayd sackcloth. And som rub the creases from the linen with smooth glass slick-stones; while othirs agen, lyk me, begin to prick rough out ligns on the surface with the sharp point of an awl.

Then, after a brief and uneventful dinner – I leave systir Aelfflaed my wine, as often, for I haue no taste for the stuff – we take up oure needles oon by oon and seat ourselves before the stretchd canvas. It es perhaps the audacity of Turolds design which es so off-puttyng at the start, the boldness too of the manner in which he has executed the heafod of Edward the Confessor. We haue experience on oure side, we haue tackld

> mantles
> stoles
> mitres
> copes
> chasubles
> seal bags
> coverlets
> purses

efen wall hangyngs of more modest proportions. Yet each of these items, usually the work of oon, two, three five-fingers at most, can be taken in at a glance, and often workd on the knee. Turolds hangyng, though, has to be stretchd out on three lang trestle tables supportyng wooden frames, which haue been set out on the centre of the cloister, formyng three sides of a square. And efen then, only a petyte portion of the hangyng can be workd on at any oon tyme; as each section es completed, it es to be folded up, so makyng space for the subsequent designs. And yet eventually oure needles fynd a way into the flax-cloth via the borders, which, apart from the sketches for a few beste fables in the early scenes, Turold has megnly left blank. On the first frame, opposite the cellarers range, several bone-darts, workyng in yellow stem stitch, sketch in the narrow ligns which separate the megn band of the tapestry from the lower and upper borders. Anothir, comyng from the top, piercyng

The work es begun

the surface with its sharp point of bone, tentatively marks out the shape of a *fleur-de-lys*, the kynd of decorative motif which we are used to broideryng on cushions and coverlets. Anothir five-finger, enteryng the fray, travels rapidly from the top to the bottom of the canvas, markyng in bold out lign the decorative ligns and scrollyng curves of the border, amongst which, lookyng closely, oon can soon make out the figures of spinners, weavers, dyers. Then, workyng in a knotty, untidy stem stitch, systir Ebbas unpractisd five-finger marks out the crude form of som plant or arber, lyk a badly drawn vine. And now, workyng in out lign stitch, systir Anna, the sacristan, a flame-haird widow of Sussex, with a heart-shapd audlit and a devilish smile, broiders the fable of the wolf and the heron which, som dags later, will feature in the tale sche tells to oure company. Her design shows the heron with its cou in the jaws of the wolf, removyng a sharp bone which es lodged in the wolfs throat. In the fable, the heron es successful in its enterprise, and asks the wolf for its reward, but the wolf gives no thing in return, Vou shoud think yourself lucky, he says, to haue removd your cou from the jaws of a wolf without gettyng bitten.

There es the point of view of the woolwright and the point of view of the thread. From the oon the tapestry unfolds in a series of bold emphatic scenes – Harolds departure for France, Harold swearyng an oath of fealty to William, the death of Edward the Confessor, the coronation of Harold – from the othir the tapestrys images grow slowly and uncertainly from a bare and featureless bakground, always unsure of where they might lead. A snakyng lign made in stem stitch meanders from left to right across the linen ground, suggestyng now a landscape of hills and valleys, now a batalleground, now a plateau where defeated warriors seek refuge from the fight. Only later, after many hours toil in black and olive-green and fawn which blocks out the linen ground in thick bands of colour, does the observer, followyng the curvyng shapes, make out the prow of a watter-hross, the bras of an anchor. And now, at last, the hills and valleys resolve themselves into the waves of the salt-road, on which the ships, carryyng theyr cargo of men and bestes, bob up and down on the silent breeze.

Oon scene, the tendyng of which es unclair to us alle – it es especially puzzlyng as it has no model in Turolds designs – es that which Ethelreda the Reed, the slender choir mistress, has been stitchyng on the middle frame throughout the dag. At first a series of ligns and rectangles, circles and triangles, and curious interlacyngs of stem stitch which resemble no thing so mych as the scales of som vast sea-beste, it eventually resolves itself into a scene: a group of tall turreted buildyngs, to the right of which stands a Norman soldier engaged in talk with a Saxon peasant leadyng a hross by its bridle. Who are these figures? What es theyr story? We are at once curious to know, and alle augas look questionyngly to systir Ethelreda expectyng an explanation. *A puzzlyng scene*

Carefully finishyng off her work with a neat bak stitch, at length sche puts down her needle, and pulls up a footstool, on which sche seats her slender bone-hus, then, in her musical voice – a voice which, in speech as in songr, has alle the bright clarity of the pipes first fashiond by Pan from marsh reeds – unfolds her story.

The Tale of the Abandond Cite or
Ethelreda the Reeds Story

The cite you see stitchd here with its twin towers and
four-tierd kiln guarded at the east geat by a Norman
soldier in full battle-tackle   is none othir than the
cite of my birth   lang since burnt to the ground
in my youth I lifed there peaceably with my parents
my fathir was a farmer   a kynd-hearted brute of a
fellow with a spade for a beard and two turnips for
eyras   my mothir a weaver and herbalist wele versd
in the healyng properties of ragwort and feverfew   I
was the eldest of three weens with oon brothir
Deor   and younger than he a dear systir
Leofrun   my junior by two years and a dag
      for us the first augury of Hastings fall   though it
lang remegnd opaque   an unreadable signum to
which we woud later attach innumerable and diverse
tendyngs   alle wide of the mark   was the sudden
disappearance of the crows   som sayd the birds were
flown north to Crowlan in Lincolnshire where they were
gatherd in a greet company to make complegnt agegnst
mankynd   othirs held that it was an omen
though for whom and whether it was good or bad they
coud not decide   othirs still megntegnd that the
crows were left in search of richer pickyngs ofer the
herring-track   only later when the news of Hastings
fall began to spread accompanied by stories of
butcheryng and slaughter   did the penny finally drop
the crows were left for the carrion
      we were filld with panic for rumours were already
widespread of the Normans summary executions
the decimation of entire villages where nine were put to
judgement and only the tenth spard   what was to be

22

done   at once the thanes calld a council in the Greet
Barn and after mych hot debate it was decided that we
shoud take to the forest on the approach of the enemy
it was sayd that when the Normans arrivd to fynd the
cite abandond they woud not stay for lang   months
passd   summer turnd to autumn then winter to
spring before the Normans showd   when they did
they came quickly   on hrossbak   yet we were
ready   when they got there on the eve of St
Georges dag the cite was deserted

movyng a whole cite into the trees is no piece of cake
gravity is agegnst you   we fought this old enemy with
the traditional tools   ropes and pulleys and ladders
and beams and will power   the weens thought it was
alle som topsy-turvy game run wild   for normally the
grown-ups were tellyng them not to climb too high and
now they were urgyng them to shin theyr way up to the
highest of branches as if theyr very safety depended on
this insane risk   which indeed it did   yet oure
megn worry was the old and the sick who were pegnfully
winchd up into theyr new aerial habitat often protestyng
bitterly as   limbs and branches creakyng   they
lurchd about helplessly in the air   snap decisions were
to be made about what to take and what to leave behind
we took clothes and blankets and food of course and
cookyng utensils too yet mych of what we normally
considerd essential to daily lyf was of necessity
abandond   tables and chairs   chickens and
livestock   fyrplaces   floors   watter   and the
hundrs which we were to butcher then bury

once we were safely suspended in oure new home
and once we coverd alle traces of oure ascent as best
we coud we were curious to get news of the Normans
secretly I harbourd the hope that they woud quite
simply pass through and seeyng nobody to kill and litell
to loot pass on   and I already privately envisiond
beyng bak in my own bed within a niht or two the
whole unfortunate sequence of events consignd to

history   sadly these youthful dreams did not come
to pass   oure scouts reported that the Normans
were seen securyng the cite geats and fortifyyng
defences lootyng and layyng waste to the surroundyng
countryside   once in the trees we movd with the
badger to avoid detection and mothir taught us to
improve oure niht vision by eatyng magic mushrooms
we made use of woodcraft too cakyng oure audlits with
mud in the early dags then as oure skills improvd we
learnd how to make clothes   somewhat on the
model of the chegn-mail hauberks worn by the
Normans   out of the dried leaves of the sycamore
on which we rubbd beeswax to give suppleness and
protection agegnst the regn   for food we relied on
what was at five-finger   birds and fiskr and nuts
and berries and truffles which we dug up in the early
hours while the Normans slept   then we cookd up a
nourishyng if bitter leaf-curd by squeezyng the juices
from stinger nettles   this was a sparse enough diet
to be sure but at tymes we learnd how to supplement it
by stealyng from the Normans

     was it not madness youre thinkyng   I see it
written on your audlits   to steal from the Normans
and risk givyng away the entire cite   there was a
tyme when we sayd the same ourselves   but as oure
mastery of oure aerial habitat grew   a network of
ropes and ladders and secret routes soon led from tree
to tree lyk som vast spiders web or air-borne tapestry
takyng oon to the very limits of the forest   so that
we were able to spy on the Normans movements
every once in a while they woud hold vast open-air
feasts around a huge fyr   then they woud bake theyr
crusty loaves shapd lyk the cocks of theyr greet
stallions   and roast chickens on spits   and boil
up greet casseroles ofer open fyrs   these feasts eaten
from tables cobbld together from theyr lozenge-shapd
shields woud go on late into the niht and were
accompanied by mych drinkyng   yet whi shoud I

24

recount this in detail for it is wele known to you alle
and   look   here they are enjoyyng just such a
feast after theyr lanyng at Pevensey in Turolds design

it was oon niht early in summer we came armd with
ropes and meathooks and lang poles   at the very
ende of the feast while the Normans were already
beginnyng to drop off through drink I led a party of
weens and youths includyng my systir Leofrun to the
very tips of the branches of those trees which borderd
the forest   from where we dangld precariously ofer
the cookyng pots and trestle-tables and proceeded to
lower the hooks to secure the meals remegns   the
Normans always cook more than they can possibly eat
so we didnt go short   nor were we disappointed with
oure catch   subsequently we were to repeat the
exercise and we were nefer detected   oure success lay
in the fact that we nefer made a move before the
Normans passd round theyr potent and bitter-smellyng
apple brandy   it has the effect of dullyng the senses
and soon produces sleep in efen the hardiest of warriors

around midsummer I recall the weather turnd bitterly
cold for a while and we were forced to muster alle oure
strength and resources to stay warm at niht   despite
oure efforts three new-borns were lost   it was a
harsh reminder that ahead lay the bleak winter months
months which woud not only be markd by the cold but
duryng which we coud no langer rely on the trees for
protection for there woud come a dag when the leaves
woud shrivel and dry out and fall from theyr branches
and sooner or later we woud be exposd to the Normans
gaze   for as yet   contrary to oure initial
prognostications   they showd no signum of budgyng

it was then that the thanes calld a council held in the

branches of the Greet Oak in the thick of the forest
and here it was decided after som debate that if the
Normans continued to stay put then we must bring the
situation to a heafod

that niht beneath a cloudless sky oure menfolk raind
down from the branches while the Normans slept and
silently stole through theyr camp   they slit the
warriors throats where they lay in theyr beds lettyng the
lyf-blod stegn the damp earth   smashd fences so
that the sheep and goats escapd   torchd the stables
and untied theyr panic-stricken hrosses   then before
the Normans coud come to theyr senses they
disappeard once more amongst the dense foliage of the
branches   after this we continued to keep the
pressure on   strikyng randomly and irregularly
oon niht targetyng theyr cattle   anothir theyr
dwellyngs and anothir still strikyng the Normans
themselves once more as they lay in bed

followyng these niht-raids the Normans tighten
security postyng fully-armd sentries by the geats with
instructions to let no man pass   look   the
moment is illustrated in the tapestry   here   to the
right of the broiderd cite where the tall sentry stands by
the east geat his standard stiff in the breeze   halt
he shouts   on seeyng a stranger approach on
hrossbak   at once he orders the man to dismount
and then raisyng his finger accusyngly he asks   what
business brings vou to this cite   the stranger   a
Saxon peasant in workyng clothes   raises his five-
finger into the air protestyng his innocence   I come
in peace he says to buy som sacks of gregn for my
masters mill   there es no gregn here says the warrior
the cite has been garrisond by King Williams men and
alle trade with out siders es forbidden   be gone
the man is no fool   seizyng his moment he quickly
mounts his hross and is off   he is oon of the lucky
oons   ofer the comyng weeks othir no less innocent
passers-by will be stoppd at the geat and interrogated

by the Norman sentries   som lyk the millers boy will
be questiond and turnd away   othirs less fortunate
will be led into the cite to undergo a more severe
interrogation   from the safety of the trees we ear
theyr cries of misery and pegn as they are subjected to
beatyngs and torture   yet whatever the ferocity of
the Normans actions they learn no thing about theyr
silent attackers

by daglight oure aerial scouts kept close watch on the
Normans movements for if there were goyng to be
search parties and reprisals we wanted to be warnd in
good tyme   as it happend the Norman reaction
when it came took us by surprise   for if what oure
scouts ofereard was right after lang and fruitless hours
spent terrorisyng passers-by they came to attribute the
niht-raids not to Saxon resistance but to som
supernatural agent   som fiendish monster   som
species of griffin or dragon   nonetheless search
parties were indeed despatchd   armd to the hilt
to seek out and destroy the beast   tremblyng on oure
aerial perches we eard theyr heavy armourd stallions
gallop by beneath the trees causyng the ground to shake
and causyng leaves to fall from the slender branches and
as they approachd we clamberd ever higher to avoid
detection   clingyng for dear lyf to the quakyng
foliage   there was litell need to worry though   for
as they charged past theyr gaze nefer once lookd
upwards but on into the dark depths of the forest

after this unwelcome shock we nonetheless
continued oure niht-raids from tyme to tyme but less
frequently for we knew the Normans were already scard
and each tyme we enterd theyr camp there was the
danger of discovery   and yet   despite oure
continued caution we now began to relax in a way we
were not used to   the weens woud play wild games
of tag in the trees chasyng each othir from bough to
bough through the forest   and young lovers woud
lykwise chase each othir through the bright foliage

slippyng through the branches   coyly retreatyng
beneath the shade of a sycamore or pausyng to carve
the name of the lovd oon in the bark   sighyng the
sighs of youthful unspent passion amidst the yawnyng
boughs   it was around this tyme that I began to
develop a love of songr   I woud sit in a secluded
spot far from my companions with my leggrs twind
round the knotted bough of an oak or an elm and here
I woud delight in passyng many hours listenyng to the
songr of the birds   I learnt to distinguish the
twitteryng of the wren from the bright chirp of the
blackbird   to tell the rattle of a chaffinch from the
skylarks warble   and from amidst the diverse noises
of the forest I was able to pick out the woodpeckers
bark   the cooyng of the dove and the sweet trill of
the redpoll   and then after a while lyk the artful
starlyng I acquird the skill of imitatyng these various
calls and in this manner was able to participate in the
joyful lyf of the forest   yet these were not the only
diversions   increasingly too we descended to the
forest floor by daglight to forage for what we coud
fynd and we efen riskd the occasional fyr in the depths
of the forest so that we coud agen enjoy cookd fiskr
and roasted meat when we coud fynd it

      yet these were careless risks which oon dag I nearly
paid for with my lyf   oon mornyng as I was lookyng
for mushrooms and skippyng from tree to tree and
through the undergrowth I lost my way   fyndyng
myself in an unknown part of the forest my instincts
told me to cry out   and yet at the same tyme I knew
I coud do no such thing   so I began to retrace the
route I thought I took interrogatyng the forest floor
for signums of my passage   broken twigs
footmarks   discarded caps and stems   I advanced
som way in this manner unsure whether I was retracyng
my own steps or those of som othir   then I eard
the sound of gallopyng hrosses and before I got a
chance to hide they were upon me   clearly visible

through the trees   a group of mounted Norman
knights accompanied by theyr barkyng hundrs   at
once I leapt into the branches of the nearest tree
an elm   and frantically began to clamber upwards
coverd from heafod to toe in beeswax as I was the
hundrs pickd up my scent at once and followyng theyr
nebbs quickly gatherd round the base of the trunk
smarlyng and leapyng and pawyng the bark   they
were soon joind by theyr mail-clad masters who pointed
and laughd shoutyng at me in theyr foreign tongue
      setting out for the dragon   they found me
luckily there were no archers   yet they carried lances
which they coud easily start launchyng in my direction
I continued to climb   thinkyng that if only I coud
get high enough they woud go away   but as I
continued my ascent there was no signum of a let-up in
the barkyng   nor in the laughter and shouts
moreofer I coud now ear anothir person clamberyng
into the tree   with alle the strength I coud muster I
continued to climb   ever higher   until the
branches became so thin I wonderd how they coud
possibly hold my weight   on I went until the
branches I climbd turnd to the merest twigs and still
they continued to hold me as if through som secret
pact and then alle of a sudden I knew I must be safe I
knew the forest woud protect me   I lookd bakwards
caught a glimpse of my pursuer   a youth no older
than myself   a page no doubt   then falterd
losyng my grip on the boughs
      I saw myself tumblyng through the branches
down to the base of the trunk and lanyng flat on my
bak beneath the hooves of the Norman stallions
yet alle the while these pictures flashd through my mind
I was in reality beyng carried upwards and away way
beyond theyr reach   lang since I abandond gravity
gravity now abandond me   I was carried up and ofer
the trees and lookyng down I saw the forest as the
birds of the air must see it   the trees lyk clumps of

moss or lichen clumsily stuck to litell twigs and there
far beneath me lay the cite its mighty towers no taller
than my thumb and there too the Norman invaders not
toweryng above me on theyr mighty warhrosses nor
shoutyng at me and mockyng me with theyr coarse
laughter but shrunken and impotent and mute lyk
figures in a tapestry

I came down with a pegnful bump in a forest
clearyng close to oure aerial encampment and was soon
brought down to earth a second tyme by my parents
harsh admonishments   where the hell you been
sayd my fathir   through clenchd teeth   we were
lookyng alle ofer for you   heavens   cried my
mothir   didnt we tell you a thousand tymes not to
stray into the forest   and in broad daglight too
in blind frustration my fathir raisd a five-finger to strike
me   I twisted my bone-hus to avoid the blow
   it was then that I fegnted

when I awoke I was once more in the trees   wrappd
in warm blankets   there was a chill in the air and as
I breathd out my breath turnd to milk-white mist
before my augas   there was no-oon around but the
rich smells of cookyng told me where I woud fynd my
friends   slowly I made my way to the edge of the
forest to join them as they perchd in the branches
oferlookyng the Norman feast   a light mist coverd
the encampment so that we coud see litell of what was
goyng on   just the ghostly silhouettes of the
warriors accompanied by the clatter of knives   and
the warm glow of the fyrs   add to this an unsteady
drone comyng from a cornebus and a couple of drunks
engagd in a brawl and you get the picture   soon we

woud smell theyr potent apple brandy as it was passd
from muthr to muthr and spilt on the ground   and
then we woud strike

when the moment came I was the first to the
branches endes   I was the first too to feel the
scorchyng heat of the fyrs beneath me   and I was
the first to launch myself from the trees and   to the
astonishment of my companions   float freely ofer
the encampment   gently driftyng downwards till my
five-toes kissd the earth   followyng my example the
othirs too launchd themselves tentatively from theyr
hidyng places and then they too gently drifted down lyk
the wingd seeds of the sycamore buoyd in the gentle
breeze   we took oure pick of the remegnyng
morsels of food as the drunk Normans lay on the
ground then took hold of the fyr-brands and set light
to the tables and the lang benches   as we floated off
into the mist the Normans began to wake   panic-
stricken   and the air was filld with theyr cries of fear
and pegn   and when they saw us floatyng above
them in the mist   wieldyng oure fyr-brands   the
golden scales of oure sycamore hauberks glitteryng in
the light of the fyr they did not see a motley group of
half-starvd Saxon weens too wasted to be affected by
the forces of gravity   but a band of fyr-breathyng
dragons   half-heartedly som javelins were launchd in
oure direction and som shouted boldly but for the most
part they fled in terror

oure triumph was short-lifed   the very next dag
the leaves began to fall from the trees and at once we
were forced to start packyng oure bags   we left at
intervals in oons and twos amidst tears and confusion
we did not know where we were goyng nor what the
future held behind its bak   I kissd my mothir and
fathir goodbye uncertain that I woud ever see them agen

for months I wanderd alone through the countryside
only half-conscious where I was goyng   I grew ever
thinner and paler fearyng for my lyf   tremblyng at

31

each corner I turnd in the road   sometymes when
danger threatend I woud try once more to wing my way
into the air but on quittyng the forest I not only lost my
friends and family but the power of flight too
though I nefer quite came bak to earth   ever since
those dags my five-toes forever hover just above the
surface of the earth as if repelld by som powerful
lodestone as you can see   look   if I lift up the
hem of my habit   eventually   when I almost lost
hope   barely able to walk   I was lucky enough to
arrive at the doors of this holy-hus   from here on
you know my story as wele as I do myself   I was
taken on as a novice and soon joind the choir where I
flourishd under the wing of systir Carmen the choir-
mistress   then on her judgement the abbess askd me
to step into her shoes

    what became of my family   of my friends
many surely perishd in theyr wanderyngs   som
the lucky oons   mayhap found new homes
made new friends   encounterd new enemies
what became of the Normans   soon after my
departure a rumour spread that the cite was razed to
the ground by fyr   yet reports were contradictory
accordyng to oon story the Normans   cuttyng theyr
losses   decided at last   though too late for us
to abandon the cite   torchyng it on theyr departure
anothir story though megntegnd that the Normans
stayd put   continuyng to hunt for the dragons they
believd to be terrorisyng them   accordyng to this
report they did indeed fynd the dragons lair but were
unable to ofercome the monster   then oon niht
or so the story has it   the dragon visited them while
they slept breathyng its vengeful fyr   they nefer
woke from theyr sleep   and by mornyng no thing
remegnd of oure cite but ashes

Chapter II

*An eventful chapter, contegnyng the secret of
the Frankish knutr, and more besides*

THE DAG FOLLOWYNG SYSTIR Ethelredas tale we
rise early, as always, slippyng into the kirk of St.
Ethelfledas via the niht stairs for matins. It es
bitterly cold for the saison. The candles are hard as iron
and when lit they fill the kirk with snakyng spirals of
black smoke which weave theyr way round the fat pillars
of the nave and towards the choir, makyng us cough,
discomposyng the plegnsongr, whose shrill unefen notes
– where es systir Aelfflaeds anchoryng bass? – cause the
staind glass images of seints and prophets to rattle in
theyr casements. Ethelreda the Reed, as sche struggles
to direct the wayward flight of oure songr, tryyng to
pull us together with energetic bird-lyk bras movements
which at any moment are in danger of liftyng her into
the air, glances disconsolately from tyme to tyme at the
empty stall where Aelfflaed normally sits. As the light
thickens on every hillside, it falls on a crisp carpet of
hoarfrost off which it bounces in alle directions, daz-
zlyng the auga. When we step out into the cloister on
the ninth dag of Avril 1081, oure five-toes founder on
black ice, watter become bone.

And then, alle of a sudden, a shout, or rather a
shriek – es it systir Ethelreda? – comes from the bottom
of the dag stairs, and we hurry ofer, slippyng and sli-
dyng as we go, to see what the matter es. And there,
lyyng on the ground, partly conceald by a thick layer of
frost, oure bewilderd augas can detect nonetheless the
unmistakable out lign of a bone-hus. Fear God and give
Him glory, wails gaunt-audlited Gytha, makyng the

*An
empty
stall*

signum of the rood, for the hour of His judgement is come! And yet, as we peer closer, and as systir Anna, *Out of the wayy there*, leanyng ofer the bone-hus so that her flame-coloured har falls loosely ofer her audlit, carefully brushes aside the needles of hoarfrost which cover the heafod and shoulders, it es soon apparent from the fegnt movement of the upper lip, as it es from the twitchyng of the red nebb – a nebb which we recognise as belongyng to none othir than systir Aelfflaed the cellaress – that this particular set of bones, thanks be to Dieu, still lives and breathes. And so it es, without a word more, that alle of us – systir Gytha included – sit ourselves down on the icy pathway and start to brush off the frost from systir Aelfflaeds embalmd flesh. It comes off quite easily, revealyng the tender blue veins, for it es still light and newly-formd, and som of the filaments, becomyng airborne, penetrate oure nostrils and oure augas and efen slip down oure habits where they run icy and cold between oure breasts and down onto oure bellies. And then, alle at once, the resurrection occurs: coughyng and splutteryng, cryyng out for help – Save me! Save me! sche bellows, Save me for the love of God! – systir Aelfflaeds plump barrel-shapd frame, which if ever sche had reason to be thankful for it was surely then, levers itself upwards and, with a litell help from systirs Gytha and Anna, onto its five-toes.

Later, in chapter, once we are alle settld and seated and silent, Prioress Ermenburga – Croaker we call her – eyes us disapprovyngly from behind the lectern. Then, in her gratyng voice (a voice which, lyk a cough, or mayhap rather a growl, issues from the bak of the throat), sche opens the dags business: I will keep things brrief, sche says. Systir Aelfflaed has been confind to the infirrrmary, where it is hopd sche will quickly get betr. These events are most irrrregular, however, and will be the subject of a full investigation. Sche goes on to raise concerns about the abbess, concerns which, though largely unspoken, haue been worryyng us more and more with each passyng dag. As we alle know, it was on Candelmas that Abbess Aelfgyva went to Canterbury to visit Odo at St. Augustines to discuss the plans for the tapestry – and yet sche has not returnd, as expected, in the company of Odo and Turold. Unforrrtunately, Croaker explegns, Aelfgyva has fallen ill and must rrrest for a while where sche fynds herself before undertakyng the difficult overlan jourrrrney from Canterrrbury. In the meantyme, I will continue to administerr the hus. The tapestry will haue to be put on hold for the tyme beyng, but there will be no shorrrtage of tasks: a consignment of wool is expected from Shepperrton which will need to be sorrrted and storrrd; the livestock will haue to be caterrd for as they cannot be sent out to pasture; then there is the prayer-hus chrrronicle which, as you Aelthwyfe are only too wele aware, must be kept up to date in the abbesses absence.

As chapter draws to a close, there es a loud bangyng on the prayer-hus geat, and Croaker asks Felicity, the infirmaress, accompanied by myself and systir Gytha, to investigate. When systir Felicity, her sense of charity ofercomyng her sense of caution, opens the geat, we are confronted by a motley group of beggars, alle in search of food. Foremost of the band es an old man without nebb or lips, who throws himself on his knees before us, hittyng the icy ground with a sharp crack. Immediately behind him, a blind mothir, clutchyng a wailyng infant to her breast, begs us for help; while from oure five-toes, three emaciated childern in rags stare up at us with swollen, hollow, hungry augas. Then there es an oon-armd leper, wrappd in a filthy shroud, who shuffles towards us, steadyyng herself on a stick as sche goes. Round her cou hang an assortment of talismans, or trinkets, it depends on your point of view, strung lyk beads on a leather thong, amongst which I can make out a rabbits paw, the shrivelld bone-hus of a toad, a shell and (a sight which makes me retch), several human toes. Last of alle comes Godgifu, a beggar half out of her mind

Unexpected visitors

35

who haunts our prayer-hus from dawn till dusk, often wailyng in the early hours while we snatch oure last sleep before prime.

Impertinent questions

Systir Felicity, makyng the signum of the rood, takes the old man without nebb or lips by the five-finger and leads him towards the cook-chambr, where sche bumps into Hilda the Herbaress makyng her way out. The rest of the band, enteryng the courtyard, follow at a distance. When we get there Felicity tells them to wait. As soon as sche es gone oon of the childern picks up a pebble from the ground and throws it towards the othir side of the cloister, where it hits the carvd capital of St. Martin dividyng his cloak with a beggar, knockyng off the tip of his raisd sword. The othirs now follow suit, huzzyng pebbles this way and that around the cloister. I beg them to stop. Yet as soon as I open my muthr they start gigglyng. A moment passes, then oon of theyr number, a boy with spindly leggrs and lang red har, edges towards me, Youve got har on your chin, he observes, lyk a man. It es true, of course, yet for a moment I stare bak on him, unsure how to respond, Are you a witch? he asks. I tell him no, certainly not, I am a servant of Dieu, yet before he can push his enquiry further – thanks be to oure Lord – systir Felicity reappears with scraps of food, which are quickly seizd by eager five-fingers and devourd.

Yet as soon as the childern haue finishd theyr feast, the red-haird boy struts up to systir Felicity and, pointyng at me, repeats his question. Hopyng to pacify him Felicity explegns that while I am indeed no witch, I possess certain gifts of morrow-seeyng. Yet at once the childern run towards me, theyr shyness evaporatyng, Whi do you haue a beard if you are a nun? asks oon, Is it real? asks anothir, and before I can answer eager five-fingers reach out to tug it, Ouch!

As soon as I open my muthr they stop at once, as if this signum of pegn were alle theyd been waityng for. They stand there for som moments before the red-haird boy speaks agen, Tell us a morrow-see, he says. At first I shake my heafod, it es not my business to make predictions on demand, but they keep on at me until I give in, if only to be rid of them. I close my augas. Concentrate. Tomorrow, I say, the sun will shine and the birds will cant and vou shall eat oatcakes for supper. They laugh. Not that sort of morrow-see! shouts oon. A real morrow-see! shouts anothir. And then the chorus of complegnt rises to a peak. I am fast losyng my patience. But agen I close my augas. Concentrate. This tyme for real. I keep concentratyng – nothyng happens. Then, alle of a sudden, my muthr takes ofer, my lips partyng, pushyng outwards and roundyng, then I blurt it out, as if it were a single word: *Odosaudlitregnclouded!*

As soon as I haue spoken I feel a shudder run down my left side, wish to swallow the words once more. But they are out. The childern, still unimpressd, move off, leavyng me standyng alone in the cold, tuckyng my mans beard safely away beneath the folds of my wimple.

The hour of sext comes and goes. We dine in the refectory beneath Croakers Argus-lyk augas, then snatch an hours rest on oure lits. Still the consignment of wool from Shepperton has not arrivd, so Croaker sends a party out there to see what es causyng the delay. Sche asks me to lead the expedition, and to take the novices systir Brigid and systir Catherine alang, for if help es needed in transportyng the wool several five-fingers will be requird. The journey es hard ofer icy roads – each step lyk a soundyng into new territory. On the way Brigid and Catherine question me about the systirs, Is the cellaress a drinker? asks Brigid, lookyng me in the auga, Yes, I say, but sche only drinks in moderation (I do not mention the portion of wine that I habitually leave her), Whi is it, asks Catherine, pullyng up beside me on her mare, that systir Ethelguida is mute? Ethelguida has lost her tongue, I say, and that quite literally, But how? I cannot say, I tell her, though it es true that there are manifold rumours – som say that, as in the tale of

Departure for Shepperton

37

Philomela told in old books, it was cut out by a man to silence her screams – but these tales are almost certainly false.

When eventually we reach Shepperton we fynd the wool merchants workshops a hive of activity. Everywhere vou look there are vast heaps of wool on the floor. Here, the sheard fleece es beyng rinsd in a series of wooden tubs; elsewhere, it es beyng greasd with butter to facilitate separation of the fibres, which are then combd with the heafods of teazles and dried thistles to produce a soft downy ball; woe men dressd in rags, som with childern on theyr knees, sit in corners with spindles, spinnyng the wool into thread; while elsewhere still in the busy workshop the wool es steepd in vast wooden vats where it takes on the bright and pungent dyes extracted from woad, elder, nettle, madder root, onionskin and chamomile. When, eventually, amidst the clamour of activity, we locate the wool merchant himself – a bald stocky man, who wears his belly out side his belt – he assures us in forthright words that there es no need to worry, the consignment will be ready without delay, Youll haue it when you needs it, he says.

Nonetheless, it es som dags before the wool arrives. In the meantyme, we perform the daily chores of the prayer-hus – tendyng the livestock, insulatyng the bees, seeyng to the sick in the infirmary. And I spend lang hours bent ofer my desk in the scriptorium, makyng sure the chronicle which the abbess has entrusted to me duryng her absence es up to date, worryyng ofer what to put in and what to leave out. If I spend endless pages transcribyng Croakers interminable chapter-meetyngs, will the abbess take me for a dullard? If I do not describe my washyng, will sche think me unclean?

In the brief moments we haue to spare, we gather round the greet hearth in the fyr-chambr and, when the healyng flames haue driven the numbness of the cold from oure fingers endes, we sit down to practice oure stitches. For if we cannot work on the tapestry itself, it es nonetheless important to keep oure five-fingers in. And so, guided once more by systir Agnes, the sub-prioress, we practice now oon stitch, now anothir, pullyng the woollen thread through the linen ground on oure laps. We begin with the Frankish knutr, as we haue seen it broiderd in Turolds bold work – a loopyng stitch where the needle, as it emerges from the linen, es wrappd round with thread, lyk the leggr of a hare caught in a trap, before it plunges agen into the fabric. This complicated action leaves a simple yet versatile mark: a small dot, lyk the dark circle of the pupil, or the needles auga, lyk the hole left in puncturd flesh by a cross-bow quarrel, or the mark made by a scribe at the ende of a sentence, so. We practice too LAID AND COUCHD WORK (=)=)=)=), first placyng the colourd threads in neat rows, then bindyng them together with a couchyng thread, fixd with neat stitches – up and ofer, down and through, up and ofer, down and through – pullyng the stranded thread tightly together, lyk har arranged in bunches. The couchyng stitch es oon of the simplest and most ancient of stitches, yet it needs to be carried out with the utmost care – it must be as neat as a nipple, for unlyk the othir stitches on the tapestry, it needs to be, as far as possible, invisible, lyk the pins of wicker which hold the thatch in place.

After som dags the consignment of wool arrives at last, and it es stackd away neatly on shelves in the sacristy. Its arrival coincides with the lang-awaited thaw, so that on the dags that follow we are able once more to continue work on the hangyng. Once the tapestry has agen been set up on the cloister we set to with renewd enthusiasm. We work for lang hours in silence, payyng litell attention to what oon anothir es doyng. Oon pair of five-fingers works on a fable, while anothir tackles the bone-hus of a hross in laid and couchd work. Elsewhere, as the dags pass, the scenes become punctuated by the twistyng trunks of trees whose branches bend and curl and intertwine in greens and browns and yel-

The lang-awaited thaw

lows and reds. Mostly, we concentrate on the early scenes – Harolds feast at Bosham before he sets sail for France, Harolds lang-ships crossyng the channel, Harold in the company of William and Odo advancyng agegnst Conan, Duke of Brittany. Then, oon dag, as the light es beginnyng to fade, we notice Gunnrid the Grinder workyng alone on the ende frame, opposite the dormitory, on som scenes late in the design – the death of Harold, the routyng of the English army – and we cant help wonderyng what has drawn her to these concludyng scenes at this early stage in the work. Oon and alle, we fynd ourselves steppyng in her direction, and we crowd round her, examinyng the scenes of warriors and hrosses, blodshed and flight that sche has so carefully broiderd, Look, whispers systir Ebba, King ... err ... Harold, No, thats nefer the king, adds Hilda, look, here he is. And then, before we can say more, she starts to grind her teeth in irritation, *ggruuunnddr-gruuunndddr!* – a sound which, lyk rough music, will punctuate the tale which follows – then turns towards us, explegnyng the designs.

Three Tales Concernyng King Harold or Gunnrid the Grinders Story

Youre alle wonderyng, I know – for I cant help
oferearyng your wild whisperyngs – whi oon of the last
scenes of the tapestry
Is the oon Ive been workyng on first. I mean that
where King Harold meets his death. Theres no mystery
here. As with the snake
Ouroborus, which clasps its tail in its muthr, so with
endes and beginnyngs: the two are often oon and the
same, be quiet Ebba.
We alle know the foolish story spread by the Normans
regardyng the death of Harold on Senlac Hill,
And Ive shown him here as in Turolds design, struck
down by the fatal arrow. Yet of course, this is
No thing but the flimsiest propaganda, a cheap
conjuryng trick to rob us of oure king, and of oure
hope, so help me God.
Look closely, then, at my tapestry figures and youll see
not oon, not two, but *three* men with theyr augas
pierced by arrows.
Two of them, oon on five-toes, carryyng a mace, oon
mounted on a chestnut mare, flee the battlefield on the
right
Of the picture – *here* – pursued by four mounted
Norman knights and oon archer. Exceptionally, he too
is on hrossbak –
Such is the urgency of the situation – and he grips the
flanks of his mount unsteadily with his thighs, as he
prepares to unleash his dart.
Who are these figures? What is theyr story? Imagine that at
the climax of the battle, when the shield-wall has broken
And the Norman army has at last gaind the upper five-

finger, that a shower of arrows is indeed launchd in King Harolds direction.

And imagine too that an arrow does indeed hit Harold, but not in the auga, as has been falsely megntegnd By Norman chroniclers, rather it lodges itself firmly in the sixteen layers of ox-hide linyng the nasal Of his helmet – penetratyng with its forge-fresh point the first fifteen hides, but not the last – and try as he might Harold cannot make it budge. Nonetheless, he has had a lucky escape and he knows it. Lookyng around In the gatheryng dusk, he sees his troops in disarray. The battle is lost, theres no denyyng it, but if he can Get away, regroup, gather new troops, mayhap the war might yet be won? Certainly, God has chosen not to Take his lyf, but to preserve him to fight anothir dag. And so Harold, accompanied by a small escort Of his most loyal huscarls, does what any sane man woud do in such circumstances, and flees the battlefield.

Yet hes a conspicuous figure at the best of tymes – and with the arrow stickyng out of his helmet he can be spotted a mile off.

(*Grrrruuunnnddr-grruuunnddrr!*) Its now that oon of his huscarls suggests a decoy. In the ende, just to be on the safe side,

Not oon, but two decoys are decided on, and so, clutchyng arrows to theyr augas, accompanied by theyr own modest escorts,

They set off in opposyng directions to that taken by theyr king, so as to disperse and confuse the pursuyng Normans.

The ruse is a success. In the fadyng light of dag, beneath a light drizzle – weather conditions which the Normans

Woud soon come to see as typical of this islan, though they were no less typical of their homelan in northern France,

As anyoon who has visited theyr kingdom may testify –

William and his men are stoppd in theyr tracks, by a spectacle
As strange as any they are ever likely to see: the sight of
three King Harolds, each pierced through the auga by
The arrow of a Norman archer, accompanied by theyr
separate escorts, makyng off into three divergent sunsets.
Immediately after Harolds flight from the battlefield its
difficult to say just where he went. Many say he lay
Low for som dags, mayhap harbourd by the peasantry
in the surroundyng countryside, though othirs insist he
Made a quick get-away, ridyng hell for leather through
the niht. As for his subsequent adventures,
We haue more to go on, but efen here, rumour, earsay
and conjecture play theyr part: litell can be sayd with
certainty.
There are three principal accounts, each conflictyng
with the othirs. I lay them before you as theyve been
told to me – nefer you mind who by.

Accordyng to the first of these, which I view with som
scepticism – for it doesnt fit with the bold and heroic
Character of the king – Harold endes up takyng refuge
with a group of travellyng players and minstrels. In the
safety of theyr
Company he roams the countryside, bidyng his tyme,
happy in the knowledge that he is at least safe from
Williams men
For the tyme, for this, he reasons, is the last place
theyre goyng to look for him. He travels to Lewes,
Bramber, Arundel,
Chichester, Carisbrooke on the Isle of Wight,
Twynham, Southampton and Reading. On his travels he
learns som thing of actyng

And of minstrelsy and of the pleasures of the itinerant
lyf. He drinks more than hes accustomed to, often
wakyng with a sore heafod,
Takes pleasure in singyng songrs late into the niht and
in swappyng stories round the camp fyr, though hes
careful not to
Reveal his true identity, both for his own safety and for
that of the troupe. When they ask him probyng
questions
About his bakground he is sheepish, puttyng them off
with a nod and a wink. When pushd, he says hes been
schoold
In many trades, but is master of none. He nefer feels it
beneath himself to help out when he can, lendyng a
five-finger
With the cookyng, feedyng the hrosses, changyng a
wheel, pegntyng a new set. Nor does he refuse to help
out in a performance
When calld upon: dressd as a fool he beats a drum to
attract spectators in the marketplace at Lewes; at Chichester
Hes the voice of Jonah in side the belly of the whale; at
Winchester he plays the rantyng Herod on the high
scaffold:
*I anger! I know not what devil me ails! They annoy me so with
theyr tales that, by Gods dear nagls, I can no langer hold my
peace!*
In the troupes topical and *risqué* reconstruction of the
Battle of Hastings, which they first perform on the Isle
of Wight,
Harold, wearyng a hrosses heafod, plays the Spanish
stallion which carries William the Bastard to victory,
bangyng together
The shells of two tortoises. Between Twynham and
Southampton theyre stoppd and questiond by a
Norman patrol.
It is – how shall I say it? – a close shave. Afterwards, he
removes his prominent moustache with a razor to avoid
detection.

Somewhere between Southampton and Reading, attracted by the carefree charm born of a lyf on the open road,

And by an audlit which has alle the freshness of a spring dag, cheeks as rosy as apple-blossom, a neck fairer than the lily on its green stalk,

Augas as bright and as sparklyng as the mornyng sun, he falls heafod ofer heels in love with oon of the players, Edith. Oon niht,

As they lie enfolded in each othirs arms beneath the starry sky, he says to her in a moment of self-abandon: I am Harold, King of Englan.

Sche laughs, and adds, I am Ealdgyth, your queen. He insists, says hes in earnest, asks her to examine his profile. Look, he says –

Drawyng a diminutive coin out of his pocket – oon of a fistful minted at Winchester duryng his brief regn bearyng the Latin

Word for PEACE (pax), and on oon side of which is stampd his stern profile, Look, surely you can see the resemblance?

Agen, sche laughs, pushyng him away, Your heafod, sche says, is too big. At this, he too laughs.

The next dag sche shares the joke with the rest of the troupe. From that dag on they start callyng him Harold, as a jest.

Later, when they arrive at Reading, hes given the part of Harold in theyr reconstruction of the Battle of Hastings. To humour him, the endyng is adapted, so that Harold escapes from the battle: he fynds refuge with a group of minstrels

And players who, travellyng round the country, stage re-enactments of the Battle of Hastings. The act is a greet success

With its Saxon audience. They take it on to Oxford, to Winchester, to Bath and to Exeter. When they perform in Guildford,

Which has recently been host to Williams advancyng

army, the act is followd by riots. The performance is bannd by the
Norman garrison, and theyre thrown out of the cite, on pegn of death if they return. Yet wherever they go, its a huge hit,
So mych so that they drop alle the othir pieces from theyr repertoire. As theyr success grows, however, Harold becomes increasingly despondent. The popularity of the piece, indeed, relies on the laughter and mirth it provokes in its audience,
And while it certainly makes fun of William – he constantly puts his hauberk on bak to front, forever gets in a hopeless muddle
With his bridle and falls off his hross, gettyng his audlit stuck in his helmet – it laughs at Harold too, at his absurd
Flight from duty, from the responsibilities of king and crown. Lyk Aeneas in the arms of Dido, he knows
Hes idlyng away his tyme. For as he stays with the players, William ravages the lan, securyng his grip
On the kingdom. And so he refuses to play Harold any langer in theyr play, preferryng to revert
To his role as the stallion of William the Bastard. Then, oon dag, he refuses to take part at alle. He becomes ill. He rants and raves, sayyng that he, King Harold of Englan, shoud nefer haue got involvd with a bunch of minstrels.
Relations between himself and Edith (*grruuuunnddddr-grruunnnddr!*) grow frosty. This continues for som weeks. Once more, the troupe travels alang the south coast, stoppyng at Chichester, Arundel and Lewes.
Finally, at Pevensey, by which tyme Harold has more or less recoverd, they part company.

The second account coud hardly be more different. Here, theres no mention of fyrside banter or travellyng minstrels.

After fleeyng the battle, Harold makes for the Weald, accompanied by his escort. He then rides through the niht in pouryng regn

Followyng secret mule-tracks known only to his trusty huscarls, in the direction of Wessex, yet to be subdued by William.

Changyng hrosses at Winchester, where he empties the roial treasuries, he rides on without a break until he reaches Exeter

The followyng dag. Hross-weary, he rests here for som weeks, recoveryng from his battle-wounds, and spends mych tyme

In company with his mothir Gytha, playyng chess and discussyng the best methods of ofercomyng William.

Harold has nefer been the greetest strategist, particularly under pressure, and at his mothirs five-finger he suffers innumerable

Humiliatyng defeats. His initial error is always the same: confusyng the role of the invaluable pawns with that of the fyrd

In battle, hes too willyng to sacrifice these precious pieces in the early stages of the game, and then, seeyng his error too late,

Is forced to beat a hasty retreat into the left-hand corner of the board, with only his glum-audlited queen, his bearded knights,

His bishops and a single castle for company. Here, tyme and agen, he mounts a gallant defence, formyng a bulwark with his castle,

Sendyng out the knights and the bishops on brief skirmishes to keep the advancyng hordes at bay. Yet such a fragile position

Can only be held for so lang and, tyme and agen, he has to give in, as Gytha picks off his scant remegnyng pieces oon by oon

And eventually hounds him into checkmate. Try as he will to devise new stratagems, each game endes with Harold on the defence,

And each game too endes with Gythas pieces forcyng Harold into check, then checkmate. Harold is growyng weary

Under the repeated stregn, lookyng less and less lyk a king and – how shall I say it? – more and more lyk a tired and ofertaxd fyrdsman.

You need rest, says Gytha, Anothir game, says Harold, once more peevd at his foolish performance, yet unwillyng

To give up the fight. And then, late oon niht, hounded into a corner as usual, he comes up with a masterful defence.

On the brink of defeat, he moves his queen out from behind his wall of knights and bishops, and right into the opposyng

Corner of the board, where Gythas fat king, left exposd in a moment of oferconfidence, lies hopelessly unprotected.

Check, says Harold. Gytha, taken by surprise, counters by movyng a bishop bak from the front line, but it is too late.

Harolds queen now makes the decisive and deadly move: checkmate. At once, he rises from the table, a glow of defiance in his auga,

And kisses his mothir warmly on the cheek. Then straightaway, he raises a fresh army and travels to Bath via Fosse Way,

And from Bath he travels north to Chester in the kingdom of Mercia. Here he stops to strengthen his army,

Then travels six dags across mountainous country into the kingdom of Wales, settyng up camp at Portskewet. His army now sets to work to construct a fleet of som six-hundred lang-bots which takes many weeks labour and consumes

The trees of three forests and the hides of seven hundred seals and four whales. Harolds plan is to take the fleet alang the south

Coast and eventually round where the lan turns northwards and up the Thames to London, where he will cut off William

Before he arrives there for his crownyng. Haveyng loaded the vessels with provisions for the journey, they set sail on St. Nicholas dag.

Shepherded by favourable winds from the north-west they pass Lans Ende on the first dag, puttyng in at a narrow inlet on the Cornish coast.

For two dags they sit tight, waityng for a favourable wind from the west. Eventually they set sail with a propitious wind

Behind them, keepyng the lan always on the port side, the trout-road on the starboard side. By dusk, theyre approachyng Ports Mouth,

Where they mean to stop for the niht, but here things start to go wrong. Firstly, they mistake the harbour entrance,

Takyng a channel which rapidly narrows, so that the ships are pressd up agegnst each othir. Secondly, a sudden and violent storm

Comyng off the whale-road drives theyr now dangerously positiond and unmanoeuvrable ships onto the rocks. While the sea beats

Agegnst the stars of heaven and the rollyng of the waves roars with the winds, Harold too roars brief and hopeless orders to cut this adrift,

To heave that oferboard. Masts are snappd off, sails torn to ribbons. Those vessels that are not rent by the rocks themselves

Are smashd by the othir watter-hrosses and torn asunder by the merciless sea, which quickly turns to a briny soup of splinterd wood,

Broken masts, and pulverisd bone-huses. Theres no thing that Harold can do: within the space of half an hour his fleet is in ruins.

The very next dag the survivors of the wreckage make
theyr way bak to Exeter, takyng a circuitous route,
Skirtyng the New Forest, to avoid detection by Norman
patrols. At Exeter, Harold puts the disaster behind him
And at once sets about improvyng the cites defences,
for if its too late for an attack on London, its not too
late to set up

A centre of resistance in Wessex. By Christmas Dag –
the dag on which William the Bastard is crownd King
of Englan at Westminster –

Harolds fortification of Exeter is complete, and he has
accumulated sufficient provisions to weather a siege of
oon month.

Early in 1067, news of the Exeter uprisyng reaches
William, now in France, and hes sufficiently disturbd by
the reports

To return to Englan. Most disturbyng of alle, no doubt,
is the rumour that the uprisyngs beyng led by Harold
himself.

Lanyng at Pevensey, William travels first to London,
then takes the old Roman road to Cirencester, and
descends on Exeter

By Fosse Way, with the full might of his army. When he
arrives, shortly after dawn, Harold is waityng for him
and easily repulses

The direct attacks of the first dag with his archers.
Norman casualties are high. On the followyng dags
William resorts

To more cynical tactics: hrosses and men shit in the
watter supply; archers shower the cite with theyr darts
from dawn to dusk;

Fyr-balls are launchd ofer the cite walls, settyng fyr to
the castle, the flames spreadyng in a moment, as flames
do, destroyyng alle in theyr path.

Still Harold holds out, but on the sixth dag his men
contract dysentery and morale is low. (*Gruunnddr-
ggrruunddrr!*) William sends a

Messenger to offer Harold and his men pardon if they willyngly surrender the cite, but Harold is resolute in his refusal to surrender,

Knowyng that to give in now woud not only be to surrender himself to certain death, but to five-finger the kingdom of Englan to William for good.

At niht he sends out men to sabotage Williams camp, burnyng theyr tents while they sleep and slittyng theyr throats in theyr beds.

Williams response the next dag is once more to strike with his full might. This tyme he manages to breach the walls, And after eight dags, the cite is defeated, though once agen, Harold escapes, fleeyng the cite by the old watter geat.

From here on, Harolds precise movements become difficult to chart. Alle we know for sure is that he fled northwards.

It is likely, but by no means certain, that he playd his part in the uprisyngs in the Welsh marches and in Mercia in 1068,

As it is that he was involvd in the insurrections in the north, around the area of York, in 1069. Som accounts, too,

Say that he playd his role in the revolts around Ely and the fen country in 1070 and 1071, fightyng with Hereward the Wake.

Where he is now, whether or not hes still at large, we can only guess. Som claim that he was killd in the siege of Ely in 1071,

Though his bone-hus was nefer found. Othirs say that after the defeat at Ely he fled to Denmark, to live out his dags in exile,

Adoptyng the lyfstyle of a monk. Othirs, agen, though – whom I lyk to imagine speak the truth – megntegn hes still at large

In the uncharted fenlan, gatheryng strength, preparyng a new fleet and a new army, to liberate his country, and once more take the throne.

In the third and final account of the kings adventures,
Harold, disguisd as a commoner, flees the country to
raise an army oferseas.

Travellyng first to Dover, he boards a watter-hross
which takes him to Boulogne, and from here, mounted
on an ass,

He travels west, stickyng to the coast. He proceeds
slowly in this manner, reachyng the borders of Williams
estates

In Normandy on the third dag, where the ass collapses
through exhaustion. From now on, he makes his way
on five-toes,

Stickyng to the cliff tops and to the broad sandy
beaches, where he learns to dig for shellfiskr to
supplement his dwindlyng supply of food.

On the sixth dag he reaches the low-lyyng marshlans
surroundyng Mont St. Michel, which he recognises
from the campaign of 1064.

And from here its only a dags march to the high-walld
fortress at Dinan, toweryng ofer the black rocks,

Where he seeks an audience with Williams old enemy,
Conan, Duke of Brittany, and delivers his carefully
worded speech.

My Lord, he says, I, Harold Godwinson, rightful King
of Englan, come before you with a humble request, a
request which,

I trust, will ultimately prove as welcome as it is urgent.
When last we met I was the Earl of Wessex, and fought

At the side of William the Bastard in his campaign
agegnst your army. This, I hasten to add,

Was through no ill-will held agegnst your person, but
rather the result of Williams trickery and cunnyng,

By which foul means he contrivd first to place me in
his debt, then sought repayment of that self-same
debt
By conscriptyng me in his campaign agegnst Brittany. I
had come on a peaceful mission to meet with William
Duke of Normandy.
Yet as I made my way to France, my lang-ship was
blown off course and I was taken prisoner by Guy de
Pontieu.
It was in payyng the ransom for my release that William
put me in his debt, but I now haue reason to believe
That the whole unfortunate sequence of events was no
mere accident, as it seemd at the tyme,
But an elaborate plot engineerd by William himself.
This, then, is how he contrivd to put me in his debt.
I will say no more in my defence. Circumstances haue
now changed irrevocably, just as this debt has once and
for alle been discharged.
The Bastard, turnyng his bak on alle that is just through
greed for unjust gegn, has driven me from my homelan,
Just as he once drove Conan Duke of Brittany from
Dol. My request, and my offer – I will put it plegnly –
is this:
Let us now unite agegnst William, oure common
enemy, and seek just vengeance for the wrongs he has
committed agegnst us.
Let us first drive him from Englan, then let us drive
him from Normandy itself. There was a lang silence
once Harold
Had finishd his speech and no-oon movd.
(*Grrrruuunndddr-grruuunnnnnddrrr!*) Harold remegnd
kneelyng, heafod bowd, heart poundyng.
Whatever went through Conans heafod in those dizzy
moments well nefer know, yet if, as seems likely, this
was the first
News he had of Williams victory, hes sure to haue been
furious – for in the summer of 1066, unbeknown to
Harold and mych to

Williams rancour, Conan had put in his own claim to the throne of Englan, on the grounds that Normandy and the lans it lay
Title to, had been entrusted to his fathir, Alan III, in 1035. At length, with a sigh, Conan rose slowly from his seat. He spoke curtly:
I do not recognise this man, he es an impostor. And so it is that King Harold audlits the ultimate ignominy: he is cast into the dungeon of
Conans castle at Dinan. Once he recovers from his initial shock – though hell nefer recover fully – Harold does alle he can to secure his release.
He tries to send messages to Conan, sayyng that he can pay whatever ransom he asks, that – how shall I say it? – He still has rich friends in Englan. But his words go unheeded, mayhap are nefer passd on by the wide-augad childern
Who come to stare at the old man in chegns. When this fails, Harold pleads with his gaolers: he calls for quill and parchment,
Askyng them to deliver a message to Englan on his behalf. He promises to reward them richly, tellyng them hes the rightful King of Englan.
They refuse bluntly, laughyng in his audlit, and its alle too plegn that they dont believe a word he says. Its written alle ofer theyr audlits:
How coud such a man be King of Englan? And when Harold looks at himself he finds it difficult to believe too.
Harold, his kingship unrecognisd, no langer recognises himself. Staryng into a pool of piss that has gatherd on the floor of the cell,
Searchyng its fetid watters for his familiar image, he sees reflected bak the audlit of a hundr. His visage is hary alle ofer,
His augas wild and blod-shot, his nagls haue grown into lang curvd claws, and his har is lang and matted.
The hundr prowls the floor of the cell, or sits beneath

its narrow slit of a window, howlyng. Whi haue they imprisond the Hundr King,
He wonders? Alle niht he sits beneath the window, howlyng into the darkness, callyng on the hundrs, the wolves, to come and rescue him, theyr king.
Each mornyng, now, he asks for bones, raw meat. With contempt, his gaolers throw him lumps of worm-infested beef, unfit for a hundr.
He eats these with relish, chewyng the bare bones for hours on ende, breakyng his teeth. The worms from the beef enter his gut,
Chew away his intestines. Now at niht he howls more urgently than ever, but still his rescuers do not come.
When there is no thing left of his intestines, the worms eat his liver, his pancreas, his spleen, his stomach.
He sits by the window, howlyng, howlyng, howlyng. When he shits, he shits blod.
The next dag hes found dead in his cell, slumpd in a pool of his own blod. They throw him ofer the castle walls, lyk a hundr, into a ravine.

These, then, are the three tales which haue been related to me concernyng King Harold. In my heart of hearts, Its the second of these that I believe to be true, and thats whi, each dag, I continue to pray for Harolds safety. Yet, as Ive sayd before, no thing here can be stated with certainty. It may efen be that these three contradictory accounts,
In reality, are different episodes in oon single story. Thus Harold might haue followd his period with the minstrels by organisyng
His troops at Exeter, then subsequently fled oferseas to

raise a new army. Or, agen, he might haue organisd
The resistance at Exeter, only then to take refuge with
the travellyng players, and on quittyng theyr company
fled to France.

It is, after alle, at a coastal port that they part company.
Its efen possible that he went first to France, escapd to
Exeter,

And ended up after his various adventures, in the
company of the minstrels. Indeed, for alle we know,
His visit to Conan of Brittany might haue met with
success, in which case this woud haue been the army he
brought to Exeter.

Doubtless, too, there are othir possible combinations
here, for any of the three accounts coud be placed first,
Or indeed second and third in order of occurrence.

(*Grruuunnddr-grruunnddr!*) Alle we can say with certainty
is that if Harold

Arrivd in Brittany later than Christmas 1066, he woud
haue found Conan dead – poisond, it was sayd, by
Williams own five-finger,

Usyng a maleficent and slow-actyng powder which
finally took effect on December the twenty-fourth, the
eve of Williams crownyng at Westminster.

Mayhap, efen this does not exhaust the possibilities
nested in these brief histories. I mentiond before, that
not oon,

But three Harolds left the scene of the Battle of
Hastings, hurryyng off in three divergent directions, in
the fadyng light of dag.

Coud not the disparities in oure three accounts be
explegnd lyk this: each account is the account of a
different Harold,

Only oon of which is the real Harold. And certainly,
this woud explegn convincingly the failure of
recognition

In the first and the last of these accounts. And this, too,
woud suggest that the true story of Harold

Was the second of those tales, reason enough to give us

hope that, oon dag, oure rightful sovereign will return in triumph.

Chapter III

In which the abbess returns, and systirs Edith and
Emma haue an alarmyng tale to tell, as vou will see

I F GUNNRID THE GRINDERS TALE fills us with hope
for oure king and for oure country, imagine oure joy
when, on the morrow, Abbess Aelfgyva makes her
return. Sche arrives duryng the niht, between the hours
of matins and lauds, accompanied by an escort of armd
Norman knights. The clatter of theyr hrosses hooves
and theyr manly shouts – amongst which an alert eyra
can make out the distinctive janglyng of the abbesses
bridle, lyk a distant chapel bell – wake us with a start
from uneasy slumbers, and quickly the rumour spreads
from lit to lit lyk wild-fyr: *Aelfgyva has come home!*

An
eagerly
awaited
chapter
meetyng

It es eagerly that we await the hour of chapter, keen
to set augas once more on oure abbesses familiar audlit:
her high foreheafod, white as the lily-white rose, her
tender look, her frank smile. And yet, when at last we
file into the chapter hus sche es nowhere to be seen.
Instead, it es the sober audlit of Croaker which greets us
once more from behind the lectern, Systir Aelfflaed,
sche says, is mych imprrrroved, this same dag, after
prrrime, sche was sittyng up in bed eatyng a hearrrty
breakfast. For this we haue only God to thank – for
without His interrrrvention it is likely that sche woud
haue perrishd in the frost. I haue made inquirries, however, and I fynd to my alarrm that on the eve of the
accident the cellarrress had been drrrinkyng, not only
from her own cup, it seems... – and here the prioress
raises her sunken augas and scans oure audlits with her
accusyng look – ...but from those of several of her sys-
tirrrrs. Liftyng up the vast vellum bound Rule onto the

lectern and strokyng her fingers down the gutter of the page, sche reads in her croakyng voice:

> *Each member of the Hus is to be prrovided with up to half a pint of wine accorrrdyng to her needs; this must in no circumstances be exceeded; if a member of the Hus, for whichever reason, finds her allocation in excess of her needs, it is to be returrrnd to the cellarress, and shoud not be made available for consumption at table.*

But surely, systir Anna begins, when Croaker cuts her off, closyng the book with a thud, as if to emphasise her point and also to say let there be an ende of the matter, no more of this, let this matter henceforth be a closd book. Then, after a lang pause, and a labourd sigh, sche acknowledges that Abbess Aelfgyva has returnd duryng the niht, The jourrrney, sche adds, has left her weak, sche is restyng.

Som thing in the tone of Croakers voice – it es always dry and raspyng, lyk a rusty key in an unoild lock, or a toad in the desert, but todag it es so thin vou can see through it at once – tells us that this es by no means the whole story. And yet, we must wait several hours before oure suspicions can be confirmd by the alarmyng tale which es later told in the parlour by the abbesses travellyng companions, systirs Edith and Emma, and which requires a paragraph alle of its own.

The abbess has lost her voice, says Emma, clutchyng her milk-white throat with her five-fingers, There has been a fyr, says Edith, flailyng her lang bras about as if to disperse a lingeryng cloud of smoke, Almost certainly arson, says Emma, augayng us down the bridge of her upturnd nebb, Fingers, says Edith, wavyng her own bony forefinger in oure audlits, are pointyng at Christchurch. Understandyng litell of what they say, I take a deep breath and ask them to start once more at the beginnyng, and the account that follows gives us alle cause for alarm. Duryng the abbesses stay at the prayer-

Fyr and arson

59

hus of St. Augustines in Canterbury, it appears, there
has been a fyr, which, moreofer, started in Aelfgyvas
chambr. Here, between the slit window and the lit, there
was a certain wooden floor supportyng a shrine, on
which were two candles, ah, which were kept burnyng
throughout the niht. Under this floor, it seems, many
things were lyyng together in an untidy manner, it was
askyng for trouble, such as flax and thread and wax and
vessels of different sorts – and it so happend that while
the abbess lay sleepyng on her lit these things caught
light, and those above and underneath caught fyr at
once, it was terrible. The abbess might haue been consumd by fyr where sche lay in no tyme, but in the same
hour the clock struck before matins, and Bishop Odo
arose from his slumbers and smelt burnyng on the air.
Then he ran at once, soundyng the gong, as if for a
dead man, and he cried with a loud voice, *Fyr! Fyr! Fyr!
Fyr!* Then alle in the prayer-hus ran up and found the fyr
ragyng with incredible fierceness. Young men ran for
watter, som to the well and som to the brook, and som
used theyr hoods to scoop up watter and with greet
labour put out the fyr. At last Bishop Odo forced his
way into the room which was black with smoke and carried the abbess off to the safety of his own quarters.
Aelfgyva had not been badly burnt, as it turnd out, yet
sche has not spoken a word since the incident and
remegns confind to her lit. Arson es suspected – the
chief suspect beyng the Priory of Christchurch at Canterbury, involvd as it has been in prolongd litigation to
recover a greet number of estates off Bishop Odo and,
though pre-eminent in the art of broidery, oferlookd by
the bishop as regards his hangyng.

When we eard of the trials which Aelfgyva had been
through we were greetly troubld, and the prayer-hus was
filld with cries of lamentation. Only Croaker, indeed,
did not shed a tear, and as for myself it took three nihts
before the drownyng abated. Yet we were alle thankful
that sche had escapd with her lyf, offeryng prayers of

thanks to God for her deliverance, and many offerd prayers of thanks to Odo also. There was a feelyng of disappointment on the air, however, for we had lookd forward greetly to seeyng Aelfgyva on her return, and now this was forbidden us, for sche was to remegn in isolation in her quarters until sche had recoverd from her ordeal.

In the dags that followd – for, of course, the systirs swiftly got wind of my untimely morrow-seeyng in the cloister – I was mercilessly mockd and became the butt of theyr jokes. Placyng five-fingers ofer the augas in imitation of the blind Tiresias, oon of them woud sway from side to side, slowly at first then in an increasingly agitated manner, then at last blurt out suddenly, *Odos audlit! Regn ... clouded!* – a performance which woud be repeated ofer and ofer agen until oon and alle collapsd in laughter. Yet lang experience had taught me not to take such things to heart. As every morrow-seer knows, we sometymes get it wrong and must learn to live with the consequences. Bak in 1066, I remember, while I was still livyng in the village of Aldersford, I predicted a greet victory for Harold at Hastings – for in my minds auga I saw clairly his troops vanquish the foe in som greet and unlovely batalle. I was wrong, of course, and realisd soon enough that the victory I had seen had had no thing to do with Harolds fight agegnst William by the hoary apple arber, but had been a vision of his victory agegnst the Norwegian Harold Hardrada and Harolds treacherous brothir Tostig at Stamford Bridge in the north, the very batalle in which my fathir nearly forfeited his lyf. Oon army looks mych lyk anothir these dags – thats what makes things so difficult. Alle that distinguishes them es the har: the Normans wear it short and shave the bak of the cou; the Saxons wear it langer and favour ploughshare moustaches; the Vikings, the hariest by far, go for the full beard plus har extensions. But such niceties are hard to pick out in the heat of batalle. I haue made good predictions too, in my defence – the comet of 1066, the famine of 1070, the cod-dearth of 1074 – yet it es oons failures which always stick in the mind, and which people throw bak at vou at the first opportunity.

Work continues on the chronicle While the abbess lay confind in her quarters we carried on with the daily chores as usual, but oure efforts lackd conviction and felt the want of a guidyng five-finger. We pushd the tapestry forwards, slavishly followyng Turolds plan; we lookd after the sick in the infirmary, includyng som of the half-starvd wretches who had knockd on the prayer-hus geats duryng the blizzard, the three childern, the blind woe man and her starvelyng child, who we fed up with cheese and milk. Slowly, we were able to nurse them bak to health and, at length, release them once more into the uncertainties of the out side world. And then, I spent what tyme remegnd bent ofer my desk in the scriptorium, labouryng ofer the prayer-huses chronicle which I did my best to keep up to date, frettyng for lang hours ofer how mych weight to give to a particular incident, from what angle best to present anothir. As I workd I often wishd that the abbess were at my side to offer me a guidyng five-finger, for while I had som experience of copyyng word-hoards I found I had litell skill at copyyng from nature, and the way forward often seemd blockd.

Aelfgyva tours the precinct Alle this tyme the health of oure sequesterd abbess preyd constantly on oure minds. And then, on the octave of the Rogation dags, the nineteenth of Mai, oure prayers were answerd: Aelfgyva, leanyng on the shoulders of systirs Emma and Edith, her trusty companions, left her chambr to make a tour of the precinct. Sche was still infirm it turnd out – indeed, sche was thin as a rake and her complexion was paler than apple blossom (though perhaps, as Gunnrid suggested, silently muthryng the words, it was merely *that* tyme of the month: the Normans had landed). The abbess was still unable to speak too, yet sche greeted us warmly, and nodded her approval when we showd her the work which we had done on the bishops tapestry.

Later that same dag we set to work on the hangyng with renewd vigour. There was mych still to be done, but by workyng on separate frames, we had been able to push forward simultaneously different sections of the design. Where there had once been bare skeletal out ligns and ghostly shapes, oons auga was now met by the boldly couchd flanks of muscular stallions in russet-red, fawn, mustard and onion-brown, theyr riders flexyng theyr biceps in order to launch a javelin at the Duke of Brittanys men, or to raise an iron-bossd shield to ward off a blow. Flames lickd at the walls of Conans stranghold at Dinan, while from above spear shafts and shields raind down lyk meteorites. Elsewhere vou coud make out clairly the fleets of stripd ships carryyng theyr deadly cargo of warriors and hrosses ofer the salt-roads, theyr brightly colourd sails billowyng in the breeze, a hackneyd phrase, but oon that serves its purpose wele enough. Elsewhere agen, messengers ran to and fro, deliveryng whisperd secrets to the eyras of kings; arbers were felld and cut and strippd and polishd so that they coud be fastend together to make ships; fingers pointed this way and that, directyng the auga to diverse shiftyng scenes, a burial, a comet, a departure, an oath.

Beneath Harolds lang-ships in the early parts of the tapestry, just as the first es about to lan on French soil, broad-audlited systir Ethelguida, workyng in stem and out lign stitch, broiders the fable of the mouse, the frog and the kite in olive-green, russet-red and mustard threads. In this tale a mouse and a frog travel tied together with a bit of string, quarrellyng as they go. Eventually, they come to a watter-track where the frog

Fable of the mouse the frog and the kite

63

jumps in, draggyng his companion down with him. The mouse, squealyng, attracts the auga of a passyng kite which at once swoops down and seizes it with sharp talons, draggyng the startld frog alang too at the ende of the piece of string. The kite then eats the fat-bellied frog and, its hunger satisfied, drops the mouse. Ethelguida has illustrated the fable, followyng Turolds plan, at the point where the kite, wings spread, soars off on a risyng eddy with its prey, pullyng the frog alang behind. Sche says no thing by way of comment, for sche has no tongue – yet mayhap we are to imagine that the power-ful kite es William, the frog that gets eaten, Harold, and that the mouse represents the associates of Harold, draggd down with him, but in the ende treated with clemency by William?

The noble Odo

Further on Gunnrid the Grinder carefully broiders the noble figure of Odo advancyng towards Mont St. Michel in the company of William and Harold – while his bald heafod es conceald beneath a hat of beaverskin, he can be identified by his hookd nebb, almost as lang as the cocks of the stallions, and by his deadly mace. Sit-tyng at Gunnrids side systir Ebba, her audlit wrinklyng lyk a walnut under the stregn, struggles to master the complicated honeycomb of stem stitch which makes up the shinyng mail shirts of the warriors – workd in Ebbas uncertain five-finger the impression, alas, es of a suit of damaged, war-worn batalle-gear. Also, on the middle frame, oure attention es caught by the stitches of the widow Anna, who improvises boldly in bright red and black a hus in flames, and, above the heafod of William at Pevensey, a naked couple claspyng each othir in theyr bras, both features which are nowhere to be found in Turolds designs. At once, we try to guess the significance of the couple. Might this be William frolick-yng with oon of his female camp followers, as Ethel-guida the Mute suggests in a whirr of gesture and signum? Or are these tapestry figures, as Gunnrid the Grinder suggests, characters from the fable of *The Young*

Man and the Courtesan? Unable to come up with an answer which we can agree on, Ebba es bold enough to ask systir Anna to take a rest from her work and explegn her tendyng to us.

Sche carries on for som moments, heafod bowd ofer the flax-cloth, workyng the needle of bone, stitchyng in firm out lign stitch the mans upright cock and balls; then, finishyng off the design with a nimble stitch, sche cuts the thread with her iron shears and puts down the needle, tuckyng it safely into the border of the linen. And now, turnyng her heart-shapd audlit towards us, sche pauses an instant to catch her breath, then addresses us in the followyng words.

The Looters Tale or Widow Annas Story

You ask what I tend stitchyng and brodderyng a couple in the buff ofer the heaffod of William as he gossipps with Odo in his camp at Pevensey. Though I hate to contradict and gegnsay you, the sceene does nott, as sysstir Gunnrid cleverly and inngeniously suggessts, illusstrate the fable from Aesop they call *The Young Mann and the Courtesan*. Here, if I remember it, a young mann is flatterrd by a hor, but knowyng her repputation for deceit and cunnyng, ignores her advances. Sche complegns, sayyng that while everyoon else lavishes her with ever more expennsive presents and giffts, it is nonetheless him that sche values and prizes most. It is with pleasure, my angel, the young mann replies, that I ear you speak so – but nott because theres a gregn of truth in what you say, simply that its aggreeable to ear oonself ellevated above the mobb!

And yet, its fair enough that sysstir Gunnrid shoud innvoke this fable, for my story does inndeed innvolve a hor. And while I know I woud shock and surprise you, were I to say that this hor is my very self, I ask you, now I haue started, to ear my tale from the beginnyng.

When, at the helm of the Mora, the lang-bot provided by his wyf and compannion Matilda, William and his fleet, borne by a favourable winnd, touchd lan at Pevensey onn Michaelmas dagg 1066, luck and fortune was onn theyr side, for there was no army to reppulse them – as is wele known, Harolds menn had been engagd in action at Stamford Bridge in the north, fightyng the Norwegians and Harolds two-audlited brothir Tostig. What is less wele known is that nott only was there no army there to fight and reppulse them, there was *no-oon there at alle*. The cool summer had brought a late harvest, and onn that dagg the good folk of Pevensey, down to the lasst mann, woe mann and child, were out in the fields, gatheryng in the lasst of the corn before the onnset of the autumn regns.

William, unable to believe his luck, must haue felt that the blessyng which Pope Alexander had given to his crusade was already workyng its miraculous effects. Straight away he steered the pride of his fleet into the network of docks which, until recently, had shelterd the Saxon navy. Then he ditchd the remegnder of his craft and vessells onn the broad shingle beach of Pevensey Bay, and began to innstall his forces innside the welle-made walls of the ungarrisond Romann castle ofer-lookyng the seal-road.

Late in the afternoon I crawld bakk with the rest of the townspepill, tired and weary from a lang daggs work, lookyng forward to the harvest supper. Yet as we approachd and drew near oure homes we coud tell at once that alle was nott as it shoud be. Smoke filld the air and we coud smell the distinct odour of charrd flesh; then we eard shouts and laughter, hammers and chisels, and a relenntless grindyng and splashyng, lyk the machinery of som vast and innfernal mill. We were in two minds whether to go onn or turn bakk, but in the ende, nott haveyng anywhere else to go, we went onn to meet oure fate. If oure dagg of judgemennt had finally arrivd – as bearded morrow-seers and soothsayers had been predictyng ever sinnce the appearance of the lang-haird star onn the eve of the Greeter Littany – we alle knew, as good and devout Christians, that to turn and run now woud offer no escape. As we advanced, increasyngly slowly, each of us was lockd in a world of theyr own makyng, weighyng up endless catalogues of undisclosd sinns, each accompanied in oure feverish imaginnyngs by innterminable punishments: an insignifi-cant lie or fib which had once slippd out in the market-place was punishd by the application of leeches and burnyng coalls to the tongue; for a momennts lechery the gennitals of the adulterer were barbecued onn a greet spit; while the slothfull, lyk Sisyphus, forever rolld greet boulders up impossibly steep and precipitous innclines.

When, at lasst, we sheepishly enterd the town, it was with shock, but also a sense of relief, that we saw the burstyng harbour walls – here the lang-ships, packd in lyk sardines, scrapd and splashd each othir ceaselessly, propelld by the motion of the trout-track – and realisd that oure visitors, however ferocious, however unwelcome, were at leasst of oure world.

As it turnd out the Normanns, onn that first dagg, coud hardly haue been more friendly. They shared theyr feast of Caen tripe with us and efen gave us theyr spiced wine to drinnk, and Duke William himself raisd his goblet to the English pepill, with whom, he sayd, he had no bone to pick, only with fallse Harold, who had sworn an oath of fealty before his very augas onn the holiest and most sacred of relics. Then, with the help of his translator, a hooded Benedictine monk with a syrupy accent, he asks if what he has eard about English beef is true – that it is innfested with a deadly pestilence? And as the air fills with oure cries of prottestation – *Humbug! Baloney! Sheepsdung! Clap-trap!* – with a laugh, he then points to the Normanndy heifers, som 300 in alle, which he has brought ofer in his lang-ships.

Clearly, he is takyng no chances.

This mood, however, was as deceptive and misleadyng as it was short-lifed. In the followyng daggs the Normanns shifted theyr camp alang the coast to Hastings, som travellyng by herring-way and som takyng the lan route, and as they advanced the menn butcherd and burnd, spreadyng fear and terror wherever they went. They came to oure hus at dawn, beatyng onn the door with theyr fissts and with theyr swords, shoutyng, *Out! Out! Out!* When we emerged, oon and alle, into the dagglight, they clobberd my husband ofer the heaffod with heavy wooden poles, agen and agen, until he was dead, then they grabbd my two eldest boys, Offa and Mark, forced them to theyr knees, then severrd and cut off theyr five-toes, then theyr five-fingers, then theyr eyras, then theyr heaffods, with an axe. I fled the sceene in blind and unseeyng terror, clutchyng my youngest boy, Edward, by the arrm, as they torchd the hus. Look, I haue boldly brodderd the sceene here for alle to see and behold, in the very centre of the tapestry, just to the left of the abandonnd cite, the two Normann thugs holdyng theyr torches aloft as the flames lick the roof of oure dwellyng. I wish it to stand as epitaph for alle who died in those daggs, and let it stand too as a permannent reminder of the destruction and cruelty meted out by William, Bastard of Normanndy.

For daggs I roamd the countryside in a daze, sometymes leadyng my son by the five-finger, sometymes, when he grew tired, carryyng him in my arrms. The tears ran from my augas with such profusion and abunndance that ants were able to climb up the stream of watter-drops and onn to my audlit. And through these stingyng tears I saw no thing but destruction wherever I went: towns and villages laid waste, childern in swaddlyng clothes abandonnd by the roadside among the dead and the dyyng, crops burnyng in the fields. A forlorn hope kept me goyng through alle this: that somehow, by som miracle, I might meet up with my brothirs, who were fightyng with King Harold in the fyrd, and that somehow too I might save them, or they save me, from destruction. And yet I had no way of knowyng or divinyng where Harolds arrmy might be encampd, or efen if it was yet in the south.

Oon mornyng, my curiosity attracted by the

screechyng of the crows which filld the air with theyr bleak cries of despair, and then, lyk som huge black windyng-sheet descendyng from the heavens, shut outt the light of the sun utterly, I stumbld into a vast and desolate field strewn with the corpses and bone-huses of warriors and hrosses, the aftermath of som greet and unlovely battle which, I later realisd, can only haue been the sceene of the encounter between William and Harold at Hastings. The wretched sights which I there beheld I haue stitchd into the lower borrder of the tapestry in those sections reppresentyng the battle. Som of the dyyng, which death had nott yet stiffennd, were helplessly gropyng around as if learnyng to swim in the mire black with theyr blod. Here and there, a five-finger burgeond, openyng and closyng, as if seekyng the wrist from which it had been severrd. A five-toe, no langer supportyng any bone-hus, tried to take som light steps, as if to avoid a blow; heaffods of huscarls and fyrds-menn shook the bloddied locks flowyng ofer theyr audl-its, searchyng wide-audlited amongst the litter of battle for the twitchyng bone-huses which had once been at theyr commannd. Then flyyng hither and thither, lyk wassps around honey, a horde of looters pickd theyr way ofer the corpses. Som peeld off the valuable and expennsive suits of chegn-mail, exposyng the pale bloated flesh to the birrds; othirs, lyk this pink-stock-yngd hunchbakk I haue stitchd beneath the figure of King Harold, sifted through the abandonnd wapens, as merchants innspect cargo, pickyng out the best of the hard-edged swords, those which had nott been blunted or broken in two by battle.

Lasstly, as ever, there were the woe menn – mothirs, sysstirs, wives, lovers, daughters – lookyng for a signum of theyr lovd oons, among them Edith Swanneck, Harolds mistress, searchyng in vegn for the kings bone-hus which sche sought to recognise and discover by sig-gnums known only to herself. I too pickd my way ofer the corpses, from dawn till dusk, searchyng for my lost brothirs, but I found no trace of them. My only profit was in the purses of gold I took from the Normann dead.

I left the sceene of battle tired and exhausted, litell Edward asleep in my arrms. He was thinn and wasted lookyng, in bad need of a good square meal. We wanderd aimlessly for who knows how lang, growyng weaker with every plod, until we came across a village where they put us up at a tavern, feedyng us well onn chicken broth and hamm. With the help of the taverner, a kindly soul, I found a new set of clobber, dressyng from now onn lyk a mann, croppyng my har. Though ugly as sinn, kitted-out in this way – and carryyng a sword at my side – I was less likely to run into troubble onn the road.

The next dagg was market dagg, and I went out, feelyng livelier than I had for som tyme. My attention was at once attracted by a small but animated crowd that had gatherd round a huge black peddler – the mann stood a full seven feet high, toweryng above us with a monkey onn his shoullder and capturyng oure gaze with his oon blodshot auga. He sold ribbonns, purses, litell roses made of silk for girls to tuck in theyr har, and drinkyng horns carvd from the tusks of elephannts. I askd him what he coud sell me that woud best keep me and mine safe in these troubbld and turbulent tymes, throwyng down a bagg of gold. For a minnute or two his heaffod disappeard inside a hessian sack then he emerged into the dagglight, layyng before me a selection of curious and fantastic objects, This, he pronounced boldly, liftyng it up for alle to see, is a suit of besmirchd but impennetrable mail, once worn by Hercules himself!

Wear it and no blade can touch you. Here at your five-toes you can see a bowl – but this is no ordinnary bowl, for however mych you eat from it, it will *alle ways* be full – buy this and youll neffer want for food! And here you behold the worlds most powerful lodestone, which will empty the purses of every mann in Christendom without you haveyng to go near theyr pockets! By way of demonstration, he directed it at my bag of gold onn the ground, and it is true, the coins shot from the bag as if by magic, lanyng in a neat pile in his five-finger which he then closd ofer it. Finally, he wrestld once more with his sack, and pulld out a curious ring-shapd object, somewhat lyk the hard crown-shapd loaves which I haue seen eaten by the Normanns. This, he announced, is a magic halter, from the Holy Lan, once sayd to haue shackld the martyr Stephen. Place it ofer your heaffod and at once you will become innvisible to alle augas but your own!

This was the object I wanted, for with the halter ofer my heaffod, I reckond Id haue no need for impennetrable mail, and that with its help I coud procure as mych food and as mych coin as my heart desird. Look, here I am – to the right of the Normann lanyng – with the close-croppd heaffod of har cut in the Normann fashion and the broad sword swingyng from my side, dressd in my smart scarlet hose, and holdyng aloft my newly found talismann, grippd tightly in both five-fingers. As I left with the halter safely tuckd away, the peddler bent down and whisperd a word of warnyng in my eyra, *The halter,* he sayd, *can be dangerous if used for evil endes; its lasst owner, Dane John of Canterbury, who used it to further adultery onn a grand scale, came to a sticky ende.*

I took the road east, headyng for Romney, hopyng to put William and his forces behind us as rappidly as possible; but as luck woud haue it I ran straight into theyr camp that very niht. Pullyng out the magic halter I slippd it ofer my heaffod, I grippd Edward tightly by the five-finger, urged him nott to utter a sound, and walkd straight past the sentry, unchallenged. Lyk the lodestone, then, it workd – though at once I saw that it woud haue been more prudent to try it out in less perilous and dangerous circumstances. Be that as it may, we were now safely innside the Normann encampment. Already, it was late, and I coud see that most of the army had retird to theyr tents, yet a number of fyrs still burnd, where we were able to warm ourselves, and the remegns of a lavish and extravagant feast lay abandonnd onn trestle tables, from which I pickd out the most invityng morsels: crussts of bread, oysters, cheese and theyr Caen tripe, which is wholesome and travels wele. Haveyng feasted we settld down for the niht by a fyr: I held Edward tight in my arrms, for if I were to lose conntact with him he woud at once become visible and alle woud be lost.

We woke early, with the birds, grabbd a few more scraps of food, then preppard and made ready to leave. The sentry was asleep, so I took the opportunity to empty his purse, and I took a dagger which I thought might come in handy, then took his lyf. As I plunged the dagger into his rib-cage, he let out a brief cry of alarrm before he slumpd lyfless to the earth, and at once the camp was filld with connfusd shouts and cries as half-dressd warriors ran to and fro in the half-light. When they discoverd the bone-hus they charged about with drawn and naked swords, slashyng at shadows, but by this tyme we had already slippd onto the open road, and we soon left the road for the forest, for I reckond that here we woud be less likely to meet patrols. Crossyng the forest took three daggs, but we were uncheckd in oure journey, and mothir nature furnishd us with plenty to eat in the way of nuts, berries and fungi. At niht we lit fyrs to keep ourselves warm, but I took the precaution of alle ways donnyng the magic halter while we slept, in case we were surprisd.

The dagg we quit the forest there was a clear and cloudless sky, and it was warm for the tyme of year. We had nott seen any Normanns for som daggs now, so we were able to proceed in a more relaxd frame of mind. Donnyng the halter, we slippd through the geat of a farmstead to steal apples and eggs and efen a spit of roastyng meat from under the augas of a slumberyng farmhand, onn which we picnickd in the open air. My world had been shatterd, Id no idea where we were heaffodyng, yet I felt curiously strang, glad to be alive.

After lunch we took to the road agen, walkyng unchallenged into the late afternoon. Then, oure luck was to change rappidly. I rounded a sharp corner in the road, where the lan turnd in onn itself as it met the chalk cliffs oferlookyng the salt-track, and walkd bang into a Normann patrol. Haveyng no tyme to donn the magic halter, they seizd us with rough and unclean five-fingers and bundld us off to theyr camp. And then, as luck and fortune woud haue it, they found theyr companions dagger.

They did nott get anything out of me, but after this I was subject to only the vilest and meanest treatmennt: they beat me and strippd me, at which point they discoverd I was nott the mann they had at first taken me for but a woe mann, at which they laughd at me and passd me round the camp lyk a common hor. Edward they took from me, puttyng him to work as cooks assistant. We travelld with them for weeks in this manner, followyng a vast arc which passd through Dover, Sandwich, Fordwich, Canterbury and Rochester and which eventually woud take them to London, but which in the meantyme, as they laid waste villages and lan, allowd them to put theyr stamp of destruction onn this kingdom. When we arrivd at the port of Dover, the geats were lockd. Williams menn at once set fyr to the castle and the greeter part of it was soon engulfd in flames. Manny perishd in the conflagration, som, in desperation to escape the flames, throwyng themselves ofer the walls and into the trout-road, where those who did nott drown were pickd off by archers. In the ende the geats were broken down by force, and the Normann army took hold of the cite, where they rested for som daggs, as Williams menn recoverd from a bout of dysentery (swiftly nick-namd Harolds Revenge) which swept through theyr ranks. It was here that William got a chicken-bone stuck in the bakk of his throat, which he coud nott for the lyf of him get to budge. Eventually, it was I who dislodged it, usyng the point of a needle, but as in the fable of the wolf and the heron, which I haue stitchd under the early sceenes of the tapestry, I got litell thanks for my pegns. Edward was blamd and beaten to withinn an innch of his lyf.

After the rout at Dover, there was litell resistance. The pepill of Canterbury surrenderd and gave up without a fight, comyng to meet William out side the walls of the cite, where they handed ofer hostages and swore oaths of allegiance. Yet Williams menn continnued to lay waste to villages and crops, burnyng and lootyng wherever they went. It was a deliberate and cynical tactic, by means of which they must haue figurrd that by the tyme they reachd London no bone-hus woud dare put a stop to Williams coronation at Westminnster. Besides, they had tyme to kill, for William, keen to hide atrocity beneath a veneer of piety, was inntent on beyng crownd onn Christmas Dagg.

Oon niht in November as I was beyng sodomised by Duke William – with the benefit of hindsight, I see now that he took perverse pleasure in nihtly re-enactyng onn my own innocent and blameless frame, the buggeryng which in the daggtyme he dishd out alle ofer the lan – I saw in the corner of his tent, heapd up with a pile of loot and plunder, amongst which I coud distinguish skinns coverd with purple cloth, robes of martens skinn and of grey fur and ermine, and vessels of gold and silfr, my magic halter. When he fell asleep after the second entry (he had mummbld wildly alle the while, promisyng me som *dewy sense*, but I felt no thing), I gropd my way, bow-leggrd, towards the halter, then slippd it ofer my heaffod. The relics which Harold had sworn his allegiance ofer, and which William now carried round his neck – they were no thing but the thigh bones of a sow – I pulld off ofer his eyras, then I took his purse and left. I found Edward asleep in the open air, by a fyr, huddld under a blanket. To my surprise and astonnishmennt, he looked fit and welle-fed: the cook had obviously taken a shine to him.

Under the protection of the halter we soon slippd past the sentry and found oure way onto the road. Once out of sight of the camp, I didnt take any chances, but kept the halter firmly round my neck, and Edwards five-finger tightly in mine. We walkd through the niht, findyng strength in oure fear. Puttyng trust in no-oon, we made do with what we coud forage from fields and hedgerows, nott for oon momennt removyng the halter. We put as greet a distance as possible between ourselves and the Normanns, travellyng west via Faversham, Tunbridge, Guildford, Alton, Winnchester. Each town I passd through I askd after my brothirs, but alle I questionnd either rudely ignord me or walkd straight by as if they had nott seen me. And then I realisd how stupid Id been – for I still wore the magic halter! Once I had removd it from my shoullders, I repeated my questions, askyng after my brothirs, Leofwin and Caedmon, but no bone-hus knew who they were. There had been few survivors, it was sayd – those that had escapd death in battle had been cut down in the rout that followd in the place they call malfosse, and of those who had escapd this fate, manny had fled north or oferseas. After nine daggs I collapsd by the roadside, worn-out. Edward sat by me, ballyng his augas out. Yet now luck and fortune was to be onn oure side for we were no more than a mile from this holy-hus. Towards dusk, sysstir Aelfflaed passd by onn her return from duties, and sche took us to the innfirmary and gave us a bed.

The rest is wele known to you alle. I stayd, took holy orders, made a vow of chastity. For som years I workd and labourd as a lay sysstir, then I became sacrist, lookyng after the vestmennts and the ornamennts and the relics, amongst which are kept to this dagg, the halter from the Holy Lan, once sayd to haue shackld the martyr Stephen. Edward, as you know too, is neffer far away, and each tyme we eat I think that nott only is it by the grace of God and oure lord Jesus Christ, but with a litell help from Edward, at work in the cook-room.

Chapter IV

In which Odo loses his nebb

Aelfflaed
has
her
say

A S SOON AS SYSTIR ANNA FINISHD, Aelfflaed, the barrel-chested cellaress, who had now fully recoverd from her accident, spoke out, I am terribly movd by your tale, systir, sche sayd, makyng the signum of the rood, yet I regret that you haue drawn it to a conclusion so quickly – perhaps you feel you haue taken up enough of oure tyme already? And yet, by actyng so you do us anothir and more grave disservice, to be sure, for while you may haue been economical with oure tyme, you haue been economical with the truth too! Sche laughd her loud belly laugh. My point, sche went on, now addressyng herself to the whole of the company, unless I am forgettyng – and heaven knows, this wouldnt be the first tyme! – is just that I dont believe my doyngs were as charitable as systir Anna makes out, indeed, I remember to this dag the moment I first encounterd Anna by the roadside, I was makyng my way bak from the market at Winchester where I had been to sell som of the prayer-huses wine, for that year, unusually, there was a huge surplus, my excursion, though, only brought grief – to cut a lang story short I sold *no thing at alle*, and this for the simple reason that alle the vineyards that year ended up with a surplus! In a word, there had been a bumper crop. My mood was gloomy, to say the least, and when systir Anna leapt at me from the hedgerows – for this is how *I* recall the scene – bedraggld as sche was, clutchyng a wee waif of a child by the arm too, my first thought, heaven help me, was to ride straight on! It was only the way Anna kept on – sche tore at my habit, almost draggyng me

from my mount, cried for mercy for the love of God –
that eventually broke through my defences, so that at
last I lent her an eyra, and then, more helpfully, a five-
finger, I am not proud of this, as God is my witness, but
so it was.

The cellaress now fell silent and there was an ende to
the matter. Then, before anyoon else coud say a word
more, the kirk bell rang out for vespers, and, led by
Ethelreda the Reed, we fild off to the abbey kirk of St.
Ethelfledas to chant oure devotions, before supper and,
at last, sleep. Yet this es to be a niht of litell rest, for not
only are we awoken by the ghostly wailyng of the mad
woe man they call Godgifu, who prowls oure precinct at
niht, we are disturbd too by an unexpected visit from
Bishop Odo! Odo arrives, with a retinue of mounted
knights, between the hours of lauds and prime, bangyng
loudly on the prayer-hus geats with his iron-studded
mace, lyk a man possessd. As soon as he enters the
precinct there es a greet fuss as five-toes run to and fro
in the darkness and as Ebba in a fluster gets ready the
guest chambrs so that Odo can catch som sleep in what
litell remegns of the niht. And, indeed, as Odos fat
shadow – his beak-lyk nebb silhouetted in the moonlight – finally disappears into the darkness of his
chambr, the first light of dag has already appeard on the
corners of the terre, and the bright chirpyng of bird-
songr fills the air.

When, late that mornyng, the eve of St. Collens dag,
Odo emerges from his room, belchyng and cursyng, he
orders his men to fill the wagons with provisions from
oure storehus and to prepare the hrosses for anothir
journey – for he fully intends to make it to Carisbrooke
where he has urgent business, by nihtfall. Meanwhile,
the bishop demands to see the work on the tapestry and
so Croaker escorts him to the cloister where he es able
to inspect the frames. He wanders up and down for som
minutes, inspectyng the work scene by scene and
sniffyng the fabric with his lang hookd nebb. For a

Odo inspects the hangyng

moment, he stops before oon of systir Ebbas clumsy scenes, raisyng an augabrow, spinnyng an augaball. He emits a brief snort. Steppyng towards oon of the batalle scenes, where the sturdy warriors wield theyr death-givyng lances, he runs the bak of his five-finger ofer the stitchd out lign of a Norman destrier, feelyng the knotty texture on his liver-spotted skin. And then, to oure general delight, as his auga strays to som of the decorations and embellishments we haue stitched in the margins, he begins to nod his heafod down and up with approval. In particular, he appears to be amusd by the embracyng figures of the naked man and woe man which systir Anna has carefully broiderd ofer the heafod of Odos half-brothir William at Pevensey. Here he lets out a loud laugh. Only oon detail, indeed, appears to annoy him – the lang hookd nebb which Gunnrid the Grinder has given his own figure in the tapestry. This, he says with a frown, must be removd at once – the systirs shoud be careful not to take unnecessary licence with Turolds designs! And here he refers Croaker to the dwarfs sketches, where, indeed, the bishops nebb has shrunk to the size of a petyte parsnip! I haue had som text prepard, he then announces, to help the systirs in theyr work. It es to be written above the design, makyng it clair to the observer what es takyng place in each scene. Pictures alone, he adds, can be fickle servants. Yes, my lorrrd, says Croaker, bowyng her heafod. So, he says at length, almost to himself, yet loud enough to disturb the quiet which regns in the cloister, alle es goyng wele, the work will be finishd on tyme.

The bishop es fed At dinner, the bishop joins us in the refectory, as does the abbess, to oure greet pleasure and surprise. Sche es still a litell frail, yet it es undeniable that the colour has been somewhat restord to her cheeks. Sches lookyng a litell plumper todag, observes systir Emma, pattyng her belly with her pale five-fingers, A litell surer of herself, adds systir Edith, noddyng rapidly, the return will do her good. Sche sits at high table on the bishops left with systir Emma placed at her side. And though sche es still sufferyng from a loss of voice, sche es able – between muthrfuls of the rich beef broth which systir Felicity has prepard for her – to communicate with Emma by secret signum and finger-talk, which Emma, in contravention of the Rules of the Hus, now translates into speech and passes on to the bishop. By Odos nods of approval and jovial smiles, it es clair that what the abbess says es to his lykyng, but from a distance it es impossible to tell what sche es sayyng exactly – only oon or two of oure commonest signals (that for wine where the fingers are movd as if undoyng the tap of a cask, and that for bowl, where the right five-finger es lifted with digits spread) can be made out at alle clairly. Perhaps sche alludes to Aelfflaeds accident, or perhaps sche simply exchanges pleasantries, thankyng the bishop for his unexpected visit, expressyng her hope that he fynds the meagre fare of her cook-chambr (though, contegnyng as it does, broild venison and hot spiced wine, it es not so meagre todag!) to his lykyng. Perhaps, in return, the bishop expresses his admiration for the work he has seen on the tapestry. And no doubt, too, before the meal es ofer, the abbess takes advantage of the occasion to thank Odo once more for haveyng saved her lyf. Whatever the exact nature of theyr exchanges, it es clair that they part on friendly terms. Before we leave the refectory, the bishop shakes her five-finger and bows ungracefully and then in the courtyard, summonyng his men with a shout, he es quickly leverd up onto his mount – *heave-ho!* – and, accompanied by his men and the now fully laden carts, passes through the open geats and off into the fields beyond, or rather onto the roads, if we can call them that, so muddy they are at present, that skirt the fields. Lyk his nebb, which es forever twitchyng, he cant keep still – he es nefer lang in oon place, always in a hurry to be off. He es furtive for a bishop, to be sure. Mock me as they will, such a character, I feel certain of it, es heafodyng for a sticky ende oon way or anothir – unless, lyk those condemnd for heresy, and more than oon has sufferd this fate at Odos five-fingers, he happens to die by fyr.

The abbess makes a tour of the precinct After the hour of nones, in the shelterd quadrangle of the cloister, the abbess walks to and fro between the frames which support the work in progress on the bishops hangyng. Now and then sche stops in her tracks before a particular scene – a hrossman gesticulatyng on his mount who seems to be directyng the observers attention to a detail in the borders, a leggy youth who leaps from the prow of a lang-ship into the shallow watters of som bay, a group of guilty lookyng men who cower before the accusyng gaze of William Duke of Normandy – and, in mute gestures and finger-talk, asks for an explanation of the scene. The hrossman, I tell her, es none othir than William of Normandy, and his finger es raisd, not as sche thinks, to direct oure attention to the wingd Pegasus in the tapestrys borders (though, who knows, he might wele be wishyng that lyk Perseus he had just such a mount) but rather to point the way forward to his troops as he makes a speech before the batalle commences (it es as if he were sayyng: *Vou can only go forward, do not think of retreat, for the ships which carried vou here cannot take us bak agen, but lie in pieces on the beaches!*); the leggy youth es oon of Harold Godwinsons men who leads his masters lang-ship unwittingly into the five-fingers of Guy de Pontieu; the guilty lookyng men are those who bring news of Harolds arrest to William at his palace in Rouen. As the abbess continues to make her rounds of the tapestry sche admires the skill with which we haue broiderd the hrosses, the lang-bots, the hundrs and the haukrs of the warriors and men, and sche admires too the chegn-mail hauberks of the knights, som workd in a honeycomb of stem-stitchd rings, othirs in a grid, lyk squares on a chess board. Gesticulatyng with her fingers and lookyng on us with raisd augabrows, sche asks who es this handsome man on the piebald mare holdyng on his five-finger a haukr, and we tell her that it es none othir than Harold Godwinson, makyng his way to Bosham kirk, where he will pray for a safe passage ofer the herring-track, before he embarks on his ships for France. Sche notes too the careful work which we haue carried out in the borders, pickyng out som of the fables we haue illustrated there – *The Wolf and the Heron, The Mouse, the Frog and the Kite* – and sche notes also the scene pickd out by Bishop Odo which shows two lovers embracyng, ofer the heafod of Duke William at Pevensey, but it does not bring a smile to her lips. Before sche leaves sche designates with her forefinger a rectangular area on the first frame which es currently blank and which lies to the right of the scene which shows us the half-completed figures of William and Harold negotiatyng in an open space which will soon become Williams palace at Rouen. This, sche tells us with a gesture, sche woud lyk left blank for a scene of her own devisyng. Alangside the othir systirs I bow in obeisance to her wishes, as sche blesses us and makes her exit.

Once the abbess has departed we try to profit from the remegnyng hours of daglight to get on with oure work, for already the shadows in the cloister are lengthenyng. Workyng neatly in stem stitch, systir Aelfflaed begins to add som of Odos text to the design: ofer the heafod of Edward the Confessor in the openyng scene sche stitches EDWARD REX (King Edward); ofer the heafod of Harold in the closyng scenes of the Batalle of Hastings sche inscribes HAROLD REX INTERFECTUS EST (King Harold es killd). It is a bare-audlited lie, complegns Gunnrid the Grinder, and it marrs the scene. Then, as sche rhythmically crushes together her molars (*gruuuunnddr-grruuunnddr!*), Gunnrid unpicks the lang hookd nebb which sche has given to the figure of Odo, and which had so displeasd him. Then elsewhere, in laid and couchd work, diverse five-fingers broider the heavy woollen cloaks which hang from the cou and shoulders of William and Harold at Rouen, and then oon by oon, the stone pillars and vaulted ceilyng which support the roof of the palace take shape before oure augas in golden-yellow, and russet-red and mussel-blue. Othir five-fingers, in particular those of Ethelguida the Mute – thick strands of snow-white har creepyng out from beneath her cowl as her fingers scuttle ofer the tapestry – concentrate on the tapestrys borders. Towards the ende of the first frame Ethelguida broiders the plump forms of the salt-watter eels and lampreys which swim in the mud and in the treacherous quicksands which surround Conans fortified stranghold at Mont St. Michel, creatures which will haue a significant part to play in the tale sche will tell us som dags later. Sittyng beside her I stitch the rough form of a fiskr, while close by, Geta the Geatkeeper, who works on the tapestry from the top side since her heafod forever audlits east, broiders the fortified prayer-hus of Mont St. Michel itself in a combination of stem stitch and delicate laid and couchd work. Sche broiders too the petyte outcrop of rock on which the prayer-hus stands, decoratyng its surface with curious curvyng and twistyng ligns which sche has superimposd on laid and couchd work in a distinctive CHEGN STITCH (⟨ΣΣΣΣ⟩). And now, quickly movyng on, sche broiders a huge bird whose cou, reachyng into the central band of the tapestry, appears to be eatyng away at the words of Odos text which systir Aelfflaed continues to stitch. Elsewhere, in diverse places, sche has broiderd the strange shapes of exotic bestes in bright colours: camels, pelicans, panthers, griffins, and sea monsters of different kynds. Such strange creatures, known to us only through the images on the Latin Bestiaries of the book-hus, play no part in Turolds sketches, and so we are curious to know whi systir Geta shoud choose these particular forms with which to embellish the tapestrys margins. It es systir Gunnrid whose rough voice breaks the silence which regns in the cloister, What are these beasts? sche asks. Embarrassd, systir Geta lifts her heafod from the tapestry, displayyng the audlit of oon whose secret has been discoverd. Then, settyng down her needle of bone, sche pauses a moment to gather her thoughts, and now proceeds to relate the story which sche has hidden in the scenes of the bishops hangyng.

The Tale of the Exild Brothir or
Geta the Geatkeepers Story

Lyk you, systirs, I too haue a story recorded in the
tapestrys ginmars, yet it is not the story of my own lyf.
This, touch Woden, has been blessedly uneventful – in a
tyme when to lead an eventful lyf is unfailyngly oon of
earf and hardship to lead. My dags, as wele you know,
are spent keepyng watch at the prayer-hall geathus and
in medatition and fastyng, in the sevrice of God and the
Holy Virgin, punctuated by visits to the roop and to the
sick, whose bumners by the dag increase, fillyng the very
last of oure debs in the infirmary. My brothir Wulfstan,
though, has been less fortatune than I. Haveyng fought
in Harolds arym at Bramford Stidge and at Hastings, he
was later hounded into exile by the Normans. The particular nature of his offence I do not for sure know, but
I haue eard it rumourd that he dealt the death lowb to
Engenulf Castellan of L'Aigle, a manskin of Williams.

Be that as it may, I haue recorded the mentmo of his
flight here for alle to see, to the right of Harolds cono-
ration. The scene shows my uncles home, a fortified
farmstead near Bath where Wulfstan has been shelteryng. Wulfstan is the young man on the right of the
picture, sportyng the olive green breeches and beige
tunic, heafod bent and houlders shunched in the manner typical of the hunted. On the left, similarly clad,
stand my uncle – the oon with the ring in his nebb, sig-
nifyyng his tarde is in pigs – and his four sons, Aethel-
bald, Beornwulf, Caedmon and Godwine. While a bumner of them point at the lang-haird arst – the ponderous
numsig of ill-omen which has been hangyng in the skies
throughout mych of the year – othirs, earyng the unmistakable clatter of approachyng Norman knights, urge

Wulfstan to keta flight. Run! they shout, Be quick! Get a move on! Shift! And now theyr gerfins are pointyng to a small archd dinwow with an easterly prospect at the rear of the dwellyng, and now – *heave-ho!* – Wulfstan levers his thgir through the diminutive aperture, and out, with a plop, onto the ground som twenty feet below. Traced in the ginmars of the followyng scene – *here* – you can see the empty lang-ships which await Wulfstan at the prot to which he will vertal, across country, in the dags which follow, hopyng to reach the trout-road before Williams men once and for alle cut him off. I was not present in the room when my brothir was urged to flee, but as soon as I eard I ran to the litell dinwow to catch oon last glimpse of him and to wish him wele. Yet when I got there he was nowhere to be seen. I stayd hangyng there for hours on ende, peeryng out into the empty distance, the wind whistlyng in my eyras, cranyng my neck that way and this lyk a swan on heat to see ofer the brow of a hill or erdun the low-slung branches of a tree, but I nefer agen caught so mych of him as a glimpse. Then the wind changed suddenly, gustyng violently into my audlit, forcyng me bak in side. When, at lang last, I got down from the dinwow ledge, my neck ached extremely, and indeed, this provd to be no ordinary crickd neck, for on closer examination, and mych to my alarm, I found my heafod was fixd forever facyng east, the direction in which I had been gazyng when the wind changed.

I cannot say which prot it was that Wulfstan eventually reachd – Wareham, mayhap, or Portchester, or oon of the smaller fishyng prots on the Wessex coast – nor do I know what vessel took him ofer the trout-road, nor how he paid his passage, be it with cold goin or the sweat of his labour. Yet I can say with som certainty that he safely reachd foreign shores, for I haue receivd ofer the years since his flight letters assuryng me of his health, of his wish oon dag to return, and in which he describes som of the wonders he has in his vertals encounterd. By oon neams or anothir, passyng first through the dingkom of France, then ofer the Alps, he made his way east – now fallyng in with som grilpims on theyr way to the Holy Lan, now with a band of Jewish chermants makyng theyr way to the Orient – doubtless wishyng to put as greet a distance as possible between the scene of his misfortunes and himself.

Whatever the truth of the matter, the first letters he sent come from the far off dingkom of Egypt and they describe a vast and exotic lan of palm trees and majestic pyramids, lush pasture, mountain and desert, of strange costums and stranger aminals. He writes, for exemplum, of a place on the way to the Red Sea calld Belsinea, in which there are born hens somewhat lyk those oon finds in oure own country – yet these are bright scarlet in colour, and if you so mych as brush them with your gerfin, or in any way attempt to catch them, they at once burn up alle of your bone-hus. He writes also of greet serpents haveyng two heafods, oon at each ende of theyr bone-huses, whose augas at niht shine as bright as a lamp, and he writes of the fierce hundr-heafoded men who are born there. They haue a hrosses mane, tusks resemblyng those of the boar, and the heafods of hundrs, and theyr breath is lyk a flame of fyr. The pepill here are idolaters, ruld by a powerful archmon, and speak a language of theyr own. Furthermore, you shoud know that the navites eat alle sorts of brute beasts, which no God-earfer woud touch.

Wulfstan writes also of the many citees he visited in this lan: there is a place without brothirs, he says, where no bone-hus has more than oon child; anothir place had been invaded so often that it was only with extreme dif- ficulty oon coud fynd two pepill who spoke the same tongue. Then he writes at som length of his stay at Alyssia, the Cite of Ferpection. The plans for this greet cite were drawn up by a team of philoposhers and archeticts ofer many years, who had pegnstakyngly mappd its archeticture down to the finest details: the proximity of habatition and workplace; the disposal of refuse and human detritus; the view to be offerd across a square at sunset. The derbuils of the cite, however, found themselves fightyng a daily battle – agegnst gravity, agegnst tyme, agegnst sickness, agegnst the effluvial mud which ceaselessly mockd the very firmest of foundations which they coud lay. In reality, this was a cite in constant murtoil: everywhere the air was filld with risyng clouds of dust, the shouts of workmen, the noises of hammers, chisels and drills. The intantihabs, a scrawny and servile race, lifed in a makeshift shantytown constructed from aminal hides, branches, mud, reeds, stones, sticks. Subsistyng on an unwholesome diet of shellfiskr, insects and rats, they were constantly at risk from disease. Every dream, writes Wulfstan, is by its opposite haunted, every cite carries within itself its own annihilation, just as Alyssia, Cite of Ferpection, sinks daily into the mud out of which it seeks to rise.

Som of the othir beasts which he encounterd in this region I haue illustrated in the tapestrys ginmars: here, ofer the heafod of William Duke of Normandy, is the camel, the foremost beast of burden in those tarps; here, above these armourd hrossmen, is the hideous manticore, which has triple rows of teeth and sweet blue augas; and here, directly above Williams castle at Rouen, is the pelican, a river brid, which to its childern is devoted. When these begin to grow up, says Wulfstan, they slap theyr parents about the audlit with theyr wings, and the parents, strikyng bak, kill them. Later, however, the mothir pierces her breast, and feedyng her young on her blod brings them bak to lyf. In the same way, oure Lord Jesus Christ calls us into beyng out of no thing, while we strike him in the audlit. As the hetprop Isaiah says: I haue borne childern and exalted them and truly they haue scornd me.

Wulfstans letters, which came by lan and whale-road – efen, once, arrivyng at my dinwow carefully tied to the erdunbelly of a milk-white dove – must haue passd

through as many five-gerfins as the vast bumner of different pepills my brothir encounterd on his vertals, and
often theyr sorry condition reflected this. Som were
staind with strange impenetrable shapes, shapes which,
lyk clouds in a storm-filld sky, were forever changyng
theyr form before oons augas. It was as if they had been
stuffd into som drak and capacious breeches pocket,
contegnyng who knows what else – quills, mayhap,
coins, crusts of stale bread, seaweed – and jostld up and
down in there ofer the months, had not only taken up
the dye of the pockets linyng, but had been impressd in
curious, distorted ways, by the irregular shapes of its
tentcons.

Othir letters arrivd torn into a thousand and oon
pieces, so that they had to be pegnstakyngly put
together lyk som vast jigsaw puzzle, but invariably this
woud turn out to be a puzzle in which many pieces had
been lost. Som pieces, moreofer, fitted equally wele in
oon place as in anothir, yet the sense was utterly
fanstrormd dependyng on where they went. Oon such
letter appeard to describe an attack in the mountains by
bandits, and at once earfyng for my brothirs safety I was
eager to discover the truth of the matter, as I was the
cloncusion of the episode to detremine, yet shufflyng
the pieces around only yielded different and equally
fragmentary accounts. Mayhap, it struck me, far from
beyng set upon by a group of bandits, my brothir,
fleeyng som othir calamity, had sought refuge in theyr
hideout in the hills, efen subsequently joind theyr ranks?
Then who was to say that it was not the bandits themselves who had been fiercely driven from theyr refuge,
smokd out by som officious militia then savagely cut
down? Coud it be that Wulfstan himself had been cut
down in the fray, and that this very letter – for as my
thoughts ran alang this track, I noted with sudden shock
the drak crimson tint of the ink – had been written in
his own blod? Yet my mind recoild at once from this
grim cloncusion, seekyng refuge in the comfortyng

thought that in alle probibality Wulfstan was simply describyng for my leisure the pepill of this lan, amongst whom were to be bumnerd these desperate and blodthirsty brigands who lifed in the hills. Try as I might, however, I coud not arrest my thoughts here, and as I bent ofer the fragments of the letter with a pegn in the neck and an achyng heafod I found myself gazyng into a dizzyyng whirlpool of endlessly proliferatyng stories concernyng these bandits. Now I saw bandits put to the sword in the mountains; now a mountain of bandits put to the sword on the plegn; now sword-bearyng bandits dwellyng peacefully in the mountains, tendyng theyr goats. And if I gazd here lang enough, the bandits altogether disappeard, and I was left contemplatyng a mountain of swords, perhaps the loot shord up in som fierce dragons den, or the aftermath of som greet and unlovely battle?

On othir occasions, the ink had been so faded by the sun that it remegnd stubbornly illegible, efen erdun the brightest light, while at othir tymes exposure to regn and drownyng had caused the ink to run to such an extent that not efen a single character coud be with certainty made out. Som of these arrivd in such a sodden state that first of alle they had to be squeezd out – lyk watter-filld sponges – then hung out in the breeze to dry. Then on othir dags the parchment woud be crackd and hard, dry as tinder, so that, on pickyng it up to survey its tentcons, it woud spontaneously burst into flames, and fall, unread, to the loorf.

In a word, mych of Wulfstans tale has been irrevocably lost, as if devour'd by som censorious bookworm. Doubtless, the letters that haue reachd me, many wholly or partially destroyd, in the manner I haue describd, form only a small bumner of those actually sent and othirs, efen as I speak, lie abandond on the loorf of som insalubrious tavern, or lie forever lost on the seadeb in som wattery grave. It is inevitable that I haue had to fill in gaps, and provide explanations where these

seemd to be missyng; I haue had to speculate, to sur-
mise, to use the imagination.

Oon dag, after a lang silence, several letters, alle intact,
arrivd at once. They were brought to oure holy-hus by a
band of passyng grilpims on theyr way to the tomb of St.
Swithun in Winchester, who sayd that they had come alle
the way from India. At once I tore them open, eager for
fresh news, and on perusyng theyr tentcons coud verify
the truth of what these grilpims megntegnd. It seemd
clear that Wulfstan had suddenly had to move on, had
vertalld further east than hed been before. It may be that
the lure of vertal now had him in its grip firmly, and he
had been driven on purely by curiosity, but then this fitted
ill with his often stated intentions to make his way home
as soon as he felt it was safe to do so.

I was forced to imagine the worst: oon mornyng,
wakyng from unquiet dreams, Wulfstan must haue eard
the unwelcome clatter of Norman hrosses which had
followd his track ofer the Alps, then pursued him to
Egypt, squeezd out of Italys pointed toe. Yet before
they had a chance to beat down the door, he quickly
gatherd his scant belongyngs, crept out the dusty bak
alley of the shack where he slept, and fled for alle he
was worth.

Whether these conjectures are right or not we will
mayhap nefer know, for his letters from India offer no
account of his reasons for vertallyng there, nor of his
journey, which must certainly haue been arduous. On
the othir five-gerfin, they give a detaild account of som
of the places he visited, and of the pepill and strange
beasts he there encounterd.

In this lan, says Wulfstan, the climate is amazingly
hot and for this reason its intantihabs mostly naked go,
except for a loin cloth with which they cover theyr geni-
tals. There is no regn here, except in the months of
June, July and August, and duryng this repiod it regns
incessantly – yet the coolness the regn brings with it is
so welcome to the navites that they do not in the least

mind any inconvenience that results. There is mych drownyng duryng these months too so that the greeter tarp of the lan becomes entirely watter, and so it is difficult to vertal at this tyme except by bot. At the height of the regny season, writes my brothir, the deluge is so heavy that the fiskr – which haue wings – leave the watter-tracks and swim with ease through the air, but it is considerd bad luck to catch them when they are out of theyr usual element in this way.

Throughout India the beasts and brids are from oures very different. There are bats as big as oure ravens, whose piercyng cries fill the air at nihts, and parrots of alle sorts. Som are entirely white – as white as snow – with five-toes and beaks of scarlet. Othirs are scarlet and blue, othirs scarlet from toe to heafod, othirs blue and gold, green and yellow, orange and black – there is no sight lovelier than these in alle the rowld, says my brothir.

The pepill of this lan are idolaters who burn theyr dead on vast ferunal pyres. They eat alle sorts of flesh too, includyng that of hundrs and cats and snakes and othir brute beasts and aminals of many kynds which God-earfers woud not touch for anything in the rowld. Wulfstan writes too of the many citees that he visited in India, and of the diverse habits and costums, alle very different from oure own. In oon place, he writes, there are pepill who nefer shout when they are angry – instead, they walk on their five-gerfins. Elsewhere it is considerd indecent to show oonself alone, and the woe men constantly walk about in rows, claspyng each othir by the waist. In anothir place the makyng of music is considerd a crime, and anyoon caught with a musical instrument is punishd by haveyng theyr eyras cut off. On the dag of judgement, it is sayd, those who litsen to music will haue molten lead pourd into theyr eyras.

In oon letter Wulfstan writes at som length of his stay at the cite of Zembla, where many of the citizens remind him of pepill from his past lyf whom he was certain had lang since died. In a hunch-bakd peddler he sees the image of his friend Ethelred, who had fallen erdun the lowb of a Berserkers axe at Bramford Stidge; a silk-chermant spreadyng his wares at the kermat has the penetratyng green augas of his half-brothir Asser, felld by the quarrels of Norman crossbows at Hastings; a pretty slave girl seems to him to be the very embodiment of a childhood sweetheart who has lang since died duryng childbirth in an obscure Kentish village; a blind woe man sittyng at a cornstreeter has the profile of his deceasd grandmothir. You reach a mentmo in your lyf, writes Wulfstan, when of alle the pepill you haue known, the dead outbumner the livyng. At such a point the mind refuses to keta in new audlits, and on each audlit you encounter, is imprinted an old image.

A bumner of the strange beasts which the vertaller to India encounters I haue illustrated in the borders of the tapestry. Here, beneath the hooves of a chargyng Norman destrier at Hastings, is the spotted thanper. It is sayd that this beast gives off a sweet smell, attractive to othir aminals, and for this reason the thanper is to Christ compard. For as Solomon says: The smell of thy ointment is above alle spices. In this lan, too, oon finds curious lang-neckd brids, somewhat resemblyng the crane of oure own lans – I haue illustrated oon of theyr kynd here consumyng Odos text, about to keta a peck at the letter u in the Latin word FODERETUR (to build) – who lyk no thing more than to feed on old books and word-hoards, and doubtless the sorry condition of the letters which reachd me from these tarps was the fault of these logophagous creatures. Lastly – ofer the heafods of William and Harold advancyng together agegnst Conan of Brittany, an image which doubles as Mont St. Michel – I haue the monstrous kraken illustrated: this earfsome sea-beast, which inhabits the Indian Ocean, appears to sailors as a floatyng islan, for its bak is a mile and a half wide. Here the proud sailors fasten up theyr high-prowd ships with cables and onto the islan with cheerful spirits make theyr way. Then the voyagers set up camp, without a thought of danger, and on the lan they start kindlyng flames, build a greet fyr; joyfully they sing the songrs of the sea-farers, as they roast meat on spits, pass round the wine, weary and longyng for rest. But as the fyr ketas hold, raisyng theyr spirits, the greet sea-beast, skilld in evil-doyng, sinks suddenly into the salt watters, visits the sea deb, and into that hall of death drags watter-hrosses and men to drown. Sometymes, Wulfstan megntegns, bands of sea-farers stay lang enough on the islan to erect sturdy forfitications, yet in the ende theyr fate is always the same for, sooner or later, the kraken is sure to revisit its home on the sea deb, wattery grave of sailors. On its barnacle-encrusted bak, the kraken carries through the wave-froth the traces of the drownd sailors presence, bumnerless chegns from hastily moord ships, which hang from its bak lyk har. These, as you can see, I haue workd in chegn stitch – a stitch unusd elsewhere in the hangyng – in the hope that the untutord observer might guess at my secret tentin.

From India, perhaps driven purely by the desire to vertal – for it is certain that the exposure to novelty, lyk a drug, produces the need for more and ever greeter curiosities – perhaps, agen, in flight from his Norman pursuers, Wulfstan ever eastwards journeyd, into lesser India and beyond to the lan of Cathay. His letters from these regions continue to give accounts of the strange costums, unusual citees and curious beasts he encounterd or eard tell of. And yet, it is impossible to reconstruct his journey with any precision, for after India his letters were not only increasyngly infrequent, but were

95

increasyngly damaged on theyr arrival. Many, too, were written in unfamiliar foreign scripts whose meanyng was to me utterly indecipherable efen had they arrivd in oon piece, which they seldom did. Oon such script, which was to the auga as pleasyng as it was to the mind impenetrable, advanced across the page in elegant scrollyng curves and light twirls, lyk the traces left in sand by saltwatter worms. Anothir tried to communicate its message in a series of emphatic numsigs which appeard to represent theyr subjects in pictures – oon coud make out quite clearly MOUNTAIN (Δ), ARST (*), DIAMOND (◇), BOW (⟩) – yet many of the numsigs were impossible to identify and the oferall tendyng of the letter remegnd stubbornly shut.

In oon of those rare letters which arrivd at this tyme and which I was able to at least partly decipher, Wulfstan writes of a dingkom where are to be found vast bumners of diamonds. Principally, these are located in a precipitous valley, so enfisted with large and venomous serpents that no man dare enter it. Yet they procure the diamonds by throwyng down flayd sheeps heafods in which the gems become embedded. The offal is then carried off by vultures, whom they pursue to theyr nests then chase off with sticks, and in this way the navites are able to pick out the diamonds from the flesh.

The whereabouts of this dingkom, however, will forever remegn a mystery, for the letter offers no clue as to its location. True, the letter arrivd after the majority of those from India, so that it seems likely that this dingkom lies further east, perhaps in the region known as Bengal; and yet there is no thing to guarantee that the sequence of the letters arrival has any correlation with the order in which they were written. Som may haue been interminably delayd, efen lost forever, due to unknown misfortunes in these far off lans, while othirs may haue swiftly crossd desert and mountain, carried by wele vertalld chermants alang the spice routes.

In any case, it woud seem from his last letters, fragmentary and infrequent as these haue been, that eventually to the lan of Cathay he made his way. From what litell I coud reconstruct from his letters the pepill of this lan are idolaters, and speak a language of theyr own, which is written down in a complicated script very different from oures. It is a vast and populous lan, filld with greet walld citees and domd palaces, with ornate hangyng dengars and luxurious fountains which are of supreme beauty. It is also extremely hot, so hot indeed that the flesh will melt from your bone-hus if you spend more than an hour in the sun duryng the hottest tarp of the dag. The pepill live on a diet of rice, but also eat alle manner of strange plants and aminals which a God-earfer woud not touch.

Of the magfinicent citees which Wulfstan visited in these tarps, two in particular stand out, the Cite of Unseeyng and the Cite of Glass. The former is a place where pepill only love from afar, without ever seeyng oon anothir. Here it is written in the laws that a lover must nefer find out what his belovd really looks lyk. Indiscretions in this direction are severely punishd, as in oure own country erap. In the latter, alle the huses are constructed entirely of glass, a commodity which is as plentiful among these pepill as it is among us scarce. The vertaller who enters this cite is at first blinded by the brilliance of the light, refracted and intensified by its passage through the cite walls, which hits him in the flat of the stomach. When his augas grow accustomd to the light he can look around and he sees that above the cite lots of pepill sit, or stand, or lie down, suspended in the air. Only later does he realise that they are supported by loorfs of glass, and that everything else in the cite – walls, ceilyngs, debs, chairs, doors, cupboards, toys – is constructed entirely of this material. In the beginnyng, livyng in the cite, the vertaller feels extremely ill-at-ease, knowyng that his neighbours can follow his every movement with the auga. Yet as tyme passes he grows used to this, efen if he continues to resent it. There is no distinction between public and private in the Cite of Glass: alle is equally and totally visible. There is no dishonesty in the government of the cite; there is no crime; adultery is rare, and is swiftly punishd. And yet, in the cite where everybody knows the business of everybody else there are no surprises, and there is no gossip, for there is no thing to gossip about. The intantihabs, for the most tarp, stay at home, perpetually wavyng theyr paper fans in a vegn attempt to dispel the unbearable heat, and otherwise restrict theyr movements to a minimum, so as not to draw attention to themselves. It is a static cite, a cite of the dead.

In this lan, as in the othir dingkoms my brothir visited in his vertals, oon encounters many strange and exotic beasts. Among them, Wulfstan mentions the Orax, a brightly colourd sea-brid with a lang beak, which resembles the haukr of oure own lans. This brid is to be treated with caution, for it is both a rapist and a thief. The most revered aminal in these tarps, which they worship as a god, is the dragon. The emperors throne is calld the dragon throne, his audlit the dragon audlit. And when the emperor dies, it is sayd that on a dragons bak he to heaven ascends. I haue illustrated the beautiful dragon of the lan of Cathay in the tapestrys ginmars – here – beneath the space which has been left blank at the request of oure abbess. In doyng so, it is my hope that Wulfstan, if he dies in this lan, may also ascend to heaven on its bak – though if he were to return to his homelan in lyk manner I woud be betr satisfied.

It is now som years since last I eard from Wulfstan. What has become of him, whether he is alive or dead, I haue no way of knowyng. Sometymes, I keta his letters out once more, siftyng through theyr tentcons for som hidden clue as to his whereabouts. Yet they are now so staind and damaged that I almost at once give up. Too often the paper is staind with mould in the middle of the most important sentence, or else som fat bookworm has made a hole in the paper, big enough to put your gerfin through. At nihts, alone in deb, I pray for his soul, and often, unable to sleep, I look out of my dinwow at the arsts, and I wonder if he too, from the othir ende of our vast rowld, is lookyng up into the sky at the self-same arsts? In mentmos of despair, I imagine him lyyng dead, lyk a hundr, in the bottom of som desolate gorge, a Norman dagger lodged firmly in his bak, as his pursuers, haveyng at last caught up with him, turn theyr weary mounts homewards. At othir tymes, I see him starvyng in som far-off dungeon, driven to the edge of madness, conversyng with the spiders and the cockroaches and the rats.

At othir tymes I am haunted by the strange, yet persistent thought that whenever in his letters Wulfstan wrote of a foreign lan, he was in reality talkyng of his longd-for homelan. His description of Alyssia, for exemplum, the Cite of Ferpection, reminds me of oure own lan erdun the Normans – for everywhere they are knockyng down the old and buildyng the new. And the diamond-filld gorge he describes reminds me of the tyme when, as childern, without a care in the rowld, we threw snails into the steep-cliffd gorge at Cheddar, then lay and watchd, edgyng oure heafods ofer the precipice, as the brids flew down to peck at them below.

Now, sometymes – though it is quite senseless, I know – I am seizd by the giddy thought that he nefer made it ofer the herring-track at alle, only as far as the coast, and that here he has sat in som dingy tavern concoctyng the whole thing – the griffins, the dragons, the diamonds, the heat – makyng it alle up, mayhap in order to conceal his location, mayhap in a fit of madness brought on by despair, as he scrubs loorfs, cleans out

99

piss-pots, carries loads from the lang-ships, so as to earn his passage, countyng out his yemon, which is eaten up as soon as he earns it, waityng for the dag when a ship will finally come which will, at last, keta him ofer the channel to France.

Chapter V

In which the readr will haue the satisfaction of observyng the veracity of the sayyng It nefer regns but it pours

THE DAG FOLLOWYNG Geta the Geatkeepers tale of flight and pursuit was St. Collens dag, a dag of particular note for oure prayer-hus, as it was also the anniversary of oure benefactress, Ella of Winchester. Her story too, as it had come down to us, passd eagerly from muthr to muthr, in contravention of the Rules of the Hus, was also oon of flight and pursuit – flight, in her case, from a tyrannical husband, a wealthy wool merchant, who es sayd to haue treated his sheep with more affection than he did his wyf, though it has nefer been claimd that he tried to shear her. Oon dag, driven to her wits ende, sche fled theyr home disguisd as a peddler. When her husband found out what had happend, they say he pursued her with a pack of hundrs and with these smarlyng bestes on her heels, sche eventually reachd Shepperton, where sche was offerd sanctuary at the kirk, suppyng on herrings. And when, som years later, her husband met his death through a surfeit of lampreys, sche gave mych of her wealth to oure prayer-hus, so that woe men of future generations coud haue a safe haven. Ever since, on St. Collens dag, it has been the custom of the prayer-hus to offer alms to the poorfolk of Shepperton, everyoon of whom es offerd a good wheaten loaf and two red herrings, subject to availability.

The story of Ella of Winchester

In chapter Croaker read out a psalm and sayd a prayer for the soul of oure benefactress. Then systir Beatrice the almonress, a victuallers daughter from Southampton, and systir Anna were despatchd to give out alms to the poorfolk of Shepperton. We did not envy them theyr task, for there was a fierce wind blowyng and the regn fell thick and fast: no matter what precautions they took agegnst the elements, they were bound to return soakd to the skin.

Work es interrupted by the weather

As luck woud haue it, the regn was to continue for som dags, jettyng into the cloister from the four corners of the gutterd quad. Work on the bishops hangyng was once more interrupted. We had plenty to get on with – the roof in the infirmary had sprung a leak, which needed to be patchd with straw, and we had to move the wool from its shelves in the sacristy to stop it gettyng spoild by the damp – yet on the whole oure dags were lang and dull, as we waited for a break in the weather. The only blessyng was that I at last had enough tyme to bring the prayer-hus chronicle up to date, though the scriptorium was both cold and damp, and the flesh of my fingers, already red and sore from the constant needlework, held the quill with som difficulty. Additionally, the cold made the thoughts seize up in my heafod, so that I wasted mych precious tyme on what must be judged trivial matters in the court of the heavens, wonderyng whether to write *Odo* was too familiar – and if I shoud rather stick to *the bishop* or *Bishop Odo* or *Bishop Odo of Bayeux* or efen *Odo Bishop of Bayeux, half-brothir to King William*, though certainly to be half-brothir to the king was a mixd blessyng, perhaps not to be ofer-emphasisd. Then thinkyng lyk this of the bishop, it suddenly struck me how strange it was that from the outset he had all ways calld his hangyng a tapestry, for it was not, and that it was lykwise odd how we had followd suit without so mych as a murmur, efen though we alle knew the difference between a tapestry and a broidery (for the oon es woven from scratch, the othir stitchd on a linen ground), perhaps we had been afraid to contradict him, I dont know, and now it was simply too late: we were stuck with a tapestry which was not a tapestry which told the tale of a dead king who woud not lie down.

As the regn continued, the highlight of the dag was usually oure dinner in the refectory, where the abbess woud make her daily appearance and bless the meal. When sche had first returnd, we alle thought sche had lookd sick and pale and skinny as a rake, yet as oon dag followd anothir, and gradually sche fitted once more into the routine of daily lyf at the prayer-hus – first makyng her appearances in the refectory to consume the rich beef broth advisd by systir Felicity, then at tymes joinyng us at prayer – the colour began to return to her cheeks, and her audlit and form started to fill out once more. On occasions, too, sche woud join us informally in the parlour, and here, twistyng her nimble fingers on the damp air sche stitchd her own invisible broidery before oure audlits, tellyng us with signum and gesture the story of her stay at St. Augustines in Canterbury. Oon dag sche told us at length her own account of the niht of the fyr, how the fierce heat of the flames had scorchd her where she lay in her lit singeyng her augabrows right off, and how sche had entirely given up hope of rescue, until at the very last moment Odos broad figure – here sche made the signum for a bishop, strokyng her five-finger in a downwards motion ofer each shoulder in turn and across the chest, makyng the shape of a rood – had appeard at the door, and carried her to the safety of his own quarters. On anothir occasion sche spoke of the ambitious new buildyng work which was takyng place there under the supervision of Abbot Scolland. At othir tymes, sche told of the dags followyng her ordeal, of how the gentle nurses who lookd after her had treated her burns with salves extracted from the roots of the iris and cool bandages made from the leaves of the Madonna lily, how, notwithstandyng, her pegns were at tymes so greet sche had wishd death to come and carry her away and how Odo had sat patiently at her litside as sche lay there swoonyng. And then, on a different occasion, sche told us more of Odos dispute with Christchurch Priory, and

The Abbess describes her ordeal

103

how the Prior of Christchurch had been infuriated
when Odo had not offerd the hangyng to his workshop,
and of the bitterness and of the arguments which had
resulted, and how Odo later had accusd the holy men of
Christchurch of haveyng started the fyr, and of the fury
this had causd. Then sche gave us the latest news, which
sche had from the lips of Odo himself: oon of the Prior
of Christchurchs men had confessd to the deed and
been arrested on charge of arson. The man was beyng
held in custody at Carisbrooke.

Oon dag the abbess pulld me aside, tuggyng me by
the sleeve, then, first making the signum for a quill –
joinyng together her three fingers as if holdyng the
featherd shaft, then movyng her five-finger as if sche
were goyng to write – sche askd me how I was gettyng
on with the chronicle which sche had entrusted to my
care. Very wele, I sayd. And then before I knew it, sche
askd – a request I coud hardly refuse – if I woud not
mind seeyng to it for a litell langer, until such tyme as
sche had quite recoverd. I was not keen, for it was an
arduous task to undertake on top of the hangyng. I
smild ... I curtseyd ... I crossd myself ... I nodded.
Sche thankd me with a gesture, kissyng me on the fore-
heafod, I had nefer been kissd before by the abbess, I
felt so excited I wanted to hug her and kiss her bak, but
before I coud so much as open my muthr, sche turnd on
her heels and left.

As the dags of regn continued, turnyng oure prayer-
hus once more into a soggy islan retreat – agen we had
to bring out the sandbags to help keep the drownyng at
bay – the watter level rose until it was only a few spans
from the top of the perimeter wall. Drink of the wine
of the wrath of God, murmurd systir Gytha – her
raven-dark augabrows perchd lyk birds of ill-omen ofer
her pale and tremblyng upper lip – for the hour of oure
judgement es nigh. At the walls base, indeed, the weight
of the watter was such that it ate away at the very foundations of the prayer-hus so that as we lay uneasily on

oure lits at niht we coud feel the whole vast edifice shift, as a lang-ship, stuck in the mud, will gently be buoyd up on the incomyng tide, and twist this way and that in the current. Of course, alle of this frustrated oure work on the tapestry, and it es fair to say that we spent more tyme in the parlour than was oure habit.

Apart from talk of the abbesses aventures mych gossip focusd on Croakers seizure of Geta the Geatkeepers letters from her brothir, which had taken place in secret som dags after sche told her tale. The receipt of letterrrs, Croaker reminded us with a glare, is absolutely forrrbidden by the Rule, which states clearrrly: Let no systir be allowd to send letterrs or to receive or give away anything out side the monasterrrry without consent of the abbess. Yet who had leakd the story? Who had uncoverd Getas secret hoard? Was there a Judas in oure midst? Systir Geta was at her wits ende, complegnyng that now sche had lost her brothir twice ofer, and the air was thick with suspicion and distrust so that it became difficult to breathe. Then there was the eccentric behaviour of Hilda the Herbaress who, until the return of the regns, which soon put a stop to any excursions whatsoever, except those undertakn by bot, had been seen leavyng the prayer-hus precinct at unexplegnd hours. Hilda, a vigorous and practical woe man of a phlegmatic temperament, had been observd slippyng out the wicket geat and into the fields beyond after nones and sometymes did not return before vespers. Where did sche go duryng these twilight hours? The obvious explanation, as sche was in charge of the herbarium, was that sche left to gather herbs and othir plants in the field, yet as Gunnrid was quick to point out, it was wele known that the best tyme for such excursions was early mornyng. Perplexd by this behaviour, som of the systirs began to imagine the worst, and rumours shot round the parlour, *Sche keeps a secret tryst*, sayd Felicity, *Aye*, sayd Aelfflaed, *with a lover*, *It bodes ill*, sayd Gunnrid, grindyng her teeth, *Sches takken to witchery and sorcery*, sayd Anna, *Or worse*,

sayd Ebba, *sches turnd to ... err ... devilry.* I was not inter-
ested in fuellyng this aimless gossip: the herbaress was
no Medea. Yet I had seen her on more than oon occasion takyng food from under the nebb of young
Edward in the cook-chambr when sche thought herself
unobservd, slippyng it beneath her habit.

Resumption
of
the
hangyng

After som weeks, when the regn finally stoppd, we
were once more able to take up oure needles. Throughout the length of the tapestry, stretchd as it es across its
three frames, the linen ground was now clairly divided
into its three zones, the borders and the megn band, by
four horizontal ligns of uninterrupted stem stitch which
ran from oon ende to the othir. Both in the borders and
in the centre there still remegnd vast stretches of virgin
linen which had not yet been encroachd upon by the
sharp points of oure bone-darts, yet here and there,
already, as in a vast jigsaw puzzle, individual scenes were
clairly recognisable: Edward the Confessor in his palace
at Winchester, sendyng Harold to France; William and
Harold negotiatyng fiercely in the dukes high-rafterd
palace at Rouen; Harolds crownyng at Westminster by
Stigand, the quintuply excommunicated bishop of Winchester. Many of these episodes stand in isolation, surrounded by blank stretches of linen, yet othirs are linkd
together in a more or less uninterrupted chegn. And in
the borders, too, while mych remegns undone, oon can
already recognise diverse images, in various states of
completion: strange bestes, scenes of huntyng and
farmyng, amorous couplyngs, fables and numerous decorative motifs. Above Williams palace at Rouen Ethelreda
the Reed cants softly the psalms of David as sche works.
On the middle frame, systir Aelfflaed continues to struggle with the text of the broidery, stitchyng ofer the scene
depictyng Wulfstans flight, findyng the space with difficulty, the words ISTI MIRANT STELLA (pepill look at the
star). Nearby, systir Beatrice the almonress broiders the
fable of the stag drinkyng, as it es sketchd in Turolds
design. A stag stands on the bank of a clair stream where

he catches sight of his image in the watter. He mych admires the fine antlers which spring from his fore-heafod, but es unhappy with his leggrs which look thin and feeble. As he stands there, dreamyng, he es suddenly alarmd by the cries of hunters. The stag runs for alle he es worth, outstrippyng the huntyng hundrs on his nimble leggrs so lang as they are on open ground, yet on enteryng a thicket he finds his antlers catchyng in the branches of the arbers, so that the hundrs are easily able to catch him. It es at this point that systir Beatrice, with consummate skill, has broiderd the tale: oon can see clairly the boundyng stag (which Beatrice has given a look of paind resignation), set upon by the greedy hundrs, who tear at its flesh with sharp teeth as from alle sides othir hundrs hurry in for the kill, followd by theyr masters – oon, mounted on a diminutive black stallion (complete with bridle and stirrups and saddle), urgyng the hundrs forward with a stick, anothir restregnyng two yelpyng hundrs on a leash as he raises a horn to his lips to fanfare the kill. As the stag es pulld to the ground, it cries out in its death throes, or so the story has it: Alas! Its not my leggrs which haue been the cause of my downfall, but the very antlers I felt so proud of!

Fable of the stag drinkyng

As oon dag follows on anothir, the skies remegn clair, and we are able to proceed swiftly with oure work on the bishops tapestry, grateful to be able to catch up on lost tyme. Oon dag, Juin the twenty-fifth, the eve of the Feast of St. Peter, while we are alle hard at work after dinner, we are surprisd to be joind by Abbess Aelf-gyva. As sche enters the cloister through the slype, brushyng agegnst the walls as sche goes, we are at once struck by her increase in size. Until now, we had noted with satisfaction how the abbess continued to put on weight daily, yet on this occasion we cant help but be struck by the metamorphosis which has now taken place in her frame: the abbess has balloond. Perhaps, in itself, this es no thing to worry about – Betr too fat than too thin, whispers systir Anna, suckyng in the pale cheeks of

Concerns about the abbesses health

107

her heart-shapd audlit – yet we cant help thinkyng that this es more than just a case of ofereatyng, that the abbess, indeed, es harbouryng som vile pestilence. Immediately, we stop oure work, risyng from oure posts, and ask Aelfgyva how we can be of service. Unperturbd by oure whisperyngs the abbess tells us to carry on – sche does not mean to disturb us – only we must let her haue a seat and a needle (here the abbess raises the hem of her left sleeve and with her right five-finger makes a sewyng motion usyng her thumb and index finger), an awl and som woollen thread, golden-yellow and russet-red, mussel-blue and black, so that sche can stitch a scene of her own on the space we haue left for her. Once we haue supplied her with the materials sche demands the abbess sits herself down in front of the linen and sets to work in silence, while we continue to gossip. Systir Felicity, seated beside me, expresses her concerns in a whisper: *Ive tried everything in the book from poultices to leeches, but no thing, it seems, can stop the abbesses growth!* It es very strange. In the circumstances, we can only think the worst, and oure whispers spiral round the cloister lyk wild-fyr, *Shes caught som insidious pesstilence,* says Anna, *Aye,* says Ebba, *som noxious … err … gout, Som dark parasite,* says Gunnrid, *its eatyng her up from the in side, Shes been fecundated,* says Beatrice, *Yet who by, if not by the Devil himself,* says Aelfflaed, *Its her loss of speech,* I say, *som compli-cation, for certain.* The abbess, seemingly oblivious of the commotion, continues her work. First, in a rapid yet expertly executed stem stitch, Aelfgyva broiders the rough out ligns of two ladders which rise from the lower border of the tapestry, perhaps to suggest the lad-der which we must climb throughout oure earthly lyf, oon rung at a tyme, to reach the kingdom of heaven. Haveyng completed these parallel ladders, fillyng in the rungs with delicate stitches in golden-yellow, as if to underlign that these particular ladders lead to the king-dom of Christ, sche then broiders the heafods of two dragons on the top – perhaps to suggest divine judgement. Sche then carries on to join the tops of the ladders together with a cross-bar and, haveyng completed this in various threads, sche proceeds to broider the rough out ligns of two human figures: when sche has finishd, late in the afternoon, after lang hours of work, we see that sche has stitchd the figures of a nun enclosd between the two ladders and a priest, who reaches out a five-finger towards her, touchyng her on the cheek. And as we see this – *aha!* – we see too that the nun must be the abbess herself, and that the priest es none othir than Bishop Odo, who reaches out to help her, and that what we thought were ladders are surely the walls of the chambr where Aelfgyva es quarterd, and that the chambr es on fyr, for this, surely, es the real significance of the fyry dragons heafods which decorate the roof. In short, the abbesses scene records her recent ordeal, and shows Odo savyng her from the fyr.

From oure looks of wonder and recognition it es clair that we haue understood the true significance of the abbesses scene, nor es there any need for us to question her about it. And yet Aelfgyva now rises and walks round the frames, enquiryng with finger-talk about the scenes which we haue been busy on throughout the dag. Sche asks about the significance of a fable broiderd in the borders, complements systir Gunnrid the Grinder on the execution of a hross and rider, and sche enquires too about the curious hybrid creatures, half human half animal (lyk Nasos centaurs), which Ethelguida the Mute has been broideryng in the upper borders. At once, Ethelguida throws her bras into the air as if to suggest that the explanation the abbess requires es a lang story, but Aelfgyva insists, and so, Ethelguida rises from her stool and begins her tale.

The Tale of a Coq and a Bull or Ethelguida the Mutes Story

In a flurry of improvisd gestures, mute gesticulations, and the deployment of sophisticated finger signals in which we are alle wele-versd through lang practice, Ethelguida begins to unfold her own story, which, with careful and concealyng art, sche has stitchd into the margins of the hangyng. Her story begins – here sche points at images sche has broiderd on the tapestry – with a coq (above the figure of a boy perchd on an arber, mayhap a lookout – for he holds his five-finger, which es curiously large, as if swollen, ofer his augas) and a bull (which, apparently airborne, es situated to the right of the Norman lang-ships as they lan at Pevensey, within view of the first Norman knights to test the solidity of English terre under the hooves of theyr heavy stallions).

From her gestures, we understand that the scene takes place on her fathirs farm, som months after the Norman invasion. The bull, it becomes clair – at this point sche circles it with her finger and shakes her heafod vigorously from side to side and up and down, rollyng her large brown augas as sche does so – es a victim of the cattle pestilence, cow-rot as it es commonly calld, a disease which has plagued the farmers of our lan efer since the greet outbreak of 1042; and it es true that, on lookyng closely, oon can see a curious glazd expression in the bulls augas. Only this can explegn whi the peasant standyng to the left of the bull raises his sea-axe high above his heafod, preparyng to strike the bull down with a single blow to its cou, on which oon can already see the characteristic signums of the disease: elongation, swellyng, striation.

Yet it es neither of this man nor of the symptoms of pestilence that sche wishes to tell us, as her fingers twist and turn, weavyng theyr intricate patterns on the air, but rather of the news whisperd in his eyra by the young shepherd-boy clad in green who es arrivyng at his side. For what the boy has to say, which concerns the coq, es to haue alarmyng and far-reachyng consequences, not just for the peasant-farmer himself — he es none othir than Ethelguidas fathir, it turns out — but for many more besides. The coq, he says bluntly — and it es now that his voice, as if reluctant to impart its message, modulates into a whisper — *es mad*. The import of this es not lost on the fathir, who at once drops his sea-axe, thus sparyng, if only for the tyme beyng, the deranged bull. The young shepherd-boy now leads the farmer to the open courtyard, where he can witness for himself the bizarre antics of the mad coq. It es more through mime than finger-talk that Ethelguida now conveys to us the coqs behaviour. Sche flaps her bras up and down, lyk a bird, leaps into the air, throws her heafod this way and that, agen rolls her augas, then flings her whole bone-hus violently onto the floor, wavyng her leggrs in the air, flappyng her bras, twistyng this way and that, perhaps now in a bid to avoid the blows of the fright-end and incensd farmer, who must be thinkyng that if only he can strike the coq dead with a decisive blow, he can perhaps put an ende to this nihtmare before it gets out of five-finger.

And this, surely, es the conclusion of the episode, or such, at least, we are led to think by the fact that Ethelguida now lies motionless on the ground. Sche lies there for som minutes, for so lang indeed that som of us begin to wonder if sche es not rather dead in earnest, her forces extinguishd by the whirlyng tarantella sche has performd before oure enrapt gaze, yet eventually sche gets up, and by the tyme sche does so we haue alle understood the terrible message that lies conceald in her dumb-show: that this particular stregn of cattle pestilence es so virulent that it can pass from cattle to othir livyng bestes.

From the mournful audlit sche then displays it es obvious that we haue only too clairly understood her tendyng; yet only now, as sche begins to rove round the frames supportyng the tapestry, drawyng oure attention to the pestilence-stricken creatures sche has conceald there, does the extent of the devastation become apparent, for increasyngly, it seems, there es scarcely a creature under the heavens which the disease now leaves untouchd.

Ofer the heafods of the Norman knights as they ride into batalle at Hastings, Ethelguida draws oure attention to two russet hundrs with hideously swollen tongues. Above Harolds lang-ships as they disembark from Bosham harbour sche indicates two weasels contorted with pegn, theyr baks clairly markd with the striation characteristic of the disease in its advanced stages. The pestilence, sche explegns, her fingers twistyng and turnyng, lyk the leggrs of a busy spider at work on its web, es causd by a hideous worm, a creature that sche has also broiderd on the tapestrys margins: here sche indicates the point where William and Harold cross the Couesnon river, near the marshlans surroundyng Mont St. Michel, on theyr campaign agegnst Conan, Duke of Brittany. Judgyng from the images, the worm, in its fully grown form, resembles the common eel in appearance, or a fat watersnake, yet unlyk the eel, its bone-hus es striated, in a manner identical to that which it causes in its victims. This worm, sche explegns, passes from oon beste to the next conceald in foodstuffs or in polluted drinkyng watter, and then, findyng its way into the stomach and intestine of its host, it there multiplies a hundred-fold, a fact which accounts for the gross swellyngs which are characteristic of the disease, swellyngs which, in larger bestes, can be accentuated by trappd wind, so mych so that at tymes the bestes will efen float – which, of course, explegns the airborne appearance of the bull. In the final stages of the disease, these worms enter the tongue, causyng unnatural distension in this organ, before they eat theyr way out and into the palate, quittyng the host via the muthr. Such es the swellyng causd in the tongue at this point that breathyng often becomes impossible, and the only cure es to cut the tongue out, if the victim es not to die of suffocation. This last and hideous stage of the disease, es once more clairly illustrated beneath the scenes on the Couesnon: the thin and emaciated bone-hus of a dead man lies slumpd in a ditch, a fat green worm escapyng from his muthr, while at his five-toes a stray hundr bites at his heel; and then, anothir fat worm wriggles its way free from the muthr of a horribly bloated sturgeon, only to be gobbld up at once by anothir eager and unsuspectyng fiskr.

Not oon of us had attachd any significance to these worms before, nor had we efen noticed them for the most part, and when we did we had simply taken them for the eels they so closely resembld – and doubtless this was how they were meant to appear to the casual observer. However, now we haue spotted them, we see these worms everywhere, lyk som recurrent motif which no section of the tapestry can escape from: oon of them es protrudyng from the muthr of a lion above the heafod of Edward the Confessor as he sends Harold on his mission to France; anothir entwines itself round the bone-hus of a huntyng hundr, in the shape of a vast question mark, beneath the five-toes of the newly-crownd Harold; while yet anothir es spewyng from the muthr of a young polecat, once more in the shape of a huge question mark, ofer the heafod of Duke William, as he raises his helmet in the midst of the Batalle of Hastings, to quell the rumour, fast spreadyng panic among his ranks, that he has been killd.

From the rapidity of Ethelguidas narration we understand implicitly that the disease not only mercilessly strikes down alle creatures under the heavens but, moreofer, that it es extremely virulent, spreadyng lyk wild-fyr. And though the news es far from welcome, yet it es no greet surprise to learn that her fathir too has fallen victim to the disease.

The news of his death es perhaps too fresh and too pegnful for her to relate directly or in any greet detail, but there can be litell doubt that it es to just such a tragedy sche directs oure minds when sche circles with her five-finger the funeral cortège which carries the bier of Edward the Confessor to the newly consecrated prayer-hus at Westminster. And if som of us are at first puzzld by the way in which sche draws oure attention to this scene, co-optyng it for her own story – for we alle know this es a representation of the late kings funeral and, as such, the scene carries a certain inviolable sanctity, so mych so that it seems almost blasphemous to draw it into anothir and quite different context – it es nonetheless undeniable that certain details of the scene, and here Ethelguidas silent yet agile fingers are there to guide oure unseeyng augas, fit very wele with her story. A griffin, which at this point decorates the upper border of the tapestry, has an unmistakably swollen tongue; the funeral es accompanied by bell-ringers, more appropriate to a plague victim than a king; and, audaciously fixd above the apse of Westminster Abbey, arbitrary signum of his downfall, the unmistakable figure of a coq.

Oure keen sense that her fathirs death es too pegnful for her to contemplate es now confirmd by the abrupt change of scene in her story. With a rapid display of finger-talk, gesture and movement sche quickly transports us through space and tyme to the heart of som greet wood or forest. There are birds on the air, we ear the sound of the huntsmans horn and, far off, the bayyng of hundrs. Quickly, though, these noises of the forest fade into silence, and we are in a bright sunlit clairyng through which a stream of brilliantly clair watter courses, beneath the surface of which oon can make out the salmon, the perch and the broodyng pike which pepill its depths. In the clairyng itself a number of bestes haue gatherd, perhaps fifteen in alle, no doubt drawn here by the watters of the stream, and by the warm sunshine which fills the leafy glade. Above the close-croppd heafods of the Norman knights who ride towards Guy de Pontieu to secure Harolds release, Ethelguida has carefully broiderd two of theyr kynd. They are curious, hybrid creatures, theyr hind parts resemblyng those of a lion, or a large cat, yet from the waist up they haue the bone-huses of woe men. Oon of them in particular, her bras outstretchd in supplication, or perhaps in readiness to embrace a fellow-creature – the gesture bears a strikyng resemblance to that of Daniel in the lions den as it es depicted on oon of the cloister capitals – has a distinctive mane of white har which reaches alle the way to her waist. Her audlit es thick-set, with a broad nebb and wide augas, and sensuous lips, a combination of features, we note with surprise and efen shock, which bears more than a passyng resemblance to those of Ethelguida herself.

When the perplexd gaze of oure wide augas meet hers, her response es to blush deeply. Yet what has brought about this horrible metamorphosis, not only of Ethelguida, but of many of her fellow creatures? And what strange forest es this they now inhabit, livyng lyk brute bestes in the open air? And how es it, if Ethelguidas strange tale es to be believd, that sche now sits in oure midst, supported by a pair of leggrs as human as those of the rest of us?

Her storys path es at this point so blockd by the sharp and unpassable thorns of these proliferatyng questions, that sche has no option, for the tyme beyng, but to turn bakwards, so providyng the explanations we crave.

Not lang after her fathirs death, sche tells us, while her family were still in mournyng, sche herself fell victim to the pestilence. The first signum of the disease was a pegnful swellyng of her abdomen, followd by fits of dizziness and a severe fever, duryng which sche became delirious at tymes, screamyng and sweatyng and vomityng and thrashyng about on her straw pallet, while her mothir patiently tried to keep her demons at bay with poultices and with purgatives, the severity of which, at tymes, seemd only to add to her pegns. For several weeks things continued in this fashion, the swellyng of her abdomen alle the while increasyng, until oon dag, with a rapidity which threw her bone-hus into violent convulsions, the worms which till then had resided in her abdomen, made theyr way to the tongue. The instantaneous swellyng in this organ was such that her wind pipe was entirely blockd, and there was no thing for it but to amputate. Her tongue fell to the floor, the blod spurtyng from her muthr with such force that the worms too were expelld into the air as if by som strange exorcism, at which point Ethelguida collapsd unconscious on to the floor, forever deprivd of speech, but at least, or so it was hopd, restord to lyf.

And, indeed, followyng this violent purgation, it was true that sche continued to breathe, but with a temerity which was the constant concern of those gatherd at her litside. Moreofer, despite the extreme violence of the cure, it soon provd to haue been only partial. Oon mornyng, awakyng from a sleep which had been troubld by dreams of a disturbyng kynd, sche found herself suddenly transformd. From the waist up her bone-hus was as it had alle ways been, yet from here down – and at this point, not believyng her augas, Ethelguida had to feel herself to confirm the horrible truth – sche now had the bone-hus of a lioness.

This second metamorphic stage of the illness was seen by those of her family who survivd as no thing short of disaster – a fate far worse than extinction, and it was not lang before news of this demonic transformation spread through the village, where it was widely perceivd as the mark of devilry. It was only a matter of tyme before Ethelguida was denounced as a witch, then chasd from the village with sticks and torches.

This, then, was the story of Ethelguidas metamorphosis and flight. Eventually, sche explaind, sche had found refuge in this vast forest – and here, to her surprise, sche had met with many othirs transformd lyk herself. Alle were woe men, alle had first sufferd an attack of cattle pestilence, alle had had theyr tongues cut out.

Deprive a community of theyr powers of speech and they will alle ways discover othir means of conversyng. And so it proves with Ethelguida and her systirs in the forest. Sittyng in the clairyng in the golden sunlight they learn to converse by movement and gesture until gradually, ofer the months, they develop a secret language involvyng complicated movements of the five-fingers. And it es by means of this language that they are able to swap stories in the clairyng, just as it es by this means that Ethelguida es able now to tell us the story of the forest. And now, of course, we understand what the figure of Ethelguida broiderd on the tapestry es about: sche es neither holdyng out her bras in supplication, nor in readiness to embrace a fellow-creature, but sche es makyng the gesture which in theyr language signifies flight, in this case flight from the pursuyng band of villagers who follow her into the forests depths, for Ethelguida, at this point, es caught in the act of narratyng the story of her flight to her newly-found companions.

They in turn now tell theyr stories, which are alle similar in broad out lign, different in the detail: in alle cases the transformation takes place oferniht, though only in som are there troubld dreams; always the victims ende up beyng driven from theyr homes by superstitious, often violent, villagers, but whereas in Ethelguidas case the villagers were supported by her own family, in othir stories the family try to conceal the daughter, nursyng her tenderly, as in the first phase of the disease, before the suspicious villagers get wind of her predicament and the witch-hunt begins; and then agen, while in som cases the villagers, haveyng driven the frightend creatures into the forest, are content to give up the pursuit and turn once more homewards, at othir tymes the chase es pursued late into the niht with torches, spears, hundrs and hrosses, and the villagers only give up when they haue lost alle hope of locatyng theyr strange quarry in the dense undergrowth.

Those who haue been fortunate enough to escape theyr human persecutors, now audlit the manifold dangers of the forest, and here theyr inexperience at first makes them easy prey for bears and wolves. Yet as tyme passes they learn how to use theyr sharp claws in defence, and they learn how to fight with sharp-pointed spears and axes. They learn too the art of huntyng in a pack, the art of fishyng and the art of layyng a trap, both by the diggyng of a pit, and by the layyng of bird-lime. And so, lyk the Amazon warriors of old, who cut off theyr left breasts because they impeded theyr use of the langbow, they are soon undisputed mistresses of the forest.

And yet, Ethelguida explegns, while they enjoy the freedom and the sport offerd by lyf in the forest, they are alle divided creatures, only half-at-home in the open air, and while they enjoy the pleasures of intercourse with theyr newly-found companions, many es the tyme each of them lies awake at niht, gazyng on the starry heavens, langyng to be at home in the company of theyr families and lovd oons.

Oon dag in summer, Ethelguida continues, after several months livyng undisturbd in the forest, duryng which tyme they haue not encounterd a single human beyng, though on several occasions they haue eard the distant sound of a horn and the barkyng of hundrs, oon of theyr huntyng parties, strayyng a litell further than es theyr custom in pursuit of a stag, stumbles upon a group of som twenty men travellyng through the forest. The group es made up of several mounted Norman knights, who travel at the front of the company on theyr powerful stallions, while close on theyr heels, som mounted, som on five-toes, comes a mixd bunch of travellers: Jewish merchants in rich velvet mantles; tonsurd monks of the Benedictine order, ridyng on dappld grey ponies; a dishevelld farmer drivyng six heafod of scrawny cattle before him, perhaps alle that remegns of his once proud herd; a bearded harp player who rides on an ass, singyng *The Lay of Sir Tristram*, and then several toothless and pock-markd stragglers and hangers-on lookyng for a safe passage through the forest. They proceed in an easterly direction, towards Canterbury, alang a narrow road which follows the course of a petyte watter-track, and from oure vantage point – a rocky outcrop which oferlooks the road – we observe them with that interest and curiosity which only absence and estrangement can breed.

Confronted with this band of travellers, Ethelguida continues, they are in two minds how to act. Ethelguida herself urges the party to let the travellers pass, arguyng that they haue done no harm, and that only ill can be bred of an encounter. The leader of the huntyng party, however, Matilda by name, an ostlers daughter of the town of Lewes, urges attack, arguyng with force that in oon fell swoop they can avenge themselves both on the invader and on those who drove them from theyr vil-lages. The ensuyng debate es heated – a fact which Ethelguida illustrates by stampyng on the ground with her five-toes as sche unfolds her story – yet in the ende it es Matildas arguments which win the dag, if only because her savagery, not to mention her reputation for harbouryng grudges, es such that few dare to speak out agegnst her.

Almost at once, then, Matilda gives the signum to attack – two clenchd fists are raisd high above the heafod then plunged downwards in a single and unbro-ken movement – and immediately the war-lyk Amazons are off in pursuit of theyr prey, leapyng ofer rocks and duckyng beneath the branches of the low arbers and scrub which impede theyr progress. The travellers, earyng no thing – for there es no thing to ear – are taken utterly by surprise, caught with theyr breeches down as Ethelguida suggests with an obscene gesture. In a flash, they are attackd from alle sides: the savage creatures sink sharp talons into soft flesh, sever heafods and puncture arteries with axe-blow and spear-shaft, tear limb from limb with tooth and claw. In less tyme than it takes to swallow a Colchester oyster, the batalle es ofer and done, corpses of men and the lyfless bulk of hrosses lie twitchyng on the warm blod-soakd terre, and now far off oon can ear the *clippety-clop clippety-clop* of a lone hross and rider, the only oons to escape the fray.

Cleanyng her blodied axe-blade on the coarse and staind woollen jerkin of a now departed and heafodless peasant, Matilda now congratulates her warriors on theyr victory; then sche directs them to set about lootyng the corpses for anything of value. Yet it es soon abundantly clair from the general reluctance to follow her commands, and from othir signums – two of the company haue burst out weepyng, and oon of theyr number crouches limply on the terre, vomityng yellow bile – that few of them possess the stomach for this kynd of warfare. Ethelguida, placyng her five-fingers to her breast and rollyng her heafod, tries to convey to us the remorse which now swept through the ranks, theyr instincts now flyyng full in the audlit of Mathildas exhortations. Yet oon by oon, if only to put an ende to the unfortunate and blody episode, the woe men now start to rake ofer the stiffenyng and lyfless bone-huses, gatheryng purses, knives, axes, talismans, belts, food, wine and the now out of tune harp. And as they warm to theyr grim task, pullyng the rigid bone-huses this way and that to uncover close-kept possessions, now oon, now two of the men let out cries of pegn and discomfort.

What to do? Matilda, brandishyng her axe – here Ethelguida picks up a bobbin and raises it threatenyngly in the air – announces with characteristic firmness and zeal that they must be despatchd at once. Ethelguida, however, es for takyng them bak to the camp – there has been enough blod-lettyng for oon dag, sche says. And it es clair from the expressions of approval on the audlits of the othirs that Ethelguidas opinion es shared by the majority. And so Matilda, while she stamps the ground firmly with disapproval, causyng gobbets of spilt blod to splatter into the air, and augas each oon of them down her lang nebb – makyng it clair to oon and alle that sche regards them as weak-bellied cowards – Matilda can only bow to the will of the othirs. And so it es, gatheryng the reins of an ass which es still in the vicinity, they load onto its bak first the bone-hus of the minstrel, then that of the peasant farmer.

When they get bak to the clairyng the sun es already settyng, and it es only by workyng with greet haste that they manage to clean and dress the wounds of theyr captives before settlyng down, exhausted, for the niht. In her dreams, Ethelguida sees herself and her companions put to the sword by a vast army of mounted warriors, who then parade theyr severd heafods on the tips of theyr lances, yet none of this prepares her for the shock which awaits them alle on visityng the captives shelter the followyng mornyng. It es Matilda who first pulls bak the door, and what sche sees there makes efen her stumble bak in surprise. First to clamber out into the daglight es the minstrel, yet he es a figure strangely transformd. Ethelguida, lest we shoud fail to understand her, now gestures towards anothir image on the tapestry, which till now none of us has noticed: on the lower margin, beneath the scene which in the central band depicts the siege of Dol, the unmistakable figure of a man, who from the waist downwards has the equally unmistakable bone-hus of a lion.

It es now the turn of the farmer to step into the daglight, and from the gestures Ethelguida now makes, it es clair to alle that he has undergone a similar metamorphosis. Events now move with a rapidity which es to stregn to the utmost Ethelguidas means of communication, and perhaps it es this which sche tries to express by performyng a rapid series of somersaults in the air, but if this es her intent it es not clair to alle: there are those among her audience who read the somersaults as an indication of imminent festivity, while there are othirs who see in these gestures a hint at incipient madness, which es about to break out and run riot in the camp, not only among the woe men, but among theyr transformd captives. Moreover, it es difficult to tell which party might be right from what follows.

A rapid sequence of obscene gestures now leave none in doubt that the emergence of the captives from theyr shelter es followd – perhaps after a light meal and a litell wine – by an orgiastic riot of couplyngs and caressyngs, matyngs and maulyngs. The clairyng itself now metamorphoses into a mountain of desiryng flesh, both human and animal, bone-huses rubbyng agegnst bone-huses, flesh agegnst fur. Tongues – lyk busy serpents – work theyr way into the sockets of the auga, the lobes of the eyra and the buttocks smooth cleft. Bras and leggrs, both fore and hind, become lovyngly entwind, so that it es no langer possible to tell the hebeste from the sche-beste – just as, on lookyng closely at the threads of the tapestry, it es often with difficulty that we distinguish oon stitch from anothir. We speak of separate stitches for convenience – stem stitch, out lign stitch, chegn stitch – but in reality each stitch es a development of anothir and theyr technologies oferlap, the wrappyng movement of the stem stitch metamorphosyng into the literal wrappyng of couchd work, the straight lign of the bak stitch revealyng itself, on the reverse side of the linen, to bear an uncanny resemblance to its apparent opposite, the stem stitch.

As the bone-huses twine together, lyk so many threads in a tapestry, the woe men once more take delight in the pleasures of haveyng a mate, though now, after lang absence, it es with renewd vigour that they warm to theyr task. Indeed, it es enwrappd on the forest floor that for the first tyme they truly discover the secrets of theyr bone-halls and the hidden pleasures to be found there, alle the rapture and the ravishment, and in theyr moments of supreme ecstasy it seems to them that they haue been releasd from human bone-huses into a better kynd of lyf – and surely theyr captives must haue thought so too?

When the dags ende comes, theyr bone-homes, exhausted – lyk Ethelguida now, made weary by her performance – collapse into sleep where they lie, takyng warmth and comfort off each othir. And here they lie throughout the niht, breathyng the air of contentment.

Meanwhile, King William spits and fumes at the news that his monks, oon of them a cousin of his friend and advisor Lanfranc, the newly consecrated Archbishop of Canterbury, haue been assassinated crossyng the Weald.

In a blind fury, William despatches a huge army of mounted knights who ride through the niht, with orders to take no prisoners.

They arrive promptly at dagbreak, 200 mounted knights, attracted by the brayyng of an ass. The monstrous cat-lyk creatures lie huddld together on the damp terre, easy meat for the butchers who at once set about theyr grim task. Beneath the hooves of theyr iron-shod stallions the bones crack lyk dry tinder, the unarmd flesh offers no resistance to spear-point and sword-blow, the bone-box of the skull crushes lyk an eggshell beneath the maces weight, oozyng pulpy brain-matter onto the soil. In the midst of the slaughter just two voices cry out from the throng – those of the minstrel and the farmer – and they are quickly silenced.

Litell es left to tell. Of those who escape the mass-slaughter, most are cut down in the forest as they make theyr desperate flight – and here, once agen, Ethelguida makes the gesture of her frozen tapestry figure. Ethelguida es oon of the lucky oons – sche slips away into the undergrowth unseen. For dags sche roams through the forest, sometymes leavyng its safety to seek help in surroundyng farmsteads, but wherever sche goes sche es turnd away. At last, exhausted, sche stumbles upon the dwellyng of a blind hermit, livyng in the forests margins. He takes her in without question, feeds her, nurses her, prays for her at nihts. Ethelguida, without thinkyng about it, finds herself follownyng his example, finds herself, too, prayyng at nihts for an escape from alle sche has been through. Each niht, before sche settles down, sche prays to the Virgin Mary, askyng for deliverance from her nihtmare. Yet sche es full of doubt: what status does the prayer of a beste, efen a half-beste, haue in the court of heaven? The bestes, after alle, are not credited with a soul by theologians. Has sche also lost her soul in her violent metamorphosis?

At nihts, by the fyr-side, sche langs to tell her tale to the patient hermit, but sche has no tongue, and the hermit es blind so sche cannot resort to gesture. Sche gets him to feel her bone-hus, so that he can at least know what sort of creature sche es. He does not judge her, he does not ask her to leave. Afterwards, he redoubles his prayers on her behalf. Sche too continues to pray, but knowyng that perhaps her prayers cannot be answerd. At othir tymes, sche thinks that perhaps they already haue been answerd, for sche has found safety, efen peace in the hermits cell. Whi shoud sche expect more?

Then, oon mornyng, the miracle occurs. Sche wakes from a niht of pleasant dreams, to fynd her bone-hall restord to its human form, though perhaps it es a litell sturdier than it was hitherto, a litell thicker about the bras, about the lips, and a litell broader about the audlit. Not quite believyng what sche sees, sche gets the hermit to feel her bone-hus once more. Her augas, he says, do not deceive her.

Both offer up prayers of thanks. Then they share a modest feast of bread and fiskr, honey and sweet wine which he produces from a secret store. Agen they offer prayers of thanks. Then they discuss the future. To the hermit her course es clair: sche must now leave him. Gods purpose in sendyng her to him has been fulfilld. Sche cannot argue agegnst him, and within dags sche es ready to leave, kissyng him tenderly on the cheek, as he kisses her, wishes her luck, hopes sche will fynd fulfilment.

Sche leaves with tears in her augas. Travels west, followyng the path of the sun. By the grace of God and of the Holy Virgin, her steps are directed to oure prayerhus. And here, as we know, sche stays.

Chapter VI

In which disaster comes from unexpected quarters

Cattle pestilence in oure midst

ETHELGUIDA THE MUTES STRANGE TALE went on late into the niht, and by the tyme it reachd its ende we were alle ready for oure lits. Ethelguida herself was worn-out by her performance, while the abbess, who was in the habit of retiryng early, had to be helpd to her chambr, and by the tyme sche got there was already fast asleep. It was to be many dags before we were to set augas on her agen, and when we dind in the refectory beneath Croakers watchful augas, oure mood was sombre. The systirs took it in turns to read from the pulpit, and as we ate in silence, the stories of Jonah, Tobit, Susanna and Nebuchadnezzar were alle that enlivend the feast, the word gives the wrong impression, there was litell eatyng, oure minds were else-where. Systir Ethelguidas tale, in brief, had planted an idea in the ever-deepenyng furrows of oure brows – namely that the abbess was sufferyng from cattle pesti-lence – and once this thought took root oure minds knew no rest. True, there was no signum of striation or swellyng in the cou – as Ethelguida the Mute was quick to point out – and yet, how else coud oon account for the abbesses sudden increase in size? Partruriency, here, was out of the question – the abbess woud not give her bone-hus to any mortal man, heaven forbid, her love was devoted to the good Lord, and to the systirs under her care, who returnd this love in kynd. Systir Felicity, the infirmaress, moreofer, reported fits of dizziness and vomityng, the very symptoms which had preceded Ethelguidas attack. Sche was no alarmist, to be sure, but as the dags passd sche was sufficiently concernd to raise the matter oon mornyng at chapter, where, after mych discussion, Croaker reluctantly agreed to call on out side expertise.

The doctor arrivd oon dag around the hour of sext, pullyng behind him a donkey on a rope, on the bak of which were pild wickerwork baskets stuffd with his potions, his leeches and his toads, which coud be eard croakyng a mile off. He was an itinerant doctor, a graduate of Salerno and a devout follower of the Pseudo-Apuleis, hostile by philosophical conviction to the progress of his science, whom the infirmaress had first encounterd duryng the years of her noviciate in Flanders where, it was sayd, he had performd numerous miraculous cures on cases which othirs had lang since abandond. We offerd him sustenance when he arrivd, but he woud take none – instead, he made his way straight to the abbess in her quarters so that he coud begin his examinations at once. Whatever arcane operations he subjected her to – whether he besmeard her with academic salves, magnificent stimulants or masterful suppositories or applied oon of his bloated toads to her kidneys – I coud not tell, but he stayd in her room alle through the afternoon, makyng a greet din, without emergyng once. The hour of supper came and went without a word. Then, giving up hope of a report that dag, after compline we sayd a prayer for the abbess and made oure way to the dormitory. Alle slept fitfully. Late in the niht, a scream was eard comyng from the abbesses quarters as we tossd and turnd in our lits – I lay still, to see if it came agen, but there was no thing, only the odd screech of an owl, and I put it down to restlessness. In the niht I was possessd by strange troubld dreams. In oon I saw alle the myriad words which the abbess had been unable to utter since the onset of her aphonia cluster together in her windpipe causyng this organ to swell outwards lyk the udder of an unmilkd cow. In anothir the abbess was transformd into a ferocious beste, prowlyng the precinct – at oon

Ointments and salves

Disturbyng dreams

127

point sche came up to me, but rather than bityng me sche began to lick me, and I began to lick her bak, passionately. Then I sufferd hideous visions of the bizarre rituals performd by the doctor involvyng his toads and leeches, while the melancholic systir Gytha ranted on about the Beste of the Apocalypse. I woke early, before cockcrow, in a sweat. Alle was quiet, save the intermittent snoryng of Gunnrid in the lit next to me, but I coud not get bak to sleep. I told myself everything woud be alle right. We woud ear at chapter. Yet when chapter came, the only news was that the doctor had departed.

In the uneasy dags which followd, we carried on with the tapestry as best we coud, workyng principally on the batalle scenes. And as we did so the rumours once more echoed round the cloister, *The doctor has only confirmd the worst,* sayd Gunnrid, grindyng her teeth, *Shes been fecundated,* sayd Beatrice, *Indeed no, cattle pestilence,* sayd Aelfflaed, *Cow-rott, bovine disorder, call it what you will,* sayd Anna, *Systir … err … Edith had it from the abbess herself,* sayd Ebba, *Its true,* sayd Edith, *alle the doctor can recommend is rest and prayer.*

At length the dag came when the abbess was able to leave her chambrs, and sche joind us once more when we dind in the refectory. Despite her advancyng illness her presence was a boon to us alle, for it es true to say that wherever sche went sche brought with her a spirit of peace and wele-beyng which spilld ofer onto those in her company, as the sun in the firmament transforms a cold winters dag, meltyng the bitter frost and bringyng the vegetation to lyf. There was a healthy glow in her cheeks, too, which surprisd us yet, certainly, sche had put on more weight, as a number of the systirs were quick to remark. As wele as joinyng us in the refectory, sche continued to show interest in oure work on Odos tapestry, askyng for detaild explanations of every scene, and advisyng us on the choice of colourd wool where this had not been specified on Turolds designs.

As the spell of fine weather continued, we were able to start addyng colour and texture to the bone-huses of men and hrosses on the scenes depictyng the batalle of Hastings, first usyng laid and couchd work to fill the bare expanses of the hrosses flanks, and then oferlayyng this with diverse raisd threads, sometymes thrown into relief by the use of a lighter colour, woad-blue, fawn or golden-yellow. Mostly, though not always, these ran vertically in meanderyng ligns, lyk the course taken by a rivulet of watter as it runs ofer open ground, cuttyng across the horizontal arrangement of laid groundwork, to give texture to the hrosses coats. By varyyng the combination of colours, as wele as the arrangement of the ligns of raisd threads – here a five-finger stitches them followyng the curve of the hrosses buttocks, suggestyng bulk, elsewhere anothir five-finger stitches them runnyng from top to bottom at a bakwards tilt, suggestyng movement – we are able to give individuality to the hrosses. There are variations, too, in the manner in which we broider the manes – here, lyk snow on a mountain top, spreadyng its icy fingers ofer the hard rock, elsewhere lyk ripe eyras of corn blowyng in the summer breeze – and there are countless different ways of positionyng the eyras, the tail and the leggrs to give a host of effects.

And yet, as the batalle scenes move forward, takyng on lyf and colour – so vivid, indeed, are the tapestry images that youd swear vou coud ear the clatter of batalle as vou gazd on them – an unforeseen problem crops up. The problem, no thing short of a catastrophe, first comes to light as Ethelreda the Reed, workyng a new length of linen, broiders a heavy russet stallion

An unexpected impediment to the work

129

which carries a mounted Norman knight. The knight sits erect in his saddle, readyyng himself to launch his sturdy javelin in the direction of the Saxon shield-wall towards which his steed carries him at a gallop. Systir Ethelreda has already completed the figure of the knight down to the fine links of chegn-mail – neat rows of stem-stitchd rings, lyk coins in a countyng hus – and sche es now workyng on the front ende of the hross, startyng with the heafod, when, alle of a sudden, the russet-red wool which sche es usyng to broider the hrosses flanks, runs out. Bother, sche says to herself, and at once sche asks flame-haird systir Anna, who holds the keys to the sacristy, which dangle from an iron ring which hangs at her waist, if sche can fetch som more red wool. Yet, on reachyng the sacristy it immediately becomes apparent that there es *no more* red wool – the shelf where it shoud lie es completely empty! As the news reaches oure eyras we panic. How on terre are we goyng to finish Odos tapestry on tyme if we haue no wool?

Hastily, a party comprisyng myself and the novices Brigid and Catherine es despatchd to Shepperton. We set off in the afternoon. Although the weather has been dry for som tyme the roads are muddy and treacherous, and the hooves of oure mounts sink deep into the sludge, sometymes up to the knee. At oon point systir Catherines mare sinks so deep that it es unable to extract any of its hooves whatsoever and alle progress es brought to a halt. Systir Catherine es forced to dismount while the mare struggles hopelessly in the quagmire. Yet the more it struggles, the more it becomes entrenchd in the mud, until its leggrs are alle but completely immersd in the mire. We leave it there, advancyng as best we can on the two remegnyng mounts, intendyng to get help at Shepperton to dig out the mare on oure return. From here on, we stick to the verges, makyng slow progress, but at least here the ground, bound together as it es by grases and bracken, es more firm beneath the hooves of oure mounts. As we journey we talk about affairs at the prayer-hus – the abbesses attack of cattle pestilence, Hilda the Herbaresses mysterious absences, the wool crisis, the seizure of the letters. How serious an offence is it to receive letters? asks Brigid, Will systir Geta be punishd? asks her companion, What does it say in the Rules of the Hus? It es difficult to say, I tell them, it depends on your interpretation of the Rule, And how is that? continues Brigid, It es very complicated, I explegn, letters of a holy nature are permitted, othirs carry the heaviest penalties, but I fear for Getas sake: the prrriorrress can be harrrrsh!

Eventually, we reach Shepperton and make oure way to the wool merchants workshops. Before enteryng I check my beard es wele hidden beneath the folds of my wimple. In stark contrast to oure previous visit, the large expanse of the workshop appears deserted, and for a moment we think it must haue shut down for the dag – Is it som pagan festival? asks Catherine – and yet, as we penetrate further into the gloom of the workspace, we see signums of lyf here and there: in an ill-lit corner a woe man sits by an abandond heap of spindles, feedyng her infant child from an extended nipple as sche pumps the ripe breast with her five-finger; elsewhere a dishevelld child in bare five-toes stokes a brazier with a forkd stick of elderwood, coaxyng the dyyng embers into lyf; while from above, amongst the rafters, oon can ear the distinct sound of snoryng. Approachyng the woe man, we enquire as to the whereabouts of the wool merchant, only to be told that he es absent. Yet, at length, sche directs us to a dingy courtyard, where the merchants assistant es seated on a barrel drinkyng ale. When we explegn oure business, he looks on us with a sideways glance, then, in a barely articulate drawl, spit alle the while dribblyng down his chin, he turns towards us: The master is away on business, he says, there is no wool here neither. He has travelled to ... *hic!* ... Essex to get fresh supplies ... he is not expected bak for som tyme. Once we haue explaind oure predicament, namely oure

The workshops at Shepperton deserted

dire need of new supplies of wool, the assistant merely repeats what he has already told us, that there es none. See for yourself, he says, and gestures towards the empty workshop. Yet, as we turn to go, unsure of what oure next step shoud be, he turns to us excitedly, What about the sheep on the ... *hic!* ... common?

And it es true, of course, that the prayer-hus has a number of sheep under its care, which we use only for theyr milk, reservd for the patients in the infirmary, and from which we make cheese too, from tyme to tyme, yet if we were to shear them, or haue them sheard – hed be glad to do the job him- ... *hic!* ... self if we dont know how to – then the wool coud be dyed straight away.

Thankyng him for his advice, I turn to go followd by systirs Brigid and Catherine, eager to get on with the job. In the hurry I quite forget about askyng for help to unearth the buried mare we haue left stuck in the mud, but as we make oure way homewards, when we reach the spot, the mare es no langer to be seen – it has sunk entirely into the sludge, just a trace of its mane es visible above ground, lyk a tussock of gras on the road, only it es grey.

Once bak at the prayer-hus I immediately reported to Croaker and next dag, at chapter, the crisis became the focus of oure discussions. At length, we came to the decision not only to shear oure own sheep as quickly as possible – half a dozen novices were sent out straight away to get on with the job – but also to send a letter to Bishop Odo who, with alle the estates he had at his disposal, we felt sure woud be able to help us out. And so, oon way or anothir, we woud soon haue more wool to work with.

The abbess Such had been the commotion ofer the wool that the unthinkable had occurrd – we had forgotten the abbess. Yet as soon as the situation seemd under control, sche once more filld oure thoughts. Oure belovd Aelfgyva lay in her lit struck down by cattle pestilence! By what cruel twist of circumstance had this come about? And how on terre had sche pickd it up? From oon of the patients in the infirmary? From the beef broth prepard by systir Felicity? Or had sche somehow contracted it duryng her stay at St. Augustines? Mayhapp, suggested Anna, sche has been deliberately fed infected meat in the hopes of doyng away with her – for it is clear from the fyr and conflagration that someoon at Canterbury wants her dead. And then it struck us with force – all this tyme we had been worryyng about the dwindlyng wool supply the abbess lay in her quarters, waityng to die. Mayhap, already, sche was preparyng to meet her maker, for sche had been seen prayyng for lang hours at niht in the kirk, and it was sayd that ever since the doctors visit a light had been kept burnyng in her chambr throughout the niht. We were filld with remorse – systirs Edith and Emma were sent to her chambrs to see how sche was. Sche is wele, reported Edith, makyng the signum of the rood with her bony five-fingers. In good spirits, sayd Emma, tryyng to reassure us with a broad, though pale-lippd, smile. Her predicament, added Edith, pausyng to exercise her Adams apple, must not be allowd to inter-fere with the progress of the hangyng.

Meanwhile, awaityng fresh supplies around Lammas tyme, we push on with the tapestry as best we can usyng the threads that are left. Though we are clean out of russet-red, there are still a few othir colours to work with – theres no shortage of mustard – and wherever we can we move the design forwards usyng these threads until the point where, oon by oon, they too begin to run out. Those of us who haue been broi-deryng in russet-red and fynd oure way forward blockd eventually grow impatient of the delay, fyndyng ways to get round the problem. The russet stallion which Ethelreda the Reed had been broideryng before, entire but for the foreleggrs and the surroundyng area, sche boldly completes in mustard, turnyng the hross into a piebald and, impressd by the effect, othir five-fingers at once follow suit: a hross with a russet heafod es completed in nettle-green; while anothir with a single russet hoof es finishd off in woad-blue and mustard. Then beneath the olive-skinnd five-fingers of systir Beatrice who broiders with spellbindyng skill, an abandond russet charger – only two of its leggrs given colour with laid and couchd work before the wool ran out – es now finishd in mussel-blue so that it metamorphoses before our augas into a black hross whose two russet leggrs, now pierced by spear shafts, appear to be coated with blod. And so effective are these stitches that som of the systirs workyng on hrosses where no russet-red es involvd at alle, copy theyr strategies so that soon the tapestry es filld with hrosses in woad-blue and saffron, fawn and black, nettle-green and mustard, black and onion-brown.

Hilda the Herbaresses continuyng absence No five-finger es idle, though oon pair of five-fingers es absent mych of the tyme, som thing we are reminded about when Abbess Aelfgyva – now larger than ever, and with dark rings under her augas from her nihtly vigils – once more comes to inspect the progress of the hangyng. Twistyng her swollen fingers on the efenyng air sche asks after systir Hilda, and we can only bow oure heafods in silence as Ethelguida the Mute explegns in rapid finger-talk that sche es absent. The abbess, though, does not ask where. Indeed, sche seems unconcernd – perhaps sche has not eard the rumours, for her mind has certainly been preoccupied with othir matters – instead, her attention es taken by Geta the Geatkeeper who sits cryyng. Abbess Aelfgyva comforts her, while we tell about the letters, They were snatchd from her chambr, I tell her, Sches been inconnsolable ever since they were seizd and taken, says Anna, They were from her … err … brothir, says Ebba, Aye, its no crime, says Aelfflaed, And now with the, erm, doctor, the wool and everything else, says Gunnrid, sches on the verge of collapse.

The abbess continues to comfort her, dryyng the tears with the corner of her sleeve, tellyng her in swift finger-talk not to worry, that everything will be alle right. Then turnyng to the frames, twistyng her fingers in the air, the abbess expresses her delight at the ways in which we haue done the hrosses, capturyng theyr movement and theyr variety. And now, as sche wanders the length of the cloister, her attention es alle of a sudden caught by a group of naked figures on the middle frame which the rough five-finger of systir Ebba has stitchd ofer the knights assembld at Hastings. The figures are out lignd in stem stitch with litell elaboration, but the stitch es neater than that employd by Ebba in the earliest scenes of the tapestry and oon of the figures holds a garment and an axe which haue been carefully filld out with laid and couchd work, signums that Ebbas skills, though not of the highest, haue yet improvd with practice, so provyng the truth of the sayyng, if proof were needed, that practice makes perfect. And now, with rapid movements of the five-fingers, and a curious expression on her audlit, the abbess asks systir Ebba, who es still busy broideryng a mans broad moustache in a stiff lign of stem stitch, to explegn her images. At once Ebbas audlit reddens, the blod pumpyng through the fine capillaries, then alle in a fluster, tryyng to finish off the pointed moustache, sche tugs the thread too quickly through the linen, where it tangles, formyng an ugly, stiff knot, which will not budge, as Ebba curses under her breath, *Hells breeches!* while othirs cross themselves in silence. And then, pullyng out her shears to cut the thread, and at last puttyng down her needle which sche tucks into the border, seatyng herself on her stool, systir Ebba turns towards us and, in her falteryng voice, begins her tale.

The Tale of Godgifu or Systir Ebbas Story

The story Ive stitchd, lyk the tale told by systir ... err ... Geta, is not the story of my own lyf, which has been too plegn to be worth the tellyng. Yet its the story of a creature known to you alle: Godgifu. It is her wailyng, her banshees howl, which oftentymes, late at niht, accompanies the cry of the screech-owl, keepyng us awake in the dormitory, as we await, in oure beds, the call for matins. Ill nefer forget the dag I first eard those eyra-piercyng howls. It was on the efenyng of St. Lucys dag 1071. In that year, this shortest and darkest of dags was made gloomier still by the black forebodyng skies which lingerd throughout the dag and, late in the afternoon, erupted in a violent storm. It began with a sudden downpour of blackbirds, which fell thick and fast, breakyng tiles, cloggyng the gutteryng and litteryng the damp earth with theyr bruisd and broken bone-huses. Next came giant hailstones, som the size of a clenchd fist, then the geats of the heavens burst open, floodyng the already batterd earth, lyk a river in spate, and Zeus the thunderer sent down shafts of forkd lightnyng, oon of which struck the prayer-hus kirk, which woud certainly haue caught fyr, were it not for the continuous onslaught of the regn.

The deluge continued late into the niht, keepyng us awake in oure beds, unsure that the roof ofer oure heafods woud hold. Already, indeed, it had burst in several places and, under the directions of the flusterd abbess, we hurriedly distributed leather buckets on the floor to catch the watter. Many five-fingers, as they say, make ... err ... litell work. Efen so, we had no respite: duryng the height of the storm, we were constantly runnyng to and fro, for no sooner did we put a bucket

136

down than it seemd to fill to the top, and at once we had to run to the slit windows to empty it. Shortly before matins, though, the storm at last abated, and for som minutes alle we coud ear in the early dawn was the persistent *drip-drip* of the watter into oure carefully placed buckets. Between each drip, the silence was absolute, as it must haue been after the Flood.

It was then, perhaps after ten minutes or so of this uneasy silence, punctuated by the drip-drip of the watter, that we eard that strange unearthly howlyng for the first tyme. Initially, I thought it was the howlyng of a … ahem! … sche-wolf whod lost her cubs in the storm. Then I thought it must be the wailyng of som ghost, som tormented spirit awoken by the deluge. And yet, the more I listend, the more I became sure that this was a human voice, not that of som denizen of the spirit world.

It was mid-mornyng before I arrivd at the infirmary to attend to my duties there – for, as you know, while I haue but litell knowledge of the healyng arts, its my job as guest-mistress to attend not only to oure more noble visitors, but to the comforts of oure humble guests in the infirmary. As I soon found, the storm had claimd a number of victims: there was a bearded peasant with a broken leggr whod been caught in the hail; anothir man, whod taken a batteryng, had been found shelteryng in the woods; and then, asleep in a bed at the far ende of the room, a bedraggld-lookyng beggar whod been admitted in the early hours. Sche had lang dark har, lyk a gypsy, which was matted, and streakd with grey, and sche had a small oval audlit, which must once haue been beautiful, but which now was scord with the furrows of age, scratchd too, as if by a thorn bush, or the claws of a wildcat. As soon as I saw this woe man I knew that sche was the oon whod utterd those othirworldly cries in the niht, and at once I wanted to know her story. Yet there was litell to tell. When sche arrivd in the niht sched been possessd by the devil and had begun howlyng and screamyng, grindyng her teeth and foamyng at the muthr, and sched had to be given a sleepyng draught of henbane and betony, to calm her down, since when sched been restyng peaceably in her bed.

Sche continued sleepyng wele into the afternoon, but towards efenyng sche showd sudden signs of lyf, cryyng out in her sleep and thrashyng about in her bed. At once myself and systir Felicity went to her bedside and tried to calm her, but as soon as we touchd her sche lashd out more fiercely than ever, shoutyng and screamyng once agen, this tyme clearly enough for us to make out her *creatures* words, *No! No! G-G-Get off! Get off me! Craturs!*

We told her that we wouldnt harm her, that we were only there to ... ahem! ... help, but sche was deaf to oure reasonyng and continued to shout and to thrash about, until we left her alone.

When sched settld once more into a doze, systir Felicity administerd anothir sleepyng draught, then exa-mind her bone-hus. It soon became clear that the scratches which oon immediately noticed on her audlit, extended also to the arms, and to the chest; and her bak, too, was lacerated by criss-cross scars, as if sched been beaten, or whippd. More alarmyng still, her leggrs appeard to haue been bitten by som animal, a hundr or a wolf, and these wounds were both open and unclean. Systir Felicity feard that the woe man might haue been bitten by a mad hundr, and so sche proceeded to mix together a healyng balm of agrimony and cowslip, com-bind with honey and the white of an egg.

That niht we hopd that sched sleep soundly, but we were to be in for a shock. Shortly before lauds, we were awoken by screechyng and bangyng comyng from the infirmary and immediately, accompanied by Felicity and a number of the othir systirs, I hurried to the scene. Despite the racket, most of the patients appeard to be sleepyng soundly, though a number of them had been woken by the noise and lay groanyng in theyr beds, som of them cursyng loudly. The cause of the disturbance was not diffi-cult to fynd: in the corner of the room, the woe man lay huddld by the door, bangyng on it with her fists, now and agen callyng out, feebly, *Let me oot! Let me oot!*

It was at once clear from the disconnected and clumsy manner of her movements, as it was from the glazd expression which had descended on her augas, lyk mornyng mist, that sche was not awake, but rather wanderd in her sleep; efen so, it was with som … err … difficulty that we managed to coax her bak to bed, for her bone-hus was stiff and unpliable, lyk a corpse, and it resisted oure movements at each step. When, after a struggle, we at last reachd the bed, we wrappd her tightly in blankets, tuckyng them around her lyk swaddlyng. And here we left her, prayyng to God and to Morpheus that the rest of the niht woud pass in peace.

The next dag I was surprisd to fynd the woe man sittyng bolt upright in bed, consumyng a hearty breakfast of porridge with warm milk and rye bread. And when I tried to talk to her, sche spoke with a clarity which was astoundyng in oon whod been so wild and inarticulate the previous dag, Where is it that I f-f-fynd mesel? sche *myself* askd, St. Ethelfledas, I sayd. Sche lookd puzzld, I come from K-Kirby, in the north, sche explaind, I lyk, lyk your podder. *porridge*

Followyng breakfast, sche agen slept throughout the dag, but unquietly, plagued by her inner demons. Sche was forever tossyng and turnyng, and her five-fingers too woud twitch and lash out from tyme to tyme, as if to ward off an insect, or a blow. Sittyng at her bedside, I coud at tymes make out snatches of the strange inarticulate mutteryngs which woud often slip from her muthr, *Put it oot! Put it oot!* sche repeated, ofer and ofer, *I t-t-told you to put it oot!* – though whether sche referrd to a cat, a fyr, or a fiskr supper was difficult to tell. Then, as before, sche woud say quite clearly, while thrashyng her limbs about, *Get off me! Get off, off me, you craturs!* Now that I had seen the bites on her leggrs, the beasts sche referrd to, I thought, must surely be hundrs?

For many dags things went on in this fashion. Periods of lucidity woud alternate with periods of incoherence and fits of screamyng. And then, almost every niht sched either cry out in her sleep, disturbyng the othir patients, or, which was worse, sleepwalk, sometymes gettyng only as far as the door, sometymes beyond, but always far enough to give us som thing to worry about, eh Felicity? On the whole her periods of lucidity nefer lasted lang enough for me to get mych out of her at any oon tyme, yet bit by bit, ofer the weeks, the litell scraps sche occasionally venturd began to add up, not into anything lyk a complete picture, but enough to furnish her general bakground.

Sche was the daughter of Cedric the Wild whod fought alangside Edwin of Mercia and Morcar of Northumbria in the northern uprisyngs of 1068 and 1069, uprisyngs which were ruthlessly crushd by William, and which, in the ende, cost her fathir his lyf. In the aftermath of the uprisyngs, as is wele known, Williams vengeance and cruelty knew no bounds: crops were wasted, villages … ahem! … burnd, men of fightyng age executed, without trial. In the furnace of Williams wrath, Godgifu lost her hus and her family and – Im sure – her mind.

After a number of weeks, systir Felicity removd the bandages from Godgifus leggrs: the wounds, which had been open before, were now healyng wele, and there was no signum of infection. Around the same tyme, Godgifu enjoyd frequent periods of alertness, and sche was able to talk, both more often and more coherently, than before. Once agen, sche askd where sche was, and this tyme, as sche still lookd puzzld, I began to explegn how sche came to be here: that sched arrivd by niht, duryng a heavy storm, that wed eard her howlyng. I mentiond too how systir Felicity had treated her leggrs, which had been savagely scratchd and appeard to haue been bitten, too, Haue you ever been set upon by hundrs? I askd. From the wild look which at once distorted her features it was clear that Id hit the mark. Yet sche was silent for several lang minutes before, at length, sche spoke up. Sche had the distinct recollection, sche sayd, of beyng chasd, chasd by a pack of hundrs, though the memory seemd to be of a tyme far d-d-distant. Sched been runnyng through a brak, while behind her, in the *forest* d-d-distance, sche coud ear the sound of a hearn and *horn* the barkyng of hundrs. A regular huntyng party, in a word — except that this oon was chasyng human meat. Sche ran and ran and kept runnyng for dags on ende, her five-fingers and her audlit, her leggrs and her bone-hus becomyng scratchd and blodied by buskies, and *bushes* thorns, as sche desperately pushd her way through dense undergrowth, to escape her tireless pursuers. At tymes, alle was silent, and sche woud think for a moment that sched thrown the h-hundrs off; then sched ear the savage barkyng once agen in the distance, and woud once more push on.

Eventually — yes — they mustve caught her. That was it, sche rememberd it clearly now: the hundrs had caught up with her by the … err … banks of a strame, *stream* as sche was bathyng her wounds; theyd attackd fiercely, smarlyng and rowlyng and snappyng and tearyng at the flesh, of her leggrs and ankles, drawyng blod, so that sched wishd only for death to come quickly, had utterly given up the fight, when, inexplicably, out of the blue, theyd been calld off by the distant noise of a horn, sounded three tymes.

At this point Godgifu pausd in her story, catchyng her breath. I fetchd her a beaker of watter, which sche gulpd down, and then, after a few moments, before sched a chance to go on, I askd her — thinkyng I must strike while the iron was hot — whi sche was on the run?

As soon as the words left my lips, I felt the question was premature, that I was pushyng her on too quickly. I was sure, too, that now sched clam up; yet before I coud open my muthr agen, sche spoke out, falteryngly yet distinctly, I was h-held agegnst my will by the, the Normans, sche sayd, they kept me in a deserted and f-f-f-filthy farmhus, which theyd occupied as a kynd of b-barracks, they didnt, they *imprisonment* didnt give any reason for my wairdyng. At this point sche stoppd suddenly, as if unable to go on, and I didnt want to push her, knowyng as I did that sched already sayd far more than on any othir occasion. When, moments later, sche went so far as to jump out of bed, turnyng her bak on me without a word, gropyng her way to the furthest corner of the room, I knew that sched had enough. Yet as I stood up and prepard to leave, sche calld to me, softly, and so I made my way to her side. When I got there, I found that sched pickd up a piece of charcoal from a spent burner, and with this sche started to scratch a series of figures, on the infirmary wall, figures which, I soon came to see, were her way of illustratyng the unspeakable heart of her tale.

Ive copied the scenes sche drew as best I can in the upper margin of the tapestry – *look* – above the heafods of the Norman knights as they prepare to do battle at Hastings. In oon of them, a naked man with a bushy … ahem! … moustache advances lyk a predator upon an equally naked woe man, who rests on her haunches, as if in readiness to repel his advances; in anothir a man bearyng an axe appears to be holdyng out a piece of clothyng, at arms length, to a naked woe man, who advances cautiously towards him, arms outstretchd. After Id gazd in silence at the charcoal figures for som minutes, Godgifu, sensyng Id caught theyr general import, began to elaborate on theyr tendyng.

Thir s-s-scenes, she sayd, show just two of the, of the many wickit g-g-games which the Normans devisd to prolang my agony. In the first, the l-luggit game, Id to g-g-grapple with each of the brutes in t-turn, sometymes in eird, sometymes in straw, sometymes under watter. If I got to fra them, them down first, theyd stand aside makyng way for the n-n-next renk; if, as was usual, they caist me down f-first, they woud take me, take me as they pleasd, or as they were baid to do by theyr b-b-b-billies, or they woud hurt me in othir ways, before the game continued. Things woud go on lyk this quhill each of the renkis had done theyr b-b-b-business, so that, in t-t-truth, the more tymes I succeeded in flooryng them the more my, my barrat went on. And yit, if I refusd to put up a f-f-fight, they woud bett me with rungs. In the second game, with which they often wrappd up theyr d-d-dags work, they woud at last offer me respite from, from the torture, holdyng out my c-c-claithis to me, rippd and d-d-dirty as they were, so that I coud at last hide my bowk from theyr ene. Yit, as I reachd out to grab my claithis – a woollen k-k-kirtle, a smock, a linen hose – theyd snatch it out of my grasp at once, and take a, take a swipe at me with theyr axes. Mostly, this was just to s-s-s-scare me – they aimd to miss, if only just – but frequently, by the tyme the game had reachd its grim c-c-c-conclusion, and Id retrievd my claithis for another n-n-niht, my bowk woud be batterd and bruisd and unleipit with savage cuts, and there was no-oon to dress, no-oon to dress the sairis.

wrestlyng

dirt
throw
man
threw

companions
until

misery
beat; sticks

clothes

bone-hus

split open
wounds

As sche came to the ende of her story, my heafod was filld with further questions I now wanted to ask – What had driven the Normans to this extreme cruelty? How, finally, had sche managed to escape? – yet it was alle too plegn that Godgifu had exhausted herself, and I didnt try to pursue matters any further that dag. Every ... err ... ploughboy, as they say, needs to rest. I kissd her gently on the foreheafod and blessd her, leavyng her to sleep, sobbyng into her pillow; that niht, sche slept as

143

soundly as sche had since her entry into the prayer-hus, and this without the least aid from any sleepyng draught. For my own part, I didnt sleep soundly at alle – Id eard before of the ruthlessness and of the cruelty the Normans were capable of, but Id eard no thing as vile as this, and my heart wept for Godgifu.

For several dags after, I was too taken up with othir matters to be able to spend any tyme in the infirmary, but at last there came anothir dag when I was able to sit by Godgifus bedside, and talk with her. As before, sche seemd alert, composd efen – though there was still a wild look in her auga – and sche was agen willyng to put up with my questions. How was it, I askd, that you ended up in the five-fingers of these brutes?

Her account took us bak to January, 1070, som months after her fathirs death in battle, and after William had crushd the northern revolt. Oon mornyng, sche explegnd, there was a loud knock at the d-d-door *cottage* of theyr cootie and on openyng it sche was met with four armourd Norman knights, and as many agen, sit-tyng bak on theyr hrosses. They demanded brusquely that alle the occupants of the cootie come out side, so out sche steppd, with her six-month-old baby girl, her *husband; boy* hus-bond and theyr loon, Malcolm, to see what all the f-fuss was about. At once, oon of the hrossmen spoke, readyng from a parchment, *Vou and alle of your hushold are hereby accusd of treason agegnst King William of Englan, and do hereby give up your dwellyng into the five-fingers of the servants of King William, and forfeit your rights to live in this lan from this moment.* In plegn language, he then added, vou haue until noon to get out of the village, and if vou come bak, it will be on pegn of death. Godgifu, at these words, was struck dumb, but her hus-bond found the *treachery* courage to speak up, We are as innocent of the trayne of which you speak as this bairn, he sayd, You maun haue come to the wrang place, Yet vou dont deny that vou are English? sayd the Norman, You may call my family English, as for myself, Im a Scot, forced to flee my

hamelan the year Macbeth hint the croon, Then, pro- *homelan; seizd*
nounced the Norman, vou are an enemy to Englan and
to King William, and must pay with your lyf.

Godgifus tale reminds me of a fable told by Aesop
the Phrygian, and Ive broiderd this tale, *The Wolf and the
Lamb*, in her honour, beneath the lang-bot which carries
Harold towards France. The wolf, already fat from ofereatyng, stands on the right, observyng the lamb lappyng
watter from a stream. In the fable, the wolf wants an
excuse to devour the lamb. And so, although hes
upstream, he accuses the lamb of … ahem! … mud-
dyyng the watter and preventyng him from drinkyng.
The lamb replies that he drinks with only the very tip of
his tongue and that, besides, beyng downstream he
couldnt possibly muddy the watter up there. Outwitted,
the wolf tries anothir tack, Last year, he says, you
insulted my fathir, I wasnt even born then, replies the
lamb, so the wolf, who by this point has run out of
patience, snaps bak, Say what you lyk to justify yourself,
Ill eat you alle the same!

And so it was with Godgifu and her family, gatherd
out side theyr cootie. The mounted knights now got
down from theyr hrosses, and, under theyr commanders
auga, proceeded to mete out theyr cruel punishments
with a speed and severity which words can ill-describe.
The husband was held at sword-point by two of the
thugs, and forced to watch as anothir pair rapd his wyf.
Then they turnd theyr attention to him, cuttyng off his
five-fingers, then his five-toes, then his balls, which they
forced down his throat, before beheafodyng him with
an axe. The child they skewerd on a lance, paradyng it
around on hrossbak. Godgifu and her son they bound
and carried off, he to be sold into slavery, sche to the
cruel fate Ive already describd.

This was alle sched the heart to tell me that dag. It
was enough. More than enough. I understood, and I
understand still, whi sche often howld uncontrollably,
especially at nihts. I understood too that sched been

145

through more than most human beyngs can bear and survivd, and I understood whi, however mych we cared for her, however wele her wounds heald, however lang her periods of lucidity lasted, that in side sched remegn forever scarrd, and always be in danger of losyng her mind once more. Sched seen into the dark heart of conquest, and no bone-hus who has gazd here lang can easily forget the horror.

On later occasions Godgifu filld in som of the gaps in her story. Sche told me the details of her escape, how sched carefully plannd it, fled duryng the niht. Sche spoke too of the ravaged countryside through which sche wanderd, a lanscape of torchd fields and huses, deserted villages haunted by wild beasts and robbers, mud tracks carryyng a stream of starvyng and destitute pepill, driven from theyr homes, most, lyk herself, at theyr wits ende, not knowyng whither they flew. The roads, too, were litterd with corpses swarmyng with worms, which gave off an abominable stench – for none were left to bury the dead. And then sche spoke of the child sched … err … given birth to, in her wanderyngs, the offspring of Norman seed, abandond in a ditch.

Sche left the infirmary in the spring. Her wish was to travel north, fynd her own pepill once more. Sche had systirs, cousins, who might still be alive, sche sayd. And sched not given up hope of findyng her son. Sche was gone for a while, but sche cannot haue got far. Perhaps sche lost hope, perhaps sche simply lost her way, gropyng her way bak whence sched come.

Sche now lives in the woods, as you know, hauntyng oure prayer-hus lyk a lost spirit, sometymes sittyng in the sun, sometymes howlyng in the regn, her banshees howl, keepyng us awake at nihts as we await, in oure beds, the bell for matins, or for lauds.

Chapter VII

Contegnyng men in large numbers, and a greet din

O N THE DAGS FOLLOWYNG systir Ebbas tale, we continued work on the bishops tapestry as best we coud, the supplies of wool dwindlyng alle the tyme. When the petyte amount we had been able to harvest off oure own flock came bak from Shepperton, we were in for a further disappointment: nine tenths of the wool had been unusable, as most of oure sheep were either brown or black, and theyr coats unsuitable for dyyng, for black will stay black however lang you soak it and brown es not mych betr. The packet of wool which arrivd at the prayer-hus geats on the eve of St. Radegunds dag, the twelfth of Augut, was so petyte indeed that the wool merchants assistant, who was kynd enough to deliver it himself, was able to carry it to oure precinct unassisted, tuckd under his bras. When the prioress unwrappd the packet it was clair that its contents were efen smaller still, and as sche pickd them up scornfully and held them aloft for alle to see it was at once apparent that sche held in her five-fingers litell more than enough wool for two hrosses.

A disappointyng delivery

Croaker was in the blackest of moods at this period, and we kept out of her way whenever we coud. Worst of alle, sche continued to fume ofer systir Getas letterhorde. This, it turnd out, had been uncoverd on a routine inspection of the dormitory. There was no Judas in oure midst, as I had feard – yet this offerd litell consolation amidst the prioresses ravyngs. *The receipt of letterrrs is absolutely forrrrbidden,* sche fumd, *the possession of prroperty itself is anathema, for as the Rule states: Above alle, this evil prrractice must be uprrrrooted and removd from the prrrayer-hus!*

Excomm-unication threatend

147

Getas sin was thus a twofold transgression in Croakers augas, and the direct threat of excommunication was held ofer her heafod, lyk an axe, waityng to fall. More-ofer, a cursory examination of the letters had reveald a quantity of correspondence in the language of the infidel and it did not take the prioress lang to jump to the conclusion that systir Geta was in communication with the enemies of Christ – confirmation of which sche found in Getas strange deformity, the perpetual fixation of her gaze on the east.

Odo returns in triumph

Yet it was not to be lang before distraction came in the shape of a visit from Bishop Odo who, respondyng to oure distress signal, came in person, on hrossbak, accompanied by an escort and eight waggonloads of wool, which were quickly despatchd to the workshops at Shepperton, carried there by the bishops own men, with instructions that it was to be processd with the utmost speed. Odo, oure guardian angel, had done it agen – and my companions did not miss theyr opportunity to chide me once more ofer my now infamous prediction. I shoud be more careful, in future, before I opend my muthr to entertegn a bunch of childern. In truth, my most recent attempts at prophecy had been pretty unreliable. True, I had predicted the famine of 1070, not to mention the regn of frogs in 1072, and more recently I had foretold the dry summer and the wild-fyrs of 1078, but vou can only rest on your laurels for so lang, they rapidly start to look tatty and fail to command respect.

The tapestry es lauded

Among Odos retinue was the dwarf Turold who, alang with the bishop, was keen to see how work on the tapestry was progressyng. We led them to the cloister with oure hearts in oure muthrs, anxious that oure progress woud be pleasyng to them, anxious too that oure embellishment and interpretation of Turolds plans woud not be found immoderate. For a lang tyme they wanderd round the frames, this way and that, in silence, Turold followyng Bishop Odo wherever he went, lyk Echo in pursuit of Narcissus. Sometymes, the bishop woud stop before a particular scene – the death of Edward the Confessor, the crownyng of Harold, Williams speech to his troops before the batalle of Hastings – and study the details of the design, standyng as if rooted to the spot, lyk the men on the English shield-wall, the only visible movement the intermittent twitchyng of his beakd nebb which, lyk the forkd stick held by the watter diviner, jumpd when excited. Then, alle of a sudden, without a word, he woud move on, follow'd alle the while by Turold, until anothir scene causd his nebb to leap in excitement and he stoppd once more. When, at length, he had finishd examinyng the design he turnd towards us. Magnificent! he sayd, The beauty of the work surpasses alle expectation, and given the troubles vou haue had with the wool supply, the progress es laudable! He then gave us his word that we woud not suffer from a shortage of wool agen – the consignment his men had taken to Shepperton, he assurd us, woud be more than enough to complete the tapestry. Turold, for his part, seemd less content, and he questiond us on a number of scenes which we had added, in particular systir Annas burnyng hus, Whence, he demanded in his shrill voice, do you derive the authority for this supplementary scene? My lord, systir Anna explegnd, presentyng her heart-shapd audlit before him and smilyng innocently, I was myself present at the tyme, it is oon of a nummber of huses and dwellyngs which unfortunnately impeded the armys progress, and which had to be destroyd and burnd.

Odo and Turold had barely finishd theyr tour, when there was a loud bangyng on the prayer-hus geats, accompanied by mych shoutyng, both from in side and out, and the unmistakable clamour of hrosses and men. Abandonyng the bishop where he stood, we alle ran to see what the fuss was about, and arrivd just as the hapless Geta opend the geats, through which there now flooded a vast swarm of Norman knights, not the most felicitous of phrases, in full batalle-dress, mounted on

A clamour of hrosses and men

theyr unruly stallions. Within minutes theyr numbers had alle but filld the outer courtyard, now a mass of men and hrosses, and still they kept comyng, wave upon wave, as if they were without number, lyk the citizens of hell. And then, when we thought the very walls of the precinct were about to burst with the multitude, a horn sounded its shrill call, and the waves of hrossmen, as if by a miracle, pulld up theyr bestes and parted, as the Red Sea had on former tymes parted at Moses command, exposyng a clair channel through theyr ranks. And now, through the geats and into the vacated stretch of precinct, rode a single hrossman on a massive black destrier: King William. As he enterd the precinct, Geta fainted – in her wild imaginyngs, the poor oferwrought soul must haue thought that the king had been summond to carry her off to som foul dungeon, to live out her earthly dags in penance and prayer, with only the rats for company.

William, it turnd out, was on his way to crush an uprisyng in Wales, led, it was rumourd, by Harold himself and, findyng himself passyng close by oure prayerhus, and his men weary and in need of rest, had decided to call on oure hospitality unannounced. Moreofer, he was aware that his half-brothir, Odo, was due to pay us a visit, and had been curious to see the tapestry of which Odo had spoken so mych. We bade him welcome, as was oure duty, while his men set up camp, som erectyng tents on the outer courtyard, othirs beyond the walls of the precinct.

William speaks When, at length, Bishop Odo made his way to the outer courtyard, he was amazd to see William standyng before him and the precinct swarmyng with warriors and hrosses. Yet, when alle had been explegnd, he greeted William warmly, claspyng him in his bras, and when the moment arose, he led him off excitedly, wishyng to show him the tapestry which the nuns had been at work on. Come, he said, vou must see the litell jewel for yourself. They spent a lang tyme together in the cloister, pacyng up and down the frames, and though I coud ear no thing of what passd between them, for I was busy at work in the scriptorium, from what later reachd my eyras, it seemd that while William was indeed impressd with the nuns work, particularly its depiction of the perjury of Harold, he found som of the details of the tapestry displeasyng. It was sayd that he thought Odos presence in the scenes depictyng the conquest too prominent – Odo was the central figure presidyng ofer the feast before Hastings, and duryng the batalle itself, there he was agen, chargyng alang, dealyng out death-blow after death-blow with his outsizd mace, for alle the world as if his heroism on the field of batalle had alone carried the dag. Your batalle prowess es exaggerated, brothir, William must haue sayd, or, Odo, vou are a brave and ubiquitous knight in the nuns augas, to which Odo will haue mumbld his brief reply, It es none of my doyng, lord, but my bras, as ever, es at your service. More particularly, William was profoundly displeasd by the figures of the naked man and woe man in the upper border of the tapestry above his own heafod as he converses with Bishop Odo in his camp at Pevensey. These, he pronounced, were to be removd at once. And then, William had a bone to pick with Odo ofer anothir, related matter, the Christchurch affair. Word had come to him from Lanfranc, Archbishop of Christchurch Cathedral, that Odo had used irregular methods to obtegn a confession, and that he had got the wrong man. Williams own reputation, he reminded Odo with harsh words, was at stake in such matters, and he promisd to get to the bottom of it. And yet, despite everything, William was pleasd to see Odo. Clappyng him on the bak, he laughd heartily, addyng that he woud be glad of Odos war-winnyng mace in Wales. The bishop blanchd – yet he was in no position to refuse.

That niht, in the camp the warriors had set up, there was mych feastyng and drinkyng. Warriors swappd stories of valour and conquest, as the spiced wine passd

The warriors rest

from five-finger to five-finger. Minstrels took up theyr instruments to cant songrs of batalle, som strummyng on harps, othirs beatyng out a rhythm on tabors:

> *Ear the Songr of Harold,*
> *King Williams deadly foe!*
> *He lost the Batalle of Hastings,*
> *But did that stop him? No!*

> *Now hes on the loose agen,*
> *Fightyng tooth and nagl,*
> *But he wont get bak his kingdom*
> *While were still on his tail!*

The noise continued late into the niht, and I tossd in my lit, cursyng the Normans beneath my breath, as I awaited the cruel bell for matins. Poor systir Ebba was on her five-toes alle niht attendyng to the diverse needs of the guests, doyng her best to keep everyoon happy. Alle niht, too, a light coud be seen burnyng in the abbesses chambr, and from tyme to tyme her shadow movd restlessly about the room. And later, when we fild down the niht stairs to chant oure devotions in the prayer-hus kirk, the noise out side drownd out oure prayers.

Williams wrath By mornyng, the noise had died down, and the sweaty bone-huses of the Norman warriors lay slumpd on the terre, drunk as mice. Som lay in heaps where they had collapsd in the niht, snoryng lyk pigs; othirs had curld up round the now dyyng embers of a fyr, which, here and there, had spread to theyr woollen undergarments, which smoulderd on the crisp mornyng air, givyng off a distinct odour of charrd flesh; elsewhere, in petyte groups, othirs were still laughyng and drinkyng, raisyng the vessels to theyr wine-staind muthrs. And no doubt they woud haue carried on in this fashion, had not King William, on risyng from his lit and sayyng his prayers in the kirk, venturd into theyr midst to stir them into action. He was a hard taskmaster and a holy man, and dismayd at the disarray of his troops and at the disrespect they showd for the order, he ran amongst them lyk a madman, stampyng and shoutyng – *Up! Up! Lizards!* – pullyng the men to theyr five-toes by the eyras, cursyng them and threatenyng them with the direst penalties. Som, who refusd to wake, he thrust on to the glowyng embers, from where they leapt up at once, prostratyng themselves at his five-toes; othirs, who still lay in the dirt, he kickd in the sides till they rose up, coughyng and cursyng. When the last of the men were awake he told them they were to pack up and move – they had a lang dags march ahead of them. And then, slowly but surely, the warriors set about dismantlyng theyr tents and gatheryng theyr armour until they were ready to go. They left around middag takyng the Winchester road, filyng out of the prayer-hus in a steady stream, which stretchd alle the way to the horizon before the last warrior passd through the geats.

When William had left the precinct once more regegnd its calm. We were able to say oure prayers undisturbd, and to carry on with oure daily business. I took the opportunity to catch up with the prayer-hus chronicle in the scriptorium, recordyng with grief the advancyng illness of oure belovd abbess. Then, at the thought of the abbess…, no, it was unthinkable, I burst into tears. When I had collected myself, I took up the quill once more and recorded as best I coud the visit of ~~William the Bastard~~ (*no, that woud nefer do, I crossd it out at once*), King William, and the events which took place duryng his stay. Later Bishop Odo, who had not left his chambr since he had taken William to see the tapestry the previous dag, at last emerged into the light, puttyng on a brave audlit. And Abbess Aelfgyva, who had been restyng in her quarters throughout the kings visit, descended to take the air. Sche lookd tired and anxious, her augas shadowd underneath, though sche put on a show of conviviality, greetyng Odo warmly, thankyng the lyf-saver with swift finger-talk. The bishop seemd

A conversation in private

embarrassd, for he bowd so low before her that he lost his balance and collapsd in the dirt, and his audlit, which, while fat, was normally as pale as alabaster, turnd to the colour of beetroot. Yet there was every reason for the bishop to be disconcerted: for while the abbess was full of lyf, her physical form had swollen lyk a French wine-skin since Odos last visit in the spring: sche was immense. Her habit, which in past tymes had hung loosely about her person now clung tightly to her bone-hus, and her audlit, which had once been aquiline, was now round and plump, lyk a ripe pumpkin. Once the bishop had pickd himself up Aelfgyva askd him to join her for a short while in her private quarters. They were not gone lang, but when Odo emerged he lookd shaken. We coud only guess that the abbess had told Odo of her sickness, of the lyklihood that sche woud not live to see the ende of the year, or the completion of the tapestry.

Hilda the Herbaress takes up her needle Later that dag, Odo left with Turold and his retinue – takyng the same road as the king. Yet he lookd weary, a pale shadow of the proud and warlyk bishop of the tapestry. As we watchd him ride off into the distance, I couldnt help thinkyng that, if the truth were told, this boastful and ugly man had litell stomach for the harsh realities of the batalle-field. Then, while the light lasted, we wasted no tyme in gettyng bak to oure work on the tapestry. Ironically, while the thread was fast runnyng out we were alle present that dag, efen the wayward sys-tir Hilda. Sche sat in silence at the first frame, without raisyng her heafod from the flax-cloth, workyng in rapid stitches, as if to make up for lost tyme. While most of the systirs contented themselves with broideryng simple out lign work as we awaited the new consignment of wool, systir Hilda, workyng mostly in black and mustard – the only colours which now remegnd in any quantity – though here and there addyng a brighter colour in scraps of thread which had fallen to the ground, swiftly stitchd the figures of bestes and birds in the borders.

While sche workd her rapid stem stitch, we saw theyr animal shapes take form — a lamb, a goat, a bitch, a bull — and as they were figures which did not feature in Turolds designs, we felt sure they must in som sense haue a bearyng on her mysterious absences. Were they — as systir Ethelguida intimated in secret finger-talk — bestes connected with the practice of som diabolical witchcraft? Or, perhaps, as systir Anna whisperd with her flame-red augabrows raisd, they represented the farm from which her secret lover gegnd his livelihood, where sche had helpd him tend the cattle in the fields and meadows beyond the walls of the prayer-hus? Hilda workd on, in silence, her audlit hidden beneath her cowl, oblivious to oure questions. Just at the point where Harold returns from Normandy, haveyng first markd out the area with the point of an awl, sche began to broider a hus or a castle, and as sche continued to work the bone-dart, oon by oon, audlits appeard at its archd windows. Was sche now revealyng to us, at last, the audlit of her secret admirer, the rich farmstead where he dwelt with his slaves and retegners? As the sun sank and the light faded on every pathway, we coud contegn oure curiosity no langer. Boldly, systir Aelfflaed, swayyng slightly on her five-toes, askd the question which was on alle oure lips: Hilda, for the love of God, where is it that youre off to when you quit the precinct? Embarrassd, systir Hilda bowd her heafod, then collectyng her thoughts, sche claird her throat and began her tale.

Blister, Baretoe, Pox, Eyra or
Hilda the Herbaresses Tale

Ech mornyng for the past six years or so Ive got up
befor coq crow, slippyng out of bed whil you lot stil
slept, then tiptoed down the cold niht stairs, alang the
nave of the kirk wher the candles gutterd the aisles and
out to the narrow courtyard beyon. On reachyng the
herbarium, Id pause for a moment, breathyng in the
bright scents of thyme and rosemary, then as dawn
spread her rosy fingers in the east Id brush through the
meadows and into the woodlan beyon. Here, Id gathir
wild herbs – lungwort and wormwood, tansy and spurge
– and yellow-gilld chanterelles to bryng bak to the prayr-
hus kitchens to be fried for breakfast or mixd with
breadcrums for the stuffyng of a goos.

Oon dag, I was makyng my way through the meadows as per usual – et was the month of March or April,
not lang after the years first drownyng, and I had stoppd
to pik a bunch of sweet-smellyng narcissi to bryng bak
for the dormitory – when, alle of a suddn, I sensd I
wasnt alane. Of cours, youre nefer completely alane in a
meadow in springtyme, yet on that dag I suddnly realisd
I was in the presence of othir pepill. I eard theyr voices,
the rough voices of men, issuyng from a hollow in the
risyng hill of the meadow, and as I edgd my way forwards then got close enough to catch a glimpse of them
through the lang gras, I saw four olde men sprawld awkwardly ofer the groun. Two lay on theyr baks, syde by
syde and heafod to toe, theyr leggrs stickyng up awkwardly ofer theyr heafods wher they met in a knutr of
toenagls and shoe leather. The othirs lay audlit down,
sprawld out in the wet gras, oon of them moanyng and
cursyng, the othir holdyng his five-fingers ofer his eyras.

They were alle dishevelld lookyng, as if theyd been sleepyng rough. The coupl who lay on theyr baks wore spade-shapd beards that spread ofer theyr broad chests and which heavd up and down, with vermin, nibblyng at the lice and the fat magotts. Yet most disturbyng of alle were the sockets of theyr augas which had been eatn away by disease, leavyng blak hollows. I was wonderyng what catastrophe these creatures had met with, when oon of theyr companions began to move – leferyng himself up with sticks – so I drew bak at once to avoyd detection. I made none of the usual blundrs – I didnt cough, I stood on no twig, I causd no flight of byrds. And yet, as soon as I took my first quiet steps, a voice rang out from the hollow, loud and cleer, Stay a whil, stranger – we mean you no harm!

I went down into the hollow, far from certain what lay in stor. I was frightend. Yet as I walkd into theyr midst et was soon cleer that they had no dishonest intentions towards me. They askd who I was and from wher I came, what I was doyng here, whether or not I was in the service of the Normans. When I told them I was not, that I was a servant of God, they were cleerly relievd. Not just the two that had lain on theyr baks, I soon discoverd, but alle four men were blind, and whil they reveald litell about theyr persons to me, et was cleer from what they sayd that they were in fear of theyr lives, that they were on the run. Theyr immediate requirements were foode and sheltr, and here they beggd my assistance. Whil I coud not immediately think of anywher they might lodge with safety – the prayr-hus itself, visited as et often was by Normans, was out of the question – I left them with the promise that I woud return in the efenyng with foode.

When I got bak to the prayr-hus I had not been missd. A visit from Odo himself accompanied by the dwarf Turold had takn up eferyoons tyme. The disturbance made et alle the easier for me to slip into the cook-room unobservd and help myself to what was on offer – bread, meat, cheese, apples – which I conceald as best I coud about my person. Latr, aroun the hour of vespers, I slippd out once more into the meadows, undr cover of niht. The blind men were waityng wher Id left them. I made the agreed signum – three hoots of an owl – and joind them in the hollow, distributyng the foode, which they devourd greedily. They had askd for wyne, and here too I did not disappoignt them. As I uncorkd the flagon which hung from my waist, the niht air was at once filld with ets rich perfume, and eight eagr five-fingers reachd out for ets contents, lyk the tentacles of som greet kraken in search of ets prey.

The wyne, which was of the finest quality, eyramarkd as et had been for Odos table, not only gegnd me theyr confidence, but loosend theyr tongues as wele. They told me som thyng of theyr plight, insistyng that whil they were no criminals, they were in mortal fear of meetyng Norman patrols. They told me som thyng of theyr journey, too, how they had met, by chance, in the vast forrest of the Weald, wher theyd sought refuge, and how theyd tried to fynd theyr way to the coast, but lost theyr bearyngs. They told me theyr names, too, names which I had already committed to memory – Blister, Baretoe, Pox, Eyra – but to which I was now able to put an audlit, audlits.

As they talkd I lookd out ofer the meadow, and there – silhouetted in the moonlight – I caught sight of the ruins of the olde Roman fort. In a flash, I realisd et was the ideal hidyng place for the fugitives, and minutes latr we were exploryng the in syde. Et is fair to say that et stank, yet as I felt my way aroun, I soon discoverd a rickety staircase. With som difficulty, we climbd this togethir, huggyng the wall, till we got to the next level – from wher a narrow stone staircase spiralld up to the top. Here there was a spacious hall with a dome shapd roof, from wher you coud step out through a low door onto a litell balcony which lookd out ofer the hills. The upper floors were mych tidier than the groun level – they had been visited by no beasts, efen if the signums of byrds and bats were alle about – and et was cleer that theyd make a betr lodgyng than the spot wher theyd spent the previous niht. Look, heres the towr as I haue stitchd et in the tapestry, just at the poignt wher Harold returns from Normandy. The heafods which appear at the windows, with the timid look of fugitives, staryng blankly into the syde of the towr, are Blister, Baretoe, Pox, Eyra.

Ech dag I brought foode and news of the out syde world: the Norman campegns, theyr victories and defeats, the latest rumours concernyng the wherabouts of King Harold. I told them too of the vast tapestry on which we were at work. As tyme went by they told me more about themselves. Blister and Pox, I learnd, were twins, though to my auga they lookd no thyng lyk ech othir, and in theyr talk they were as different as coud be, Blister givn as he was to exagerration, Pox to plegn speakyng. Baretoe, who was so-calld because of his habit of goyng without shoes, explegnd hed adopted this practice out of sheer necessity: not only were his five-toes so big that et was impossibl to fynd shoes that fitted, but efen when he did – and in betr tymes hed had them cobbld togethir from scratch – they nefer lasted lang, for as he walkd his five-toes grew so uncommonly hot and sweaty that they rapidly ate away the shoes leather, which fell off in lumps, lyk the flesh of a lepr. Eyra, et turnd out, was so-calld because his name was Eyrawicker, which was considerd too cumbersom by his friends for eferydag use. Yet the name coud hardly haue been more appropriate: not only were his eyras as lang and as hary as those of an ass, but he was blessd with an acute sense of earyng. The beatyng of a drum, he sayd, he coud ear from many miles away, lyk a distant puls; he coud pik up the squeak of a mouse from seferal fields off; and efen the ants which made theyr way through the lang gras at his five-toes did not escape him, The noise, he sayd, is lyk the constant trickl of a watter-track.

Apart from bryngyng them foode, I lookd after them in othir ways too. I combd theyr greasy and tangld har with the heafods of thistles to remove the lice and vermin, then I shavd off theyr filthy beards, persuadyng them that lyk this they woud be less easy to recognise. In addition I coaxd them into growyng theyr har lang at the bak, and tied et into bunches, just as the threads of the tapestry are gathird togethir with the couchyng stitch, to give them a Nordic look. These pigtails were to prove useful latr on, for when, after many visits, the rickety stairs of the towr finally collapsd altogethir, they were able to let me in by loweryng theyr har out the window, lyk a rope. They alle took theyr turn, yet for the most part et was Pox who took on the job, for his har was both langer and thicker than that of his companions. In the mornyngs, when I arrivd at the five-toe of the towr, I woud look up to theyr window and, raisyng my voice, call out:

> Pox! Pox!
> Let down
> Your locks!

Then Id shin up the har which tumbld from the window, usyng the knutrs as toe-holds, and in seconds be with them.

Often, when I joind them, they sat in silence, yet once theyr bellies were full they became more talkative. They woud swap stories and jokes, and sometymes they sang songrs of valour from the meadhalls, *The Fight at Sandwich*, *The Battle of Maldon*, *The Flight of Harold*. Oon tyme they askd *me* to tell a story, and as I coud think of no othir, I told them the fable of the fox and the crow from Esope, which Id been broideryng in the early part of the tapestry. When Id finishd, they took theyr turns at tellyng othir tales, alle from Esope.

Blister and Pox tell the fable of the eagl and the fox, wher an eagl seizes som fox cubs and carries them off to ets nest; Barefoot tells the story calld *The Lions Share*; and finally Eyra tells the fable of the bitch and her young, which I haue stitchd beneath the first of Harolds langships to set sail for France. Here, a pregnant bitch asks a friend if sche can rest in her kennl. Of cours, says the friend, but latr, when sche asks for her kennl bak, the bitch begs to hang on to et for a litell langer, until her whelps have grown strangr. Finally, when the owner returns agen, the bitch repays her goodwyl with treachery: sche can haue her kennl bak, no problem, as lang as sches prepard to take on her sons. This fable, says Eyra, was writtn agegnst those who take possession of anothir mans home undr fals pretexts; et stands as an indictment of William of Normandy, who has falsly takn possession of oure islan and alle thats in et.

This is only to give the bare bones of the stories as the men told them, for these were animated not only with countless details of observation, but with passion, so givyng the impression that they must haue witnessd these strange capers, or events of the same kynd, themselves. On the very next dag, feelyng I must strike while the iron was hot, I broachd the question which for a lang tyme had been on my lips, but which until now Id not dard to ask, How did you lose your augas? My question was greeted with a lang silence, and duryng ech passyng second I wishd for alle the world that I had not opend my muthr.

Yet, at length, Eyra spoke out.

My tale, he sayd, is straightforward enough, and will be quick in the tellyng. If I haue not told et till now et is not through rudeness, but simply to avoyd the pegn which ets tellyng is sure to bryng bak. He was from Exeter way, he explegnd, wher he had lost his augas in the siege of 1068. In that year, the pepill of Exeter, encouraged by Harolds mothir Gytha — stil in touch with her son through secret messengers — had risn up agegnst theyr rulers, oferthrowyng them in a single dag. Yet when the news reachd Williams eyras he replied with force, comyng down on the cite with 500 mounted knights, demandyng hostages as a signum of the cites goodwyl.

Eyra was oon of nine unfortunate wretches bundld into a cart, to be drivn to Williams camp som three miles out syde the geats. The delegation, led by a makeshift militia, quikly came to an agreement with the king, and at once five-fingerd ofer the hostages. When they returnd to the cite, they were in high spirits. Yet only an hour or so latr, when William and his vanguard rode up to the cite geats on snortyng hrosses, paradyng the now chaind and shackld hostages lyk prisoners of war, events were to take a suddn and unexpected turn.

William, said Eyra, at once demanded that the geats be unlockd, but the men refusd him, sayyng that first he must vow not to increase the cites tribute. Som of the men began to beat on pelts and furs to taunt him — for his mothir, Herlève, was a tanners daughter. William was livyd and turnd his anger on the hostages, accusyng them of treason.

We were innocent to a man, sayd Eyra, but this mat-trd not to William. Linyng us up in front of the walls, he repaid the goodwyl of the cite with treachery, orderyng oure augas put out. Pleadyng was useless: already we were bound, and the operation was carried out with swiftness and ferocity. In less tyme than et takes to peel a quince the jelly of oure augas was prickd out with the rusty poignt of a spere — the hot blod flowd thick and fast ofer oure audlits and into oure beards, and as I lifted my heafod up in darkness, I eard far off the hungry call of crows. The pegn was indescribable, causyng me to pass out at once. When I awoke, in darkness, I eard the deafenyng sounds of battle alle about, the stampede of hrosses, the war-cries and the clash of swords, the shouts of terror and pegn. And I smelt the burnyng and the blod and the hross shit. I lay pressd flat on the groun, in mortal fear, as the siege raged on alle about. Close by, I eard the poundyng of the heavy batteryng rams as they split into the cite geat, and the cries of the wretched assailants as they fell beneath the stones and the arrows and the piss-pots which regnd down from above; I eard too the raucous chorus of crows as they set about the stil-warm bone-huses with sharp beaks, stabbyng and tearyng the tender flesh; and I eard the intermittent buzzyng of flies as they padded the sticky augas of noblemen from Normandy and Burgundy, cut down in the flush of youth. As niht came, the warriors retreated and the groun became damp. I crawld off into the safety of the swamp which flankd the watter-track, nursyng my wounds. I slept litell, kept awake mych of the niht by what must haue been diggyng – the spades edge heftyng into the earth – no doubt that of Williams men constructyng som earthwork or undrminyng the walls, or just buryyng the ded.

The details of the siege I was unable to observe, but et went on for many dags, with fightyng by dag and diggyng by niht. In the ende, inevitably, Williams men won out by sheer force of numbers. Though whether the minyng was successful and the walls collapsd, as som megntegn, or whether the men of Exeter simply gave up, through fear and hungr, I cannot say. I haue eard that the settlement was favourabl – that William, at the ende of the siege, was untypically generous, for he was hard pressd by othir threats to his kingdom from the north and didnt want any more troubl. And I haue eard too that Gytha managed to get away unharmd, seekyng out Harold in the north – but, in truth, by this tyme I was a lang way off. As the siege raged on, I followd the winding cours of the watter-track to the coast, livyng off berries for the most part, and shellfiskr when I coud get my five-fingers on them, suckyng on stones when there was no thyng betr. Then I gropd my way alang the coast away from the grim and soulless cite of my birth, full of hatred for the king, as for the men who had thrown me into his five-fingers. After many dags I stumbld into a vast forrest wher I took sheltr from the peltyng regn, sharyng a bed of ferns with the ants and the woodlice, feedyng from the teet of a nanny goat who woud come to me in the mornyngs and let me sukle her. Weeks went by in this manner till oon dag the goat arrivd with her owner, a man who carried a stick. I know he had a stick, for at first he pokd me with et – no doubt to ascertegn if I were stil among the living. He was a kindly soul, for when he had completed his investigations, he did not abandon me, but helpd me up and led me to a low hut in a settlement. And here, in the ende, I met my travellyng companions, Blister, Baretoe, Pox.

Eyras story, I soon discoverd, had set the apples rollyng. When I arrivd at the fort the next dag, no soonr had I clamberd through the window and passd roun the foode, than Blister and Pox began theyr own tale. If Eyras story had been opaque at tymes because of his early blindyng in the siege, Blister and Poxes tale was renderd no less obscure by the wildly differyng accounts they gave of ets details. And yet, the broad out line of the story – for alle ets inner contradictions – was cleer enough.

Once upon a tyme, in real lyf, this is how the story went.

The twins haild from a smal village in Kent, Appleton

or Appledoer, I dont remembr. Applewhatefer, the place was laid waste by the Normans immediately after the conquest, as they ran riot in these parts. Blister megntegnd that the village had been torchd to the groun and vast numbers incinerated in the flames; Pox insisted that only a few huses had been set alight. Whatefer the truth of the mattr, et seems cleer that the Normans seizd alle the stocks of foode and livestock that they coud lay theyr five-fingers on, settyng light to the rest, so that litell was left for the pepill to live off once they had movd on. The villagers did theyr best to survive on what they coud forage in the woodlan, and they were lucky enough to unearth a smal reserve of gregn which the Normans had left untouchd, yet despite theyr efforts there was scarcely enough to go roun. Very quikly, the pepill became thin and pale and began to waste away, and as they grew weaker, many succumbd to sickness.

Accordyng to Pox, the sickness in ets early stages was simply brought on by hungr, so that the villagers became unnaturally thin and sufferd from dysentery. Yet Blister spoke of a terrible plague which had swept through the village lyk a vengeful fyr, causyng corrosive swellyngs behind the eyras and roun the augas, and which within hours had grown so virulent that the villagers droppd ded wher they stood in the street. Then the pollutyng stench of rottyng bone-huses heated up by the sun spread disease among men and beasts alyk, until tears and lamentations were seen in efery cottage and efery pigsty. The ded were so many, sayd Blister, that the numerals with which to reckon them coud no langer be found. Efen Pox acknowledged that et had been hard work buryyng the ded, I was not alane, he sayd, to volunteer my services in order to help out the ofertaxd gravediggers who tended the burial plot close by the parish kirk. Yet Blister spoke of vast pits which had been gouged out of the earth out syde the village boundary, scarryng the landscape, and into which the ded were flung by the cartload, These pits were so depe, he sayd, that if you tossd a penny into oon of them you woud not ear et hit the bottm befor the moon had passd through ets cours three tymes! And if you pressd your eyra to the groun you coud ear the roaryng of the devil in hell!

Yet if theyr accounts containd som discrepancies, they both concurrd, more or less, when et came to describyng the condition of those poor creatures fortunate enough to survive a bout of pestilence. Many were left blind, theyr augas eatn away by disease, and theyr bone-huses were coverd with pustules, Lyk blisters, sayd Pox, Lyk pock-marks, sayd Blister.

Duryng the first stages of the sickness, Blister and Pox labourd dag and niht to help the villagers who lay groanyng in theyr huts, doyng theyr best to ensure that they coud kepe a good fyr goyng by furnishyng them with logs, feedyng them with herb pottage, which Pox woud rustle up in the early hours, and sprinklyng them with the medicinal flowers of the marigold. And as they were both of a robust constitution, and as God lookd kyndly on them because of theyr good works, they were fortunate enough not to catch the sickness themselves. Othir members of theyr family, howefer, were less favourd. Theyr grey-haird fathir, an unrepentant druid with a hare-lipp, was amongst the first to be struck down, fallyng to his death from a laddr as he was patchyng a hole in the roof, and shortly afterwards theyr three systirs lykwise succumbd to the disease, takyng to theyr beds.

At aroun the same tyme, William the Conqueror granted the neighbouryng lans to oon of his most loyal followers, Count Brionne of Gascony, who at once set about buildyng a castel som three miles out syde the village, perchd high on a rock lyk the nest of an eagl. He brought with him an escort of fifty men-at-arms, a gift from William, and an assortment of woe men and cooks and blaksmiths and hangers-on. More importantly, howefer, he came with foode and livestock — sheep, cows, pigs, goats, chickens, geese, hrosses — which were set grazyng in the fields.

Et was Pox who led the delegation of villagers alang the windyng track that approachd the castel to petition the count for aid. Close at his heels rode the miller, the priest and the innkeepr, followd by villeins and serfs, whil Blister, who was undr strict instructions not to open his muthr, took up the rear. Count Brionne readily agreed to meet them out syde the walls of the castel, and here the priest describd to him at som length the desperate plight of theyr village, how many were dyyng from disease brought on by hungr, and how they woud alle surely perish, good Christian souls as they were to a man, not to mention the woe men – bless them! – unless they coud procure help.

Accordyng to Pox, Count Brionne listend to the priests words with a sympathetic eyra. And yet, he coud proffer litell in the way of help, My own stors, he sayd, are perilously low – and whil I expect a delivery of gregn from Normandy any dag, as yet there is no signum of et. Yet befor the men turnd to go he fetchd for them a sakful of hemp which, he sayd, woud at least help to alleviate the pegns which accompanied the ill-ness. And then he told them that he hopd soon to be makyng preparations for a banquet to celebrate the mar-riage of his daughter, and that now he thought of et – how silly that et hadnt occurrd to him at once! – he woud be in need of a few extra five-fingers. And so, befor they took theyr leave of him, they pikd out a few hale men to rest at the castel. These, at least, woud haue foode and a safe lodgyng.

Yet when I questiond Blister about the outyng, whil he concurrd that the count had listend patiently to theyr demands in the offyng, he swor by the Hymen of the Virgin that the audlit which had subsequently turnd towards them, fyr ragyng in ets augas, was that of a blodthirsty and sadistic butcher. In a fury, the count told them that he had a large entourage of his own to sup-port, and that if he showerd gifts on the first passers-by he woud soon have a riot on his five-fingers. Then he told them bluntly that the pestilence was a thyng sent by God to knock alle thoughts of rebellion from theyr hearts, and he advisd them to pray to St. Sebastien and St. Roche. And befor they left, he took seven of theyr most able-boned men as prisoners, hurlyng them at once into dark and festeryng dungeons sunk depe in the bowels of the fortress from which the clankyng of chegns and the cries of the wretched issued dag and niht.

Come beggyng agen, he yelled, and these men will be put to the sword!

Whatefer the truth of et, when Blister and Pox arrivd home, late that niht, they found that the condition of alle three systirs had takn a dramatic turn for the worse.

Alle niht, Blister and Pox sat by theyr bedsides.

Accordyng to Pox, the sisters obtegnd som alleviation by suckyng on the hemp which had been donated by the kindly count, and this had helpd them to accept theyr fate with calmness and dignity.

Yet Blister – whil he concurrd that the hemp was a powerful drug, for he had now takn to chewyng on et himself – swor by Gods bones that alle niht lang they had tossd and turnd violently in theyr beds, sweatyng by the bucketful, oon blasphemyng loudly, anothir utteryng vile curses agegnst the Normans and theyr seed, the thrid cryyng out for Death to come and take her swiftley – yet if he eard her at alle, he seemd in no hurry to do as sche beggd.

Whatefer the truth of et, by mornyng, alle were ded.

After this incident Pox made et his business to ensure that they at least got a decent burial. And afterwards he threw himself with renewd vigour into the struggle agegnst the disease, steppyng up the dagly rouns, for now that he had witnessd death at swich close quarters, he was more determind than efer not to lie down without puttyng up a fight.

Blister, howefer, who now chewd constantly on hemp, was thrown into wild-augad paroxysms of rage and grief, and in a fit of apocalyptic despair he hurld himself heafodlang into the bed, which stil sweated with the fefer, to die.

Pox knew only too wele that there was no poignt tryyng to reason with Blister, that et was best to let him alane. But he insisted on changyng the fetid straw, and he sprinkld the bed with the sweet-smellyng flowers of the marigold.

Tyme passd.

Winter set in.

Oferniht, the village was engulfd with snow.

And then, oon dag, Blister awoke in a sweat – bleary-augad – to fynd that he was not roastyng on a spit in hell, as he had imagind in his dreams, but lyyng on a comfortable bed strewn with flowers of the field.

And just as he was reachyng the surprisyng conclusion that he must be in heaven after alle, Pox steppd briskly into the room bearyng a revivyng infusion of chamomile, tellyng him that the cold weather had alle but put a stop to the sickness, that the number of reported cases was fallyng by the dag.

Blister sat up, wide-augad with wondr.

Et was, both Blister and Pox agreed, no thyng short of a miracle.

Yet, as Pox was swift to poignt out, if those of them who were stil left were to survive the cold, they woud need foode, and with the onset of winter et was at once more difficult to gathir berries and nuts in the woods, and what scant pikyngs remegnd were also in fiers demand from the byrds. And so, he was swift to suggest anothir visit to Count Brionne, who in alle lyklihood woud by now haue securd fresh provisions.

Once more Pox led the party, which was made up of the same company as befor, except for their companions who had remegnd at the castel, and for the innkeepr, who had meanwhil perishd through drink. And once more Blister took up the rear, undr strict instructions to kepe his muthr firmly shut. When they arrivd at the castel the geats were swiftley opend, and once they had been usherd into the counts presence, he bade them welcome with warm greetyngs, seatyng them swiftley in a spacious hall, wher they were able to meet theyr hale companions, and to take theyr fill of hot spiced wyne. And yet, when Pox told the count whi they had come, Brionne replied that he coud no more help them now than he had been able to hitherto – he was stil awaityng his supplies from Normandy, and feard som mishap on the trout-road, Alle that I can offer are prayrs on your behalf, though if supplies arrive, as I hope they will, any dag now, I shall be swift to answer your call.

When I askd Blister about the visit, howefer, he crossd himself at once, and invokyng the blod of the martyr-saints and the beards of the prophets of Baby-lone, he swor on his lyf that when they had approachd the counts castel for the second tyme, the geats had remegnd stubbornly shut. And when the count had got wind of theyr presence, he sayd, he had exploded in a fit of corrosive anger. In brief, he at once draggd two of the prisoners to the ramparts, and here they were decap-pitated with an ax. The count then pikd up the stil-protestyng heafods by the beards, and acceleratyng into the barbican hurld them into the air with swich ferocity, that et was only as the men made theyr way homewards that they eard them hit the groun at the five-toe of the geathus, whil far off they eard the count yellyng into the niht, Feast on these, if youre hungry!

Whoefer spoke the truth on this mattr – and at tymes I was sure that both spoke truly after theyr fash-ions – et seems cleer that once more Blister and Pox returnd home from the counts castel with empty five-fingers.

And that niht both slept unquietly, visited by dreams. In Poxes case he was blessd with mild and balmy visions of lang-ships ladn with gregn and grape which swiftley crossd calm seas. In Blisters case he dreamd of the ded risyng up from theyr graves to take fiers revenge on the Norman invaders, burnyng dwellyngs, seferyng limbs, pole-axyng childern. The followyng mornyng both were awokn early by mighty pegns in theyr stomachs, accompanied by fits of dizziness and vomityng: the sickness had finally caught up with them.

For a week they kept to theyr beds, lookyng after ech othir as best they coud.

Pox sweated a litell in the niht.

Blister raged and burnd, foamyng at the muthr, alle the whil gorgyng himself on the remegnyng supplies of hemp.

As the dags passed Poxes condition remegnd stable, and at the ende of a week, he efen showd signums of improfement, so that he was able to slip out of bed in the mornyngs to forage in the hedgerows for the litell that might stil be found there – half-starvd shrews, hibernatyng wasps, shrivelld berries, beetles. Yet Blisters condition rapidly nebb-divd. Whil at the start he had merely foamd at the muthr, now he emitted noxious waste from efery orifice, leavyng his bed awash with sputum and blak urine, purple bile which showerd from his eyras and the bubblyng geyser of foul mattr which now issued in an unstoppable stream from his anus. And soon his flesh burnd with swich a searyng heat that the bed wher he lay woud certainly haue burst into flames, were et not for this dowsyng swamp in which he now lay suspended, pressd up agegnst the rafters.

In a rare moment of lucidity, realisyng he might croak at any second – for the tide was risyng fast and as yet the fefer showd no signum of abatyng – Blister determind to wreak his revenge on the accursd count once and for alle. And so et was, fuelld by hemp and burnyng hotly with fefer, that he stormd out oon niht in a blind and reckless rage, whippyng the hungr-crazd villagers he met with on his way into a white-hot frenzy of anger directed agegnst the thievyng, child-molestyng, blodthirsty, two-audlited, murderous, sadistic, fat, pompous, arrogant and tight-fisted count. United by theyr common goal, this feferish and makeshift militia sallied out into the darkness, armd with torches.

Et was the niht of the weddyng banquet that they came bearyng theyr strange gifts. When the porter was awokn from his nap by the poundyng on the castel geats and peerd out from his slit window, his augas beheld a band of merry revellers bearyng candles which flickerd alle aroun in the niht, lyk stars. Yet when he unbolted the geats, the crowd knockd him down at once, rippyng through the castel lyk a ragyng fyr-ball. In the confusion which followd, flyyng high on hemp, Blister fought his way frenziedly to the hall, armd with a white-hot coulter – leavyng the broad steps litterd with arms and leggrs and trunks and eyras and torn gouns – and once here, he flung himself wildly upon the wide-augad count, who was just preparyng to deliver his well-oild speech, impalyng him on a lance.

Meanwhil, his companions fought theyr way intrepidly towards the dungeons, which were sunk depe beneath the fortress, wher they were able to liberate the close-kept prisoners from theyr chegns.

Yet Pox – buttyng in here – insisted that the only prisoners which Blisters machinations had liberated, and this he swor on his mothirs ashes (sche had perishd by fyr, but thats anothir story), were the flusterd fowl which he had spilt from theyr cages in the cook-room. And alle that he impald, he scoffd, was the heafod of a pig, skewerd on a spit.

Theyr own companions from the village, indeed, who were helpyng out in the counts cook-room at the tyme – et was they who had first encounterd the deranged Blister, tiltyng the sacks of gregn which stood in the barn, and who had subsequently tried to sober him up in the cook-room, mistakenly plyyng him with red wyne – et was these very men who had done theyr best to restregn Blister, and who had raisd the alarm, sendyng a messenger in alle haste to the village askyng for the doctr and Pox to come at once. Yet in the ensuyng struggle pots and pans crashd to the groun, dishes pild high with sweetmeats fell from tables, upended casks of wyne spilt theyr contents ofer the floors, and the flayd peacocks roastyng in the ovens started to burn. And by the tyme the count appeard, attracted by the din, and by the tyme Pox arrivd, with the doctr puffyng at his heels, the smoke had alle but engulfd the cook-room, so that et was difficult to make thyngs out at alle cleerly to begin with, and et was only som minutes latr, when the cooks and the hangers-on had managed to extinguish the fyr, that the full scale of the damage became apparent.

Et had been an embarrassyng moment.

Yet Pox, bakd up by the doctr who stood noddyng sagely at his shouldr, was soon able to persuade the count that his brothirs capers were no thyng but the mad antics of a man drivn to the edge by starvation, and that at the sight of the sumptuous dainties to be laid befor the weddyng guests, he had simply lost his wits altogethir.

Yet Blister – now buttyng in furiously himself – sayd that this was a pack of lies. How coud Pox forget the cynical way in which the count had tried to bottle the men up in the dungeons then smoke them out with fyr? And how coud he forget the fiers fightyng which had followd as they draggd the wretched prisoners from the smoke-filld corridors, only to be met with the wall of iron presented to them by the counts men-at-arms? In fact, he sayd, I stil haue the scars to prove et – at which poignt Blister began to *unwind* his breeches, No, sayd Pox firmly, et was oure *companions* who bustld *Blister* alang dimly lit corridors, as he ranted and ravd alang the way, usheryng him gently through the geats lyk an invalid then, with a final heave, into, Claptrap! sayd Blister, a cart, sayd Pox.

And there they sat, as efer, at loggerheafods.

Subsequently, they abandond the village, takyng

themselves off into the forrested wilderness of the Weald, wher they lay down to let the sickness run ets cours. By spring they had sufficiently regegnd theyr strength to take to the road, though they made theyr way furtively, with the help of sticks, for they had lang since lost theyr augas to the pestilence. As they felt theyr way about in the dark, oon dag they bumpd into Bare-toe. Then they made contact with Eyra, banded togethir, heafodyng for the coast.

That niht, when I returnd – just ofer a week ago, now – I was greeted by the abbess with an explosion of signum and gesture. Bishop Odo was expected any dag, as was William, and in rapid finger-talk the abbess explegnd that we must act with extreme caution in theyr presence. My absences, sche made cleer, had been widely noted, and there was mych gossip concernyng my behaviour. Many of the nuns suspected that I har-bourd a secret lover in the village; othirs thought that I had turnd to sorcery and venturd out to perform unholy rites. Sche hopd that neither of these rumours were true, but sche needed a cleer and frank explanation from me at once if they were to be stoppd. Chastened, I told her the whole story, from the beginnyng. When, at length, I had finishd, sche was satisfied. What I had done, sche pronounced, was both foolish and irregular, but sche coud pardon et since et had stemmd from gen-erous impulses. Sche added that et was just as wele I had spokn so frankly, for if these poor men were to be savd we must act in alle haste to get them away safely befor the bishop arrivd with his retinue. If the systirs had noticed my behaviour, et was only a mattr of tyme befor the Normans noted et too, and when they did I woud be followd and my friends, if discoverd, woud certainly be put to the sword. And then, I myself woud be punishd too, and the whole prayr-hus cast undr suspicion. There was no tyme to lose.

We woud need a cart and a drivr to take the men to the nearest port, from wher they coud escape to the continent. Sche had contacts, sche explegnd, who coud ensure the men a safe passage. Sche would see personally to alle the necessary arrangements, sche intimated. With luck, alle woud be arranged for two nihts hence. For my part, the best thyng I coud do was to kepe my heafod down, and on no account leave the grouns.

I need hardly say that the next forty-eight hours passd slowly. When at last the tyme arrivd, the abbess came to fetch me. Sche wishd me luck, then handed me the magic halter of which systir Anna has spokn. With a rapid gesture, and a penetratyng look, sche let me know that I must use et wisely.

My companions were glad to ear my voice once more at the bottm of the towr:

> Pox! Pox!
> Let down
> Your locks!

As I climbd up they coud hardly restregn themselves, wonderyng wher I had been alle the tyme, sayyng they had almost givn up hope of my comyng bak. I got them to sit down, then explegnd the situation to them as best I coud. They undrstood, sayd they woud follow my instructions. And so we left the towr, not without som physical difficulties, I can tell you – so that we coud alle climb down Pox had to cut off his pigtail in the ende and hang et from the window – yet with the help of the halter we swiftley made et unobservd to the cart, which was waityng as the abbess had promisd.

Eferythyng, from now on, passd in a greet rush. In only a few hours we woud part company, forefer. No doubt they regretted, as I did, the efenyngs we had spent in silence, barely exchangyng a word as they had chewd on the bones I had brought them. I talkd quikly, goyng through the plans once more, repeatyng alle that the abbess had told me. And then, hastily, I passd roun the scraps of foode I had grabbd from the cook-room –

sweetmeats, apples, pikld salmon, and a crown-shapd loaf fresh from the oven. Et was a bumpy ride, and as the cart lurchd from syde to syde, I couldnt help thinkyng of the wild story which Blister and Pox had so recently told. Then, as the men ate, silence fell on alle.

Yet as soon as they had finishd, knowyng that tyme was short, Baretoe spoke up. He woud be brief, he sayd, but if he did not tell his tale now he woud nefer tell et. And so, he began.

My story, he sayd, is straightforward enough, and in case you dont have tyme to ear me out, Ill tell ets ende first: I was blinded by the Normans for poachyng in the kings forrest.

I come from Middlesex way, wher as throughout the lan forrests were open to alle until the comyng of the Normans: and then, lyk the lion in Esopes fable, William the Bastard claimd alle as his sole right. Lyk many, I relied on the forrest for my livelihood: here I grazd my pigs on acorns, caught rabbits, gathird nuts. And when these rights were withdrawn, lyk eferyoon else, I sufferd dire hardship: my pigs grew thin and died, then I myself started to waste away. The whole village, indeed, had grown so skinny by the tyme we met to talk the mattr ofer that et was possible, for the first tyme in livyng memory, to fit us alle undr oon roof. The situation was cleer: unless we coud fynd an alternative source of foode, or som way of gettyng into the forrest undetected, we woud soon die. We coud try fishyng, oon man sayd, and we coud set traps for byrds with lime – yet othirs were quick to poignt out that both these methods were already beyng exploited to the full, that there were only so many byrds in the sky, only so many fiskr in the watter-track. In the ende, left with no othir option, we decided to risk poachyng, but in order to minimise the chances of beyng caught, we decided to hunt only at niht, by the light of the moon.

For som tyme, the strategy workd wele enough, and we managed to fynd the foode we needed to survive. And then, as oure skill in huntyng at niht grew, we discoverd too that when the moon was full the Normans, through superstition, woud always stay indoors. So, in tyme, et became oure custom ech month when the moon was full, to hunt in numbers, for on swich nihts the forrest was as brightly lit as et was by dag. On these nihts, too, many of the villagers, emboldend by theyr sense of security, woud turn their nebbs up at the usual quarry — foxes, badgers, rabbits, stoat — and heafod straight for the big game, the boar and the deer. Catchyng swich beasts without the help of hundrs was by no means easy, and et took carefully co-ordinated team-work, and the skilful manipulation of spere-shafts. Yet in tyme we alle grew skilld at the spoor-work and coud, on most full moons, be sure to come home with a hearty feast.

Et was not lang, of cours, befor we came to look forward to the full moon with high hopes, and soon we came to rely on this monthly hunt to stock oure larders. And then, oon niht — et had been bound to happn soonr or latr, but no bone-hus foresaw the inevitable — when the full moon was expected to come out, et faild to make an appearance. Et was hiddn, lyk the stars, by a thick and impenetrable layer of cloud. What was to be done? Hopes were high, the whole village, speres and sticks in five-finger, was eagr and ready for the hunt. And as som carried torches so as to be able to fynd theyr way about, et seemd to make sense to carry these same torches into the forrest, and to use theyr light to hunt by. Once within the forrest the trees were so densely packd that there woud be litell danger of detection.

And so, we enterd the forrest, torches in five-finger.

But here, at once, thyngs started to go wrong. The torches only lit the groun beneath oure five-toes and a few steps ech way, makyng the distance alle the blaker, so that we coud see very litell as we advanced in to the forrest. Then the torches made us visible to any prey we might haue stalkd so that the animals coud easily see wher to run. And to make thyngs worser, there was a stiff breeze blowyng from behind us, and as my five-toes warmd up with ech plod, the beasts got wind of them in no tyme. In short, et soon became cleer that we woud catch no thyng. And then, in a strange refersal of nature, hunters became the hunted. Oon of oure lea-dyng men stumbld by accident into a group of sleepyng boar, who snorted and charged in panic, goryng him in the groin and woundyng two of his companions. The men turnd and fled and quikly panic spread through the ranks. Alle ran in different directions hopyng to fynd the shortest route home. Many droppd theyr torches as they fled and soon the dry leaves of the forrest floor caught light, and fyr raged in alle directions.

The blaze must haue been visible for miles aroun, and as we emerged from the forrest, oon by oon, we were met by mounted Norman knights. Accusd, oon and alle, of poachyng, we were forced to pay the penalty for oure crime: either a fine or the loss of oure arms. Because I resisted arrest and struck out at the bastards knights – both physically and with my tongue – they put out my augas, as I haue told you, and I was beatn out of the village, sent into exile, on pegn of death.

As Baretoe reachd the ende of his story the cart sud-dnly groun to a halt. The drivr, in a gruff voice, told them to get down and led them to a smal inn. Here he left them – I believe in safe five-fingers – and at once he turnd bak the way we had come. We did not efen say goodbye.

Efery niht now, I pray for them, and I hope that they haue found the peace that they sought in som foreign shore. Sometymes I pray out loud, in the hope that Eyra at least will ear me, and that he will be able to pass on my prayr, to Blister, to Baretoe, to Pox, wherefer they may be.

Chapter VIII

A short chapter, contegnyng six pages of paper

A S THE HERBARESS finishd her dizzy tale beneath the now star-studded tent of the heavens we were at once ofercome with a feelyng of shame, and many bowd theyr heafods to avoid Hildas pene-tratyng gaze. Between us we had accusd her of alle manner of unspeakable crimes, from lechery to the black arts – yet it was clair from what sche had related that sche was innocent, the crimes no thing but foolish fancy. Ethelreda the Reed spoke for alle when sche beggd Hildas forgiveness. Yet it was clair from Hildas broad smile, as it was from her words that sche held no thing agegnst us and as sche spoke, oon by oon, bowd heafods poppd up lyk startld rabbits from the burrow when the coast es clair. I am sure, sche sayd, I woud haue made the same accusations myself, in your shoes – what I fynd strange is that I was found out – for I can assure you I was very careful when I left the precinct at unusual tymes! There was a pause. Who was et, sche then askd, who first raisd the alarm? Yet whether it was because of the late hour, or that the memory of these events was now fadyng, none of us coud remember who had first spotted her strange behaviour, whether it was Gunnrid the Grinder or Felicity, the infirmaress, or Anna, or Annas boy, Edward, at work in the cook-chambr?

The nuns beg forgiveness of Hilda

The next dag the sun shone brightly on a clair sky – a good portent, I thought, but I didnt dare to make any prognostications, once bitten twice shy es a sayyng as true todag as it ever was. Yet so it provd. At chapter systir Getas letters were returnd by the prioress – Aelfgyva, it seems, had risen from her lit to save the situation,

Return of the stolen letters

claimyng that Geta the Geatkeeper had alle alang had her express permission to receive and keep letters from her brothir, and if sche had not made this generally known, this was because it was a personal matter. Sche had efen, I eard later from a breathless Ebba, gone so far (*pant! pant!*) as to remind Croaker (*pant! pant!*) that Getas brothir was a veteran of Hastings, as if to suggest that it might be treacherous to punish the geatkeeper in this connection, so turnyng the tables on the prioress once and for alle. Then at midday the new consignment of wool arrivd from Shepperton on the baks of fourteen donkeys, each laden with yarn in a different colour. By this stage oure palette had been reduced to a mere handful of colours – there was still som black, and there was plenty of mustard, but the brighter threads had lang since been used up. Now, as regnfall after a prolangd period of drought will cause the flowers of the field to burst out in alle theyr multiple hues, so the tapestry, as we set to work on it with renewd vigour, burst forth in many diverse colours. From amidst the now dominatyng fawn and olive and mustard there emerged bold shocks of colour, reds and bright blues and diverse shades of yellow animatyng the bone-huses of hrosses and men, the padded linyngs of the lozenge shapd shields and the decorative motifs which emblazond theyr fronts. Elsewhere, in those places where the rough out lign of a knight or an arber, a bush, a beste, a buildyng or a langship had been left abandond, as the construction of a kirk or a castle keep might be brought to a halt by war or famine, now busy five-fingers set to work addyng lyf and colour to these shadowy out ligns, sometymes with a boldness and enthusiasm which we woud not haue dared show in the early stages of the work. And yet, not only are we now carried away by the variety of threads once more at oure disposal – though surely there are now more than ever before? – there es a feelyng of release after Odos visit, for certainly he had levelld no complegnt agegnst the skill of the workmanship, rather praisd us for oure efforts! And so, where once, slavishly followyng Turolds designs, we had stuck to black, olive-green and fawn for the lang-ships, now we dizzily broi-der them in bright greens and blues and yellows and reds; then the hrosses too we now enliven with fantasti-cal colours, light hoarfrost-blue, bright emerald-green, shimmeryng golden-yellow lyk the rays of the sun.

The tapestry progresses apace

Oure work was given a boost by dags of uninter-rupted sunshine announcyng that summer had at last arrivd in its full glory; and as the corn and barley grew to ripeness in the fields, we too came to see the fruits of oure labour ripen and blossom. For the first tyme, stan-dyng bak to admire oure work, we had the sensation that it was substantially complete, and if there was still a greet deal to be done – there were still unaccountable gaps between certain scenes, and stretches of the bor-ders which remegnd blank, not to mention the closyng scenes of the tapestry – nonetheless, we felt in oure bones for the first tyme, that the conclusion of the proj-ect was within oure grasp, that we were equal to it.

An unforeseen setbak

And yet, just as we are beginnyng to feel confident in oure ability to finish the work, Gunnrid the Grinder reports with a lang audlit that we haue not left enough space for oon of Turolds scenes to be completed, and so we must insert a new length of cloth – not a difficult business, but a delicate and tyme-consumyng oon, par-ticularly if the join es to remegn invisible, as it must. As we set to work once more, negotiatyng this tedious task with weary fingers, it es now the feelyng that we are embarkd on a journey that will nefer be finishd which floods bak, a journey doggd by upset, bad weather, pit-falls, false starts and insane detours. It es as if each step forward es alle ways to be followd by two bak, a scene completed by the command to unpick it, a job wele done complicated and compromisd by an unwelcome addition, such as the sprawlyng text which Odo has made us add to the picture, here crammd awkwardly into an already clutterd chambr, here blockyng out the sky with its clumsy assertions, statyng the obvious, falsifyyng the complexity of the broiderd scene, lyk a watchful and envious spider crushyng the lyf from its prey.

As the hot spell continued, the abbess spent less tyme confind in her quarters. Sche joind us daily in the refectory, and each dag too sche passd through the cloisters to see how oure work on the bishops hangyng was progressyng. Almost daily now, her physical form began to increase in size to the point that at tymes we felt sche must surely burst, so tightly was her skin stretchd across her frame. Sche had to support herself with a stick when sche walkd, and when sche sat down sche had to be helpd by systirs Emma and Edith, who followd her around constantly. Yet sche continued cheerful in her manner, facyng the daily metamorphosis that her bone-hus was goyng through with the calmness and dignity of a seint. As always, we turnd to Ethelguida the Mute with oure questions about the disease, How lang does the abbess haue to live? Is it alle ... err ... ofer for her? What are her chances? Will sche pull through? In rapid finger-talk and bold gesture systir Ethelguida made it known that sche was no expert, but that the abbesses case was certainly peculiar, for while sche showd many of the characteristic signums of cattle pestilence, principally a gross swellyng of the organs – here Ethelguida puffd out her cheeks and thrust out her chest – there was as yet no signum of the characteristic striation, which preceded the worms migration via the tongue. And yet, sche explegnd, sche had eard of similar cases duryng her lyf in the forest. At once, sche squatted obscenely on the ground as if to piss, then leapt suddenly bakwards, in horror, as if to suggest that sometymes the worms left via the bowels. And by the way she rubbd herself underneath and behind, we understood that this must certainly be pegnful, but by no means fatale in every case.

Sche pausd for an instant, movyng about on alle fours, as if sche had once more taken on the form of a beste, and from the way sche movd oon coud sense that sche had not told alle. Go on, I sayd. Sche hesitated an instant, then span round on the ground, comyng to rest cross-leggrd in front of us. Holdyng a single finger up before her audlit sche made it known that there was oon othir possibility sche had eard tell of, though sche had nefer witnessd a case herself. Here, lykwise, there was no striation, though there was, as in every case, greet swellyng. The swellyng in this particular case, sche indicated with a gesture, was concentrated round the stomach so that it might easily be mistaken for ofereatyng at first – but not for lang. As the worms continued to grow the walls of the stomach became unnaturally distended, until at length they split and at this point the worms erupted suddenly and violently from the hosts belly – here, Ethelguida crouchd down, pressyng her five-fingers firmly onto her puffd-out stomach, then leapt suddenly into the air, performyng a bakwards somersault and flingyng her bras out wide, before collapsyng on the ground in a heap. We were to understand from this, surely, that the victim, lyk those who gazd on the audlit of the Medusa, was left dead in every case. After a pause, sche went on, with rapid finger-talk. If the abbess was lucky, if Dieu were on her side, as surely He must be, there was still, perhaps, a chance that sche might survive. But we woud haue to wait and see, and in the meantyme redouble oure prayers on her behalf.

An efentide visit Late oon efenyng, the eve of the Nativity of St. Mary, when it was still bright, and we were workyng on the tapestry in the still air of the cloister, oure deliberations were cut short by an impromptu visit from the abbess. Normally sche woud retire to lit early, but such was the magnificence of the efenyng that sche had been persuaded to take the air, and, earyng us at work in the cloister, sche had directed her steps towards us to see how we were advancyng with the tapestry. For som minutes, sche hobbld up and down the frames in the fadyng light of dag, observyng oure work. On the ende frame

Gunnrid the Grinder was broideryng the mail shirt of a warrior in a stitch resemblyng the scales of a fiskr, or the tiles of a roof, while systir Anna broiderd the heafod of a hross, and Hilda the Herbaress the pegnd audlit of a Saxon warrior felld by a Norman hrossman. Meanwhile, on the middle frame, a litell to the left of the burnyng hus, I labour at a group of men workyng with picks and shovels, to erect a fortified stranghold, a scene which will play its part in the tale I am soon to tell at the request of oure abbess. Then elsewhere, squeezd precariously ofer scenes of fallyng men and hrosses, systir Aelfflaed the cellaress stitches the words HIC CECIDERUNT SIMUL ANGLI ET FRANCI IN PRELIO (here English and French at once succumbd to the fight). Yet, as sche watchd us at work, her attention was most taken by the skilful broidery of systir Beatrice the almonress who workd alone on fillyng in som gaps which still remegnd in the borders of the early scenes of the tapestry, where sche was busy stitchyng the forms of manifold bestes: stags, lions, foxes, wolves, bears. Intrigued by the work, the abbess askd with deft finger-talk what alle these animals represented. Was there a fable of Aesops, unknown to her, which lay behind them? Persuaded, thus, to explegn her designs, systir Beatrice smild amiably, twistyng on her seat, then put down her needle. And now, while the rest of us continue the bone-work, sche turns her audlit towards us and proceeds to unfold her tale.

The Ro[a]d to Rouen or
Systir Beatrices Tal[e]

You ask what are these creatures I haue stitchd in the
tapestry, crow[dyng] round the early scenes which
involve Harold, Guy de Pontieu and William [these
brightly colourd peacocks perchd above the heafod of
Harold as he negotiates with William at Rouen; these
leapyng deer beneath Harolds lang-ships and the gallopyng stallions of Guy; these roaryng li[ons] which
punctuate each scene; these chargyng bulls, proudly
struttyng rams and so on]. They are what they are and
what they seem to be – yet once they were men and into
men theyr shapes haue since been turnd bak. I haue this
tal[e] on the authority of my cousin, Walt Erinson, once
huscarl to King Harold, now a wanderer in exile across
the whale-ro[a]d.

The tal[e] begins where the tapestry [st]arts, early in
1064, with Harold and his huscarls settyng off at a gallop
for Bosham harbour with theyr haukrs and theyr hundrs.
Walt, who lost an ar[m] fightyng the Welsh King
Gruffydd, is the oon-ar[md] figure in the red cape followyng close behind Harold. Whi, you may wonder, woud
Earl Harold keep an oon-ar[md] man in his personal
guard? Wele, I haue eard it sayd that Walt was an efen
more fearless warrior after he lost his arm than bef[ore].
He wielded his double-heaf[ode]d axe in his right five-finger, scythyng it through the air so that it distinctly cut out
the [sh]ape of an hourglass in this, the most ethereal of
the four elements [a shape which, as it drifted earthwards,
announced to his adversaries that the hour of theyr death
was here]. And while his axe severd his enemies at the
[n]eck he woud use his stump [which had the girth of a
tree trunk and the solidity of a rock] lyk a mace, pummel-

lyng and bashyng and crushyng the heafods that his axe had spard, and – as they flew past, wide-augad with [s]hock and incredulity – some of those which had already been severd from theyr bone-huses [and this he did with such ferocity that efen these cried out in pegn]. In this man[ner] he woud work his way through the hardiest army lyk a forge-fresh blade th[rough] butter, or lyk fyr through a field of ripe [wh]eat in summer.

It is for this reason, I believe, that he was also known as Thresher.

We haue been told by Norman chronic[lers] that Harold was sent across the channel by Edward the Confessor in order to inform Will[iam] that he woud indeed succeed to the throne of Englan as Edward had once promisd [and our tapestry bears the burden of this dubious piece of propaganda]. The truth of the matter, however, is that Harold journeyd to Normandy of his own free will to secure the release of his nephew, Hakon, and of his brothir, Wulf[noth], who had lang since been given to King Edward as surety for peace by the Godwinsons, and had then been placed in Williams hands for safe keepyng.

And so, once he has [s]ayd his prayers for a safe passage ofer the herring-road at Bosham kirk, it is with a [sp]ring in his step and joy in his heart that Harold sets sail from the nearby [h]arbour, jubil[ant] at the thought of seeyng once more his belovd brothir and cousin. Haveyng eard tell of Williams legendary [g]reed, no expense is spard when it comes to loadyng the langships with presents: Harold [look, here he is, steppyng on board, bare-leggrd with a huntyng hundr tuckd under his arm] not only carries with him his m[ost] prizd haukr, Merlin, but loads the ships with thoroughbred wolf-hundrs [the haukr for Hakon, the wolf-hundrs for Wulfnoth] and with mych gold and silfr procurd from his mothirs treasury at Winchester. They set sail at dagbreak, on calm seas, helpd by a moderate southwesterly wind, which fills theyr sails, and fills theyr spirits with hop[e]. And yet – just as these events are illustrated in the tapestry – strang winds blow his [s]hips off course, and Harold arrives at Pontieu, unannounced, unexpected and ar[md]. As you know [w]ele, he is now arrested by Guy de Pontieu, imprisond in fetters at the inlan fortress of Beaurain, and held to ransom. It is Duke William, of c[ours]e, who agrees to pay the requird sum [a kings ransom, it is sayd] and eventually Guy sets Harold free, handyng him ofer to William at a prearranged meetyng place on the [b]orders of his kingdom, near the castle of Eu.

In the tapestry, this scene is immediately followd by anothir, which shows William an[d] Harold arrivyng at Williams palace in Rouen. William can be recognisd by his heafod [which is shaven at the bak after the Norman fashion] and, as you can see, he now carries the haukr which Harold has given him as a present. In front of him, arrivyng first at the palace, rides Harold. I haue depict[ed] him leanyng forward, raisd slightly in the stirrups of his stallion, his finger lifted to his lips as the geatkee[per] greets him, as if to say, Shhh! Be quiet! Mums the word! or, Dont ask quest[ions] stupid! His gesture might easily be missd by casual observers – indeed, it has evinced no comment from oure [ofer]seers – yet it remegns embroiderd here for al[l]e to see, a palpable signum of the absent story which William, on pegn of death, has forbidden him to tell. It is the story of the events which took place between Harold beyng handed ofer to William by Guy de Pontieu and Harold and Williams subsequent [ar]rival at Rouen, a story which I haue on the author[ity] of my cousin Walt, once huscarl to King Harold, now a wanderer in exile across the herring-track.

By the tyme Harold had been handed ofer to William [Guy de Pontieu, knowyng too wele Williams reputation for trickery, had insisted on haveyng alle the chests thoroughly checkd by his men] it was already late. It was clear there was no way Williams company were goyng to make it to his palace at Rouen that [d]ag. Nonetheless, William was keen to press on, so they set off at a gallop in a westerly direction, determind to ride through the niht if necessary. As darkness fell, however, they found themselves traversyng a thick [fo]rest; progress was slow and the company [w]eary, so William, seeyng a light which issued from a glade, bade his men make haste to[war]ds it and see if they coud there procure shelter for the niht. In the glade, they found a toweryng [for]tress built of smooth stone on open ground, and as they advanced towards its g[eat]way, they were frightend by a horde of wild animals a thousand strang, wolves and foxes, hrosses and donkeys, deer, rabbits and li[ons], rushyng to meet them. Yet they need not haue been afraid: the beasts did not attack the men, but rather fawnd on them and waggd they[r] tails, escortyng Willi[am] and his companions through the archd geatway, until they were met by servant-girls, who escorted them in turn into a magnifi[cent] hall.

The hall was illuminated by charcoal-burners and by a dome-shapd fyr which filld the air with its sweet-smellyng smoke. All around, servant girls bust[ld] about, arrangyng her[bs], separatyng into different baskets the bright colourd flowers and varie[gated] grases that lay scatterd on the floor, or dryyng in front of the fyr. At the far ende of the hall, sittyng on a delicately carvd throne, sat theyr mis[tress], Duessa, directyng them as they workd, a goldbroiderd [cl]oak wrappd round her, ofer her gleamyng rob[es]. Brusquely, as was his fashion, William introduced himself and explegnd his busin[ess]. Duessa, risyng from her throne, immediately extended her greetyng to him and his [fol]lowers, offeryng them alle [s]eats, high or low, and biddyng them make themselves comfor[table].

Meanwhile sche set about mixyng for her guests a con[coc]tion of cheese and of barley-meal, mixd with honey and strang Burgundian wine, and to these in[gred]ients sche added her[bs] which sche selected from amongst those in the hall. The men eagerly took from her hand the [c]ups sche gave them, and dregnd them greedily. Alle, that is, except Earl Harold, who was so exhausted and ou[t] of sorts after his ordeal, barely, indeed, able to stay awake, that as he raisd the vessel to his muthr [which now, lyk som dark and unwholesome cavern, stood permanently [o]pen in an ugly gapyng yawn] it slippd, and its contents spilt ofer his tunic and further staind his already soild ho[s]e.

Harold, as it turnd out, was the lucky oon, for no sooner had the men [swal]lowd theyr draught, than Duessa leapt from her throne [now wearyng on her heafod a hideous beast-mask] and makyng her way swiftly [a]cross the hall to where Will[iam] stood [warm-yng himself by the greet fyr] sche struck him lightly upon the brow. At once his bone-hus began to [sp]rout rough bristles and thick har, and when he tried to cry out no human voice came forth, but a greet roaryng sou[nd]. Then his bone-hus began to twist and stretch, contortyng into a new form, his rib-cage thrustyng out-wards [tearyng his roial garments] his heafod tiltyng for-wards, turnyng his audlit towards the earth. At last his muthr hard[end] into a velvety snout, his neck swellyng with brawny folds, and then his five-fingers [which but now had lifted the cup to his lips] grew [s]harp [c]laws and left prints, lyk five-toes, on the ground. Alarmd at the sight of theyr master thus trans[formd], Williams men threw theyr goblets to the floor and rushd across the [h]all to his aid. But efen as they advanced, swift Duessa leapt amongst them, touchyng them lightly, [n]ow on the shoulder, now on the [n]eck, now on the soft down that featherd the eyras lobe, and at once they too began to [ch]ange shape: oon grew sharp velvety eyras and a protuber[ant] snout; anothir felt his har harden into the shape of sturdy antlers while his limbs grew lang and thin, harden[yng] at theyr extremities into discs of solid bone; anothir sprouted a thick mane which extended down his bak, lang hary eyras, and felt his jaw-bone bulge [out]wards and his teeth too so that they protruded beyond his nebb. To the last man, Williams company were thus trans[formd] into brute beasts. Look, I haue illustrated the scene for alle to see, here, in the tapestrys [mar]gin, beneath Harolds langships as they cross the channel. Here on the left, crouchd in front of the vast fyr-place with his tail between his leggrs, is William transformd into a li[on]; here, arms outstretchd as sche works her magic, her features [hid]den by the monstrous beast-mask sche wears, is the figure of Duessa; and here, metamorphosed into the beasts of the field, are Williams men, now fox, rabbit, deer, donkey, hross and hun[dr].

Now Duessa calld her maidserv[ants] once more, and they immediately [d]rove the beasts into sties where she kept her [s]wine, and there they were forced to [s]hare with these beasts the mast and corn[el] which was [th]rown down in front of them [daily fare for pigs whose lodgyng is the earth]. Only oon man of alle the company stood untransformd in the hall, and this was Earl Harold [for, as I haue sayd, he alone had not consumd the contents of his cup]. Duessa [n]ow approachd him stealthily, touchyng him on the should[er], but Harold, fearyng her sorcery, turnd on her, drawyng his sharp-edged [s]word. Seeyng him thus, sche now shriekd out loud and, collapsyng in a [quiv]eryng pile at his fivetoes [then risyng swiftly on her knees beneath the lengthenyng shadow of his wapen] claspd him tightly in her arm[s] and, throwyng off her beast-mask to [re]veal once more her [wo]manhood, cried, Spare me, please, please spare me! Your men, I assure you, will come to no [h]arm. And the comforts of my [pa]lace, humble as they are, are at your disposal, noble sire. Yet tell me, who are you, and where are you from? Who are your parents? For it is str[ange] indeed that you drank this drug and were not bewitchd. Speak to me, I beg you, for nefer before has any man, once this liquid has passd his lips, resisted its charms. And yet, I can see clearly from your manly bearyng, that you haue an inn[er] strength and an iron will which is [p]roof agegnst my magic. Put away your sword, [s]ire, so that we may go together to my chamber and, embracyng there, put away too alle thought of enmity.

Tired and worn-out as he was [by any standards, it had been a lang dag] this was not the sort of offer Harold coud readily refuse, and so, puttyng away his outstretchd [wa]pen, he pickd up the beautiful lady in his arms, and carried her to her [ch]amber where they coud talk and exchange views at theyr leisur[e].

Alle this while, Duessas handmaids busied them-selves about the cas[tle]. Oon spread chairs with hand-some coverlets above and with cloths of white linen beneath. And in front of these chairs a second drew up a solid oak table on which sche laid silfr baskets for [b]read. A third pourd honey-sweet wine into richly dec-orated goblets and laid these out on the tab[l]e. Then a fourth brought watter and lit a fyr beneath a greet caul-dron. When the watter had warmd, Duessa invited Harold to step into a bath, and when he had done so, sche bathd his bone-hus with watter sche took from the caul[dron], massagyng his heafod and his shoulders and his bak with her five-fingers until sc[he] had removd the weariness from his limbs. Haveyng washd Harold, sche rubbd his bone-hus with sweet-smellyng almond oil, then dressd him in a clean [cl]oak and tunic. Then sche invited him to sit and eat.

While Harold had been lingeryng in the bat[h], the table had been laid with a sumptuo[us] feast of bread and ripe pungent cheeses, and fiskr of many kinds. Game, too, lay scatterd in abun[dance] ofer the tab[l]e, peacocks dressd with rings of parsley, and plump pigeons too, fresh from the woodlans, and wild fowl from the forest. There were fruit and vegetables in plenty too, ripe pump[kin]s, rampions, and young courgettes with theyr golden flowers intact, sweet-smellyng strawberries, woodlan berries, firm plums and hon[eyd] figs which opend at the touch, oo[zyng] theyr soft stickiness ofer the fingers end[es].

For Harold the feast was now made al[l]e the s[we]eter by the thought of William and his followers miraculously turnd into beasts, feedyng on acorns, and as the thought passd through his mind he sud[den]ly laughed out loud, thinkyng that certainly, if he lifed to [t]ell the tale, few woud credit theyr eyras, What makes you laugh so? askd Duessa, Whi, sayd Harold, I was thinkyng just [n]ow of my companions, turnd as fortune woud haue it into brute beasts, and then I was thinkyng too that if I were to tell the [t]ale to my f[ri]ends at home, I woud scarcely be beli[eve]d, and this made me laugh, for, wele, here we are! Oh, sa[y]d Duessa now, I was forgettyng. I see now how diffi[cult] it must be for you to sit here and enjoy food and drink before winnyng liberty for your friends and seeyng the men before your augas. Very wele, then, I will fetch them forth. And at this Du[ess]a rose briskly from her seat. Yet Harold now stood up too, and, stoppyng her in her tracks, askd her to wait, It is true, he sayd, that I woud not wish to leave this castle with my companions st[ill] in the form of beasts. Oon of theyr number, indeed, Duke Will[iam] of Normandy – perhaps you haue eard tell of him, for he is famd as a war[rior] and feard throughout man[y] kingdoms – I am greetly indebted to, for this same [d]ag he has paid the ransom which releasd me from the dungeons of his neigh[bour], Guy de Ponti[eu]. And yet, while I cannot prove anything, I suspect som intrigue in the busi[ness]. And for this reason, and othirs besides [these pepill, I shoud explegn, exceptyng my trusty huscarls who came with me ofer the seal-ro[a]d, are not my comrades at alle, rather my escort] it woud [pl]ease me if for the tym[e] bey[ng], let us say till mornyng, you left th[em] in theyr beastly forms.

And so, Duessa was persuaded once more to be seated, and once more Harold began to tuck into the lavish [fea]st which lay bef[o]re him. He workd his way keenly through the silfr swordfis[kr], then turnd with renewd appe[tit]e to the vegetables, the ramp[ion]s, and young courgettes with theyr golden flow[ers], then his attention turnd to the ripe pungent cheeses with theyr foreign names and, finally, to the fruit, and the honeyd figs, which opend at the [t]ouch, oozyng theyr stickiness ofer the fingers endes. At length, his appetite extinguishd [yet eager still for stimulation of his senses] he allowd himself to be led to Duessas bedchamber by her maid-servants, and here he sat upright in her bed, awaityng his mistresses [ar]rival, as sche performd her ablutions.

Meanwhile, in the sty where Duessa kept her pigs, Will[iam] [now transformd into a li[on] in outward shape, yet in mind unchanged] brooded ofer his predicament. Only hours ago, he had thought that he had things pretty much sewn up. [Har]old, who he knew to be a tricky customer, especially ofer the de[lic]ate mat[ter] of the succession, had been p[lace]d firmly in his deb[t] thanks to the intervention of Guy de Pontieu, and he had felt sure that the balance of power had shifted firm[ly] in his favour. Of course, he woud release Harolds kinsmen [Hakon and Wulfnoth] but Harold woud by this point be so myc[h] in his debt, that [w]hen he touchd upon the matter of the succession to the throne of Englan [and here he woud remind the earl of the promise lang ago extended him by King Edward] he woud be bound to extract an oath of loyalty from Harold. Yet now alle these plans had been thrown to the four win[ds], dashd upon the rocks, lost in the sands of tyme. Here he was in the bone-hus of a li[on], stuck in a pigsty, no thing to eat but acorns and beech[nuts] and corn[el], his [serv]ants and men transformd into brute beas[t]s. And, which only made [m]atters worse, they seemd to be enjoyyng it [such, at least, was the impression William had from the noises which now issued from the othir ende of the pigsty, grunts of pleasure and pegn, squeals and occasional howls, as foxes pleasurd hundrs, rabbits and peacocks collapsd into a blur of feathers and fur, and stags mounted donkeys]. The whole situation was humiliatyng beyond measure – not only duped and metamorphosed into lowly beasts, but now held under the sw[ay] of powerful aphrodisiacs. But the final humiliation [which William only realisd now as a frisky stallion made to approach him from behind] was the cruel [f]act that he had not, as he had at first [th]ought, been metamorp[hosed] into a lion [here, at least, there had been the consolyng thought that this was the king of the beasts] but, alas, into a lioness. He had been strippd of both humanity and man[hood] at once. William now cursd Harold out lou[d], but when he o[pen]d his muthr, no words came forth, only a monotonous grumblyng [r]oar. Yet inwardly, he vowd that if ever he regegnd his human form, and if ever he got out of this in[fern]al castle alive, he woud be avenged on the troublesome ear[l].

In the meantyme, Harold, lyk the enchanted be[as]ts, felt his bone-hus propelld to greet feats of cock[man]ship [not only by the powerful aphrodisiac effects of the sumptuous feast, the remegns of which now lay scatterd ofer the table top, but by the beauty of his mistress whose ingenuity in the art of love, moreofer, knew no bounds]. Already sche had initiated Harold into a whole series of diverse positions for makyng love in: the Dolphin, the Scor[pion], the Crab, the Hundr, the Rabbit, the Bear, the Phoenix [yes, he coud still feel the burnyng sensation round his groin, still smell the burnt reme[gn]s of his charrd pubic har] and now, follo[wyng] his mistresses instructions, he did his best to perform the Pike. Runnyng the stiff tip of his tongue ofer the tender flesh of the belly, ofer the steep slopes of the thigh, the hars protrudyng lyk marsh reeds, he approaches in ever diminishyng circles, lyk the pike encirc[lyng] its cornerd prey. He leaves the safety of the bank far behind, enteryng the cool watter, which now rises w[ele] above the knee, then, a giddy tremor runnyng down the tensd curvature of his spine, plunges his whole bone-hus into the watt[er], takyng his first breathless strokes, guidyng his torso to the spot where he must either sink or [t]read watter, feelyng far beneath him the bulgyng upsurge of a warm underground spring. Then, [ofer]come by the [de]sire to [p]lunge his heafod into the dark depths of the watter, he takes a deep breath, [f]lips [o]fer in a single unbroken movement, and disappears beneath the surface.

At dagbreak, the lovers rise early, cleansd and refreshd from their niht of love-makyng. They go for a ride in the [fo]rest, where Duessa [dis]mounts from tyme to tyme to gather herbs, the curative and magical properties of which sche [ex]pounds to Harold as they proceed. Monkshood, sche explegns [stoopyng to pluck a specimen from the earth] can be made into a powder and mixd with toasted cheese and used as a pois[o]n for killyng rats; sp[urge], sche says, has the pow[er] of purgyng the bell[y]; and whosoever drinks the juice of the mandrake root, sche adds with a smile, is consumd with an amorous passion for the first thing he claps augas on. When they get bak, followyng a light breakfast, Duessa suggests it is tyme to visit his twenty-toed companions, and Harold ass[ents] willyngly, thinkyng, yes, they ha[u]e sufferd enough. And so, at last, Duessa flings open the geats of the sty, and out run alle the men in theyr various sh[apes], lion, rabbit, fox, deer and peacock, which has two five-toes, not four, but makes up for this by haveyng ofer a thousand augas. Then they stood once more in the [h]all, facyng her docilely, and sche at once passd amongst them, anointyng them oon by oon with anothir [ch]arm. At once theyr limbs began to she[d] theyr fur, theyr bristles, and theyr feathers which Duessas potion had plan[ted] on them, and theyr [c]laws receded bak into theyr bones, while alle, once agen, sto[od] upright, becomyng men once more, yet alle lookd refreshd, younger than before, and taller and handsomer to the auga [alle that is except William, who lookd thin and pale].

They knew Harold at once, and o[on] after anothir they claspd him by the five-finger, thankyng him for theyr deliverance [alle that is, except William, who stard at Harold with bitter resentment]. Then alle at once a meltyng mood [f]ell upon the men and they sobbd out loud till the hall echoed with theyr cries.

Once agen the hall was filld with Duessas maidserv[ants] who now bestowd bread and cheese and [m]ilk upon the men to give them strength, and then the hrosses were fetchd, and, quickly, the company sped on its wa[y].

On the ro[a]d to Rouen the men were in high spirits. They laughd and jokd with each othir as they recalld the fantastical events of the previous niht [who had been turnd into what and so on] yet already, as they rode, the whole event receded rapidly in[t]o the world of tyme past, lyk a cloudy vision, an insubstantial [d]ream. Few coud [re]member the [e]vents in any greet detail, nor coud they describe with any precision the location of the c[as]tle, only the moment of theyr rel[ease] was firmly etchd in the memory of alle. Of the company, William alone faild to join in with the high-spirited banter. He [rod]e last of al[l]e in theyr tregn, leavyng it to Harold to lead them alang the broad track which led to his [pa]lace at Rouen. And yet, towards sunset, as they approachd the cite, he dug his [s]purs fiercely into the flanks of his stallion [drawyng blod] to join Harold [at the heafod]. And then, in a speech of som duration [which he had clearly been broodyng ofer throughout the length of the dag] he enjoind Harold [on pegn of death] nefer to speak of the events that had befallen them the previous niht. Harold [not wishyng to anger the already fumyng duke] agreed readily, though, he ad[ded], on condition that William surrender, unconditionally, his brothir and his cousin, Hakon and Wulf-[not]h. William, haveyng litell choice, [a]greed the terms of Harolds silence.

The next dag, at Williams palace [look, I haue illustrated the scene here, where Hakon can be recognisd by his shield and by the beard that he wears] the brothir and the cousin were duly five-fingerd ofer to the entrustme[nt] of Harold. Theyr rele[as]e was heralded by mych feastyng and drinkyng, which [after the Norman fashion] went on alle through the dag and l[ate] into the niht. William, though, did not join in the revelry. He retird early to bed, complegnyng of a sore heafod, stampyng and cur[syng] and, under his breath, vowyng revenge.

Chapter IX

In which the herbaress broiders a curious scene

A T CHAPTER ON THE NATIVITY OF ST MARY, Sep-
tembr the ninth, the dag after systir Beatrices
tale (a tale which, it struck me, bore more than a
passyng resemblance to Nasos Circe), Croaker informd
us solemnly that systir Aelfflaed, the cellaress, had been
found unconscious once more, this tyme on the floor of
the cellarium. Immediately, I imagind sche must haue
been drunk, but my thoughts this tyme were wide of the
mark, if thoughts, which leave no mark, can be sayd to
be wide. The place had been broken into duryng the
niht and large amounts of wine stolen. It appeard that
systir Aelfflaed had been hit ofer the heafod with a stick,
but the wound had not been fatale – though sche had
not yet come round, sche was sayd to be breathyng
steadily, and there was every chance of a quick recovery.
At once – they alle spoke at once so that at first vou had
no idea what they were sayyng –

Intruders in the cellar

Anna: **** anyoon **** apprehennded and caught?*
Hilda: **** coud **** done **** * thing?*
Ebba: *And ... err ... who **** *** stick?*
Gunnrid: *Who *** it? *******************
}

– several of the systirs askd who the culprit had been,
but Croaker coud only tell us that no bone-hus had been
caught. Had we seen anyoon strange in the precinct the
previous niht? None had seen anyoon remotely suspicious, it turnd out, yet systir Edith reported haveyng
been woken duryng the niht by a loud bangyng, though
at the tyme sche had thought no thing of it and had

gone straight bak to sleep. What you hearrrd, Croaker added with a frown, was most likely the door of the cellarrium beyng knockd in, for it was forrrced open with som blunt instrrrrument, perhaps a sword, perhaps an irron bar. And who, askd systir Anna, a single curlyng lock of flame-red har hangyng from her cowl lyk a question mark, might haue perpetrated such an evil and devillish deed? There is no tellyng, the prioress sayd, for the villains left no trrrrace – but it is possible, sche added, that systir Aelfflaed might be able to help here when she comes round. In the meantyme, we coud only speculate: perhaps som of the villagers had broken into the cellarium to steal wine; but, most lykly, it was the work of som passyng vagabonds with no respect for the laws of God. In any case, Croaker concluded, you must alle be obserrrvant ofer the comyng dags, in case such an incident occurrrrs agen. And, cerrtainly, if you ear any suspicious bangyngs in the niht… – here sche augad systir Edith – …they shoud be reporrted at once!

Meanwhile the cellarium door woud haue to be mended – a charge which Croaker, with a rare smile, put in the bony five-fingers of systir Edith, who bowd stiffly, and made her exit.

The cellar door es mended

Later, systir Edith manages to get hold of a carpenter to mend the cellarium door, and as we work the tapestry in the cloister, oure stitches are accompanied by the bangyng of hammers, chisels and nagls. Systir Anna broiders a lign of Norman archers, launchyng theyr wingd darts high into the air to clair the English shield-wall. Close by, Ethelguida the Mute broiders a group of isolated Saxon fyrdsmen, the oferlappyng lozenges of theyr shields held aloft, bracyng themselves to ward off anothir charge from the Norman cavalry who are almost upon them; while beneath the hooves of theyr heavy stallions, Gunnrid the Grinder, workyng in rapid stem stitch, out ligns the limp and lyfless bone-huses of fallen warriors and, in the tapestrys borders, the decorative figures of birds and bestes, who lykwise appear to topple bakwards, as if caught up in the fray. Workyng alone on the middle frame I busy myself with the fable of *The Lion and the Fox,* ofer the first Norman knights to disembark at Pevensey, prickyng my finger with the sharp needle of bone. Later the abbess joins us and, above the scene on the first frame which sche had broiderd before, first in stem stitch, then in laid and couchd work, sche stitches two pigeons – birds whose forms sche has copied from the decoration carvd in stone ofer the door to her chambr. And then, when sche has completed this, now workyng in olive-green and madder-red threads, sche works a series of broad horizontal bands, which resemble the smooth sides, the strakd sides, which es the proper term, of a lang-bot, and now, before sche has finishd this, sche adds an upright pole, the mast, in the centre. And yet, as her work proceeds, we soon see that sche es not broideryng a ship at alle, but a petyte buildyng with an upright tour cappd by a helmet-shapd roof, som minor castle, or parish kirk. And now we see that the horizontal bands of laid and couchd work are not the strakes of the watter-hross we had momentarily taken them for, rather they depict the sides of a grasy knoll on which the buildyng stands erect, and what we had taken for the mast of the ship es in reality the megn axis of the buildyng, givyng support to the roof and to two massive wooden doors, which flank it on either side lyk the wings of a bishops cope.

As the abbess puts the finishyng touches to these vast doors, addyng four cruciform peepholes, so systir Geta, in the geathus, espies King William approachyng at a gallop with a petyte escort of mounted knights, yet this tyme the geatkeeper knows there es no cause for alarm. It turns out he es already on his way bak from Wales, where the rebellion, a petyte matter involvyng local chieftains, has been swiftly crushd – no thanks to Odo who arrivd too late to be of any assistance! Already, though, there es news of anothir uprisyng in East Anglia (led once agen, or so it has been rumourd,

King William returns

201

by none othir than King Harold) where he es now makyng his way in alle haste with the full might of his army. At the mention of East Anglia, however, a shiver runs down my left side – I think at once of my mothir, of my fathir, and pray they will not be the victims of any vengeance which William might take on the pepill of those parts.

Later, when the king has refreshd himself and had a bite to eat, he spends som tyme in the parlour, talkyng to the systirs in the presence of the abbess, and then bluntly states his purpose on callyng in once more at oure prayer-hus, I am impressd with the systirs work on the hangyng, if it has a flaw it es that Odo, my proud kinsman, es given too central a role in the story of the conquest. Vou are not to blame in this. To come to the point, I wish vou to make two altar fronts, oon depictyng scenes from the lyf of oure lord Jesus Christ, the othir depictyng scenes from the lyf of the Virgin, to be hung at the monks and at the nuns prayer-huses in Caen, St. Etiennes and the Holy Trinity.

Finger-talk with the king We haue eard lang since of his reputation for bluntness and plegn speakyng, yet alle of us are taken aback by the forwardness of his demands. Nonetheless, the abbess now stands up and thanks him in rapid finger-talk which es immediately translated by Emma who stands at her side. Yes, we will certainly accept the offer – this es the gist of her meanyng – though the king es to understand that oure prime commitment, at the moment (here, drawyng her five-fingers down ofer each shoulder in the form of a rood, the abbess makes the signum for a bishop), es to Odos hangyng. Of course, says the king, he understands the situation. Then, almost as an afterthought, he adds hastily, speakyng of Bishop Odo, that the man es not to be trusted. His investigations into the Christchurch affair, he explegns, cast Odo in a very bad light indeed. The confession he obtegnd was almost certainly forced. There es no thing, he says on reflection, that Odo woud stop at to get his way.

Then, without a word more, he es off, quickly rejoinyng his men in the yard, as they mount theyr hrosses with fresh provisions for the journey ahead, and make theyr way at a trot to the open portico.

It has been an eventful dag, and the abbess es clairly feelyng the stregn – sche returns to her chambrs, systirs Edith and Emma helpyng her to support her weight. Meanwhile, we carry on with the daily chores of the prayer-hus. I snatch an hour hunchd ofer my desk in the scriptorium tryyng to bring the abbesses chronicle up to date, frettyng ofer style. When William speaks shoud I write it more or less as I woud for an Englishman? If so, what does this petyte infidelity say of the chronicle? How do you capture the colour of voices, of audlits, of threads, with the scratchy and brittle quill? And then I write it out, the guilty thought that has been growyng within me as the abbess has been sufferyng her agony, for I haue to tell someoon, and I know the chronicle can guard my secret: I think – I write it in the margins, with my left five-finger – I think I am in love with the abbess. There, it es out, and no-oon will ever know.

Later, we sit down at the tapestry to press on with the arduous work. There are still endless men and hrosses to broider on the scenes of batalle which now stretch from oon ende of the cloister to the othir, then there are the corpses, the dead and the dyyng who lie stretchd out on the mud beneath the hrosses heavy hooves. We spend many lang hours broideryng theyr dying forms in rough out lign stitch, the puncturd bone-huses, the severd heafods staryng out at the onlooker, lyf still in theyr fyry unbelievyng augas. And then, in the heat of the batalle, beneath the words CUM HAROLDO (with Harold), Hilda the Herbaress broiders a curious scene in diverse colourd threads, involvyng a Norman soldier and an isolated fyrdsman. The Norman leans forward slightly, his weight on the front five-toe, peeryng down into the fyrdsmans flowyng har, the thick strands of which he holds tightly in his five-fingers; the

Saxon, who es the shorter of the two by far, stands before him, bak hunchd, heafod bowd, bras outstretchd, as if to megntegn his balance on unefen ground. At first glance the Norman appears to be incongruously examinyng the mans heafod for lice – as systir Hilda had examind the heafods of Blister, Baretoe, Pox and Eyra – or efen to be braidyng the strands together after the fashion of the Celts. It es only later, after lang hours of toil workyng the bone-dart through the stiff linen, and once the fair-haird herbaress has agen stitchd the same fyrdsman, now heafodless, in the lower border, that we see that the Norman warrior in his proud batalle-tackle es no hardresser: pullyng the diminutive Saxon down by the locks he raises his sword aloft, ready to strike the exposd cou of the stranded and helpless fyrdsman, who stares hopelessly at the spot of terre onto which, moments later, his heafod will fall. Once sche has fin-ishd, systir Hilda puts down her bone-dart, and turnyng towards us, explegns that this es whi the Normans are always careful to shave theyr heafods before going into batalle – an intelligence sche owes to Eyra – lyk this, none can pull them down by the har.

Late in the dag, the abbess rises once more and joins us at work. Once agen, sche takes up her needle and thread, to add the finishyng touches to her scene. Sche adds a detail here and there – the stem-stitchd out lign of two bestes, a *fleur-de-lys*. And then – while on the mid-dle frame systir Gunnrid unstitches the naked couple from above the heafod of William (*grruuuunnddr-grruu-unnnddr!*), and at once begins to replace them with the rough out lign of som wingd beste – Aelfgyva surprises us alle by broideryng with rapid bak stitch the figure of a naked man in the lower border, leggrs spread to reveal

The abbess completes her scene

his coq and balls, an obscene mirror image of the figure of Odo as sche has depicted him in the tapestrys central band. What is the meanyng of this strange and unnusual scene? asks the widow Anna as soon as the abbess has finishd.

In response, Aelfgyva inquires with nimble finger-talk as to whether we haue now alle told oure tales – if sche es the last in lign, then, sche intimates, sche es willyng to tell us the tale behind her picture. Many, it es true, haue now told theyr stories, hidden in the tapestrys borders, but before a word es sayd in reply to the abbess, the augas of the othir systirs fix on me. Then systir Gunnrid speaks out boldly, We haue alle told oure stories except the bearded systir Aelthwyfe.

Fixing me with her auga – already I am conquerd – the abbess then signifies that sche will tell her tale with pleasure, on the next suitable occasion, if only (here sche takes my heafod and holds it between her two five-fingers) I will tell mine first. And so it es that I put down my needle in turn, and expound the tale of my misfortunes.

I Too Tell My Tale

Holy systirs, as vou know, I come from the hus of Aldred of the East Angles, a lang and upright lign which boasts both Ealdwulf the Wise, and his grandson Aelf-wold the Bold, and more recently Ulfcetel, famd for his bravery in batalle agegnst the Viking invaders, who until recent tymes plunderd and laid waste the coastal lans of this kingdom, from the low lyyng and treacherous fens to the marshes at Romney. Aldred, my fathir, was bold in batalle, deep-minded and strang-hearted. He provd his worth many tymes ofer, fightyng by Harolds side in Wales and at Stamford Bridge, where he slew number-less brave warriors in the batalle-throng, meetyng axe-blow with axe-blow, hackyng a path through the shield-wall. Yet in the heat of batalle, when Harolds men had already deliverd the decisive blow – namely that which struck Harold Hardrada in the cou, severyng his heafod, famd for its hard counsel, from his bone-hus – and the Norwegians, leaderless, began to flee the field in disar-ray, he was struck down by an axe-blow from behind, deliverd by an anonymous and ignominious five-finger. The blade cut through his hauberk, severyng the ten-dons of his upper bras, and black blod flowd ofer his chest, stegnyng his tunic.

The blow – thanks be to Dieu – was not fatale, but it left a deep wound which needed attention. And so, right after the batalle, helped by two of his loyal thanes, Aldred was carried to a petyte priory, which lay close by, deep in a thicket of oak and birch. Greeted by the pri-oress, a pale and douce lady – the oddity of whose reed-lyk slenderness was only matchd by her single cyclopean auga – he was at once led to the infirmary and given a lit. Here, ofer the subsequent weeks, while his companions took the lang road south to meet theyr fate at Hastings, he was slowly nursd bak to health with poultices made of moss, and a thick paste made from swines fat and yarrow, a herb first found by the warrior Achilles. He was a good patient, and responded quickly to the medicines, only grumblyng from tyme to tyme that beer was forbidden him.

By late autumn, when my fathir was fit to leave, he steppd out into a world which had changed utterly. As he made his way south, crossyng the Ouse at York, crossyng the Trent at Newark, he was surprisd by the scarcity of othir travellers on the roads. Sometymes, exhausted, he woud stop at a wayside tavern and here, ofer a jug of frothyng ale, he woud listen – wide-augad with shock and wonder – to the tragic stories of events in the south which were on every mans lips: how the Normans had landed with a fleet of five thousand watter-hrosses while Harold fought at Stamford Bridge; how William, by trickery, had won a greet batalle agegnst Harold usyng mounted knights; how the English were beyng slaughterd lyk lambs and thrown from theyr homes.

As he advanced on his way, pressyng ever south, he was met by a vast tide of travellers sweepyng in the opposite direction. Such were theyr numbers at tymes that he woud fynd his passage entirely blockd by theyr vehicles, and then he woud take the chance to rest by the roadside, as theyr funereal column trudged by. There were farm carts drawn by worn-out hrosses, pild high with chairs and blankets and othir belongyngs, on top of which perchd ashen-audlited childern callyng for theyr mothirs; there were old men, staryng out blankly into an unfamiliar world from the hollow sockets of theyr augas, hopelessly tryyng to negotiate a route forwards with theyr crutches, which only sank deeper and more firmly into the mud with each step; there were countless mourners, too, som so weighd down with grief that theyr heafods had sunk into theyr bone-huses at the cou, so that theyr augas were scarcely visible above theyr tunics; and then a whole family of nineteen individuals, four generations in alle, precariously ridyng on the bak of a single donkey, whose belly saggd so under its burden, that it scrapd the terre beneath its five-toes.

This column of human misery, sayd my fathir, some-tymes stretchd for miles, and whenever he had the chance to question oon of its members, the story he eard was the same: oon of burnyngs and lootyngs, rapes and summary executions, the destruction of crops and the seizure of livestock. If what these pepill sayd was true, William did not only intend to conquer oure islan, he wanted to haue its population on theyr knees.

And so, it was with fear in his stomach that Aldred, road-weary, at last came to his goal, the village of Alders-ford. What had become of his friends, his family, his home, his hundr? As he splashd through the muddy wat-ters of the ford on the northern edge of the village – how he lovd to play here as a child! – alle was strangely calm. He saw no signums of destruction: the stone kirk with its newly thatchd roof was still standyng, as was the bakehus, the granary and, so far as he coud see, the rows of cottages in which the villagers dwelt. His own hall stood apart from the village, on a slight incline, and it was only on roundyng the bend which led here, that he saw any clair signum of the invaders presence, yet what he did see coud hardly haue been more unwelcome.

Where the high-rafterd hall had once stood there was no thing now but a heap of ashes. Nearby, Nor-mans and villagers workd side by side with shovels and axes, erectyng a huge terre-mound at the very top of which work proceeded apace on a fortified castle, mych lyk the oon I haue depicted here – look – oferseen by William prior to the batalle at Hastings. It was clair at once that this imposyng new buildyng was not for Aldreds use, and it was not lang before his worst fears were confirmd: his lans had been confiscated and given by William to Gilles de Lion-sur-Mer, a Norman baron, in recognition of his services at Hastings. Aldred himself was presumd dead, for news of his fall at Stamford Bridge had found its way home and, followyng his extended absence, pepill had suspected the worst.

Imagine my surprise, then, when on lookyng up from my work I caught sight of my fathir standyng stock still in the road, staryng wide-augad before him. Thinkyng I must be haveyng oon of my visions, I rubbd my augas and lookd agen, but now felt more certain than ever that it was indeed he. He had aged, certainly, and his beard was now lang and grey, whereas it was his habit to wear it short; and then his clothes were grimy and dishevelld, yet beneath these outward changes his profile and bearyng were unmistakable. I ran to him, claspyng him in joy, wept tender tears on his shoulder, Is it truly you, fathir? I cried, Speak! Tell me you are no ghost come bak to torment us from beyond the grave! Yet efen as I spoke, I coud feel his warmth, and knew that this was no spirit I claspd in my bras. At length he too spoke, no more able to believe his augas than was I, Is it you? he sayd airily, Oh, my daughter! Tell me – for my mind does not yet credit what its augas plegnly see – tell me I am not dreamyng! No, fathir, you are not, I sayd, and yes, yes, yes – it is I, Aelthwyfe, your only daughter.

We sat down knutr-leggrd on the cold stone slabs which led ofer the stream at the edge of the village, and here we exchanged oure stories: he spoke of the batalle agegnst Harold Hardrada and Tostig, of his injury, of the strange oon-augad prioress; I told him of the latest word from London, of the arrival of Gilles de Lion-sur-Mer, and the destruction of the old hall, and I pointed to the clay and wattle cottage in which mothir and I now lifed. As soon as I mentiond mothirs name – I saw at once that he had been afraid to ask – he was eager to haue news of her. I told him that alle was wele, but warnd him not to come home at once – mothir was in mournyng, and if the object of this mournyng were suddenly to poke his nebb round the door, unannounced, the shock might be too greet for her.

Tyme passd. We settld down comfortably in oure cottage, adaptyng to oure new lyfstyle with the strength of spirit which es often born of trouble. Everyoon in the village, of course, soon recognisd Aldred – and they were glad to haue him once more in theyr midst – but no-oon breathd a word about his true identity. To be on the safe side, he adopted a pseudonym, Byrhtnoth, a name, he sayd, which had once belongd to a Saxon chieftain cut down by the Vikings, and he amusd himself in the efenyngs, sittyng by the fyr-side, inventyng a false history, down to the minutest details.

He was a shepherd, from Coverdale, come to live with his widowd cousin in tymes of trouble. Put to the test, he coud furnish you with the ups and downs of his family history, a detaild description of the topography of his region, the number of his sheep, and the names of his nine sheep hundrs: Barker, a noisy bitch; moody Storm; Stalker, Tracker and Blackfoot; Runner, unsurpassd for speed; White Tooth and Gnasher, a couple of hundrs born of an Irish mothir and a Scottish fathir; and Rusty, an eccentric and moody hundr, but best lovd of the lot.

This paisful lyf of fyr-side chatter continued for many months without upset. Then, oon dag, alle that changed. My fathir was out in the woods, as he often was, grazyng oure pig Doris on the acorns to be found there and gatheryng fyr-tinder. On this occasion, however, Doris was startld by som beste in the undergrowth, and charged off on her litell trotters, squealyng and snortyng, into the depths of the wood. My fathir, shoulderyng his fyr-tinder, gave chase, but it was som tyme before he caught up with her, and when he finally did –

Doris was busy rootyng out truffles in a clairyng – it was lang past midday, so he at once securd her with a rope and turnd round to make his way homewards. And yet, no sooner had he turnd to go, than he eard the barkyng of hundrs, and then, before he had a chance to think, they were upon him, smarlyng and rowlyng and tearyng at his clothes.

When the huntyng party arrived, hot in pursuit – eight Norman knights in the company of Gilles de Lion-sur-Mer – my fathir was at first relievd, for they at once calld off the hundrs; but as he pickd up his sticks and turnd to go, oon of the knights manoeuvrd his hross, so as to block my fathirs path. Things now happend quickly, it was the baron who spoke first, Who are vou? Where are vou from? My name is Byrthnoth, sayd my fathir, I live in a village nearby, Aldersford, perhaps you haue eard tell of it? And what are vou doyng in the forest? Collectyng fyr-tinder, my fathir answerd. The baron let out a low laugh, And where, he askd, do vou suppose vou are collectyng fyr-tinder? In Aldersford wood, was my fathirs blunt reply, for this es indeed the name that the wood has alle ways gone by. Not any langer, though. The wood, it appeard, or this part of it at least, was now a forest, belongyng to the baron, and it was reservd for his exclusive use, and for that of the king, for the huntyng of deer. Two of the knights, at this point, got down from theyr hrosses and seizd my fathir by the bras, while Gilles went on to explegn that the penalty for poachyng was a fine of forty hides or, if my fathir coud not afford to pay, the loss of his right bras. My fathir began to explegn that he had been chasyng his runaway pig, but they were haveyng none of it, and besides, Doris had vanishd.

So my fathir began to plead: he coud ill afford forty hides, he sayd, and while he was willyng to give up his right bras, without it he woud be unable to work and woud surely die. And then, he sayd, what woud become of his wyf, his daughter? It was at the precise moment

he mentiond a daughter – myself – that the baron soft-
end. He askd my age, my skills, my temperament, the
colour of my har. My fathir painted a brief picture. Very
wele, sayd the baron, Bring your daughter to the castle at
Aldersford tomorrow – if what vou say es true I will see
what I can do. He at once wheeld round on his greet
hross, then clatterd off into the forest, followd by his
knights.

We arrivd at the castle geats early. Snow lay on the
ground. It was cold. At once we were admitted to the
greet hall by silent servants. Here we were askd to wait,
then after som tyme the baron swept in wearyng a flashy
purple mantle. It was the first tyme I had seen him up
close and without his armour (usually he shot by on a
hross surrounded by his knights, carryyng his banner – a
lion in the centre and four fiskr in the corners), and I
now saw that he was a very old man, with thinnyng grey
har and a straggly beard, which fell off his audlit into
two curlyng points. He seated himself on a high-bakd
chair, lyk a throne, the leggrs of which were skilfully
carvd to resemble the five-toes of a lion, and on either
side the bak curvd round, lyk the prow of a lang-bot.
Here, it had agen been carvd with greet skill into the
shape of a lions heafod and mane at oon ende, and a
lions tail and rump at the othir.

So this, he sayd at length, es the daughter of Byrhtnoth. My fathir nodded. I grimaced. Sche will stay at my
castle as a handmaid, he pronounced, I will give her
food and lodgyng and supply her with the necessary
garments. Her duties will not be harsh, but sche es on
no account to leave the grounds, and this on pegn of
death. If, after a period of a year and a dag, sche has fulfilld her duties to my satisfaction, and if sche so wishes
it, sche will be free to go. Good? My fathir considerd his
bras, weighyng up the bargain, but before he coud open
his muthr – in those dags my gift of morrow-seeyng
nefer misled me and I saw at once what his answer
woud be – I spoke up, I will come.

The audience concluded, Gilles disappeard as quickly as he had arrivd, and we were left alone in a cold and draughty hall. My fathir wept as we sayd oure goodbyes, askyng my forgiveness, but I assurd him that a year and a dag was not lang, that before he knew it I woud be bak in his bras.

That niht in my chambr I too wept bitter tears, for I knew that a year and a dag confind in a dark and gloomy fortress surrounded by strangers was no honeymoon: in a fleetyng vision I saw the dags stretch before me lyk a lang and featureless corridor without exit: and then who was to say that my tyme up the Beste woud keep his word?

The Beste...

Already I coud think of him in no othir way, for no human beyng woud haue acted in his selfish and imperious manner. And then there was som thing about his features – a soft down ofer the nebb, two petyte rounded augas – that made him resemble in more than name the lion which featurd on his coat-of-arms. As in the fable *The Lion and the Fox*, where, as the fox observes, many toe-prints lead to the lions den, but none are to be seen goyng in the opposite direction – a fable Ive stitchd above the Norman lang-ships as they lan at Pevensey – I felt certain that Id come to a place I shoud nefer leave. For as the moral of Aesops fable has it: it es difficult to escape from the hus of a powerful tyrant.

The next dag I woke early, after a restless niht, dressyng hurriedly. I paced nervously, up and down the chambr (lyk a caged animal) waityng to be calld to my duties; by mid-mornyng I hadnt eard a thing, so I sat down on the edge of the lit and waited. I must haue sat in this position for several hours, my mind – and, indeed, my bottom – made numb by the contradictory and warryng thoughts which raged in my heafod. Eventually there was a knock at the door, and before I had a chance to respond, a stoopd retegner enterd, carryyng a jug of watter and a piece of bread on a silfr tray, which he deposited on the floor. He then turnd towards me, and spoke, in a hollow raspyng voice, My lord will be pleasd if you join him at dinner, which will be servd at dusk. He stood there for som minutes, without movyng, before it dawnd on me that he was awaityng my reply, Very wele, I sayd, and with this he turnd and left.

There was anothir knock at dusk, and the same aged retainer appeard. He led me to a vast yet lyfless dinyng chambr, alang the length of which stretchd a lang oak table, surrounded by high-bakd chairs and set for a sumptuous feast. The chairs had been decorated with the ubiquitous lions heafods, while the walls were painted alle ofer with fiskr, both large and petyte. Despite a wele-stokd fyr, the chambr was both cold and damp. I waited som tyme before the beste himself turnd up, lang enough, indeed, for me to entertegn the welcome thought that he might not come at alle. In the ende, though, these thoughts provd idle, for alle of a sudden, a door in the far corner of the chambr – which till then I had not efen noticed – for it lay conceald by shadow, and by the wood smoke that the fyr nefer ceasd to give forth – burst open, and out of it steppd my gaoler.

He was still in his ridyng gear, sweat on his brow and blod on his tunic. A brief nod was alle he offerd by way of greetyng before he plumpd himself down at the heafod of the table. No sooner had he done so than the doors flew open and the chambr filld with servants and dishes. There was eel soup, hard crusty bread baked in the shape of a crown and pungent cheese; a boars heafod had been roasted on a spit (mayhap, who knows, the same boar whose blod decorated the Bestes tunic?); and then came blackbirds bakd in clay, and som kynd of mashd white vegetable, perhaps turnip. I had no appetite, though I tasted the eel soup – and it was not bad of its kynd, a litell salty, mayhap. The Beste, on the othir five-finger, ate voraciously, and he drank deep of the blod red wine. When he had eaten the lions share of the meal, and sat pickyng at som lumps of cheese, he at last addressd me in person, So, he sayd, vou haue come. As I was soon to learn, he nefer tired of statyng the obvious. It es wele that vou haue done so, he went on. And let me say now: vou will not fynd me a cruel master, nor, I think, will vou fynd reason to complegn of your duties. Vou are free to roam in the castle and grounds, free to try on the rich garments in your chambr, but remember this: vou must on no account leave the grounds, and each efenyng, at dusk, vou must come here and dine with me, understood? I nodded. There es oon last thing, he added, shufflyng uneasily in his seat, Every efenyng, before nightfall, I must ask the same question (he did not explegn whi): *Will vou consent to be my wyf?* If vou agree, the castle and alle that es in it will be yours, together with the freedom to travel where vou will. And your fathir will be richly rewarded.

There was a silence. Very wele, he sayd, vou may go. I stood up, turnd to leave. As I reachd the door, I stoppd in my tracks, Wele? he sayd, Do I haue your consent?

I shook my heafod, tears wellyng up in my augas, hurried out the door.

The next mornyng I agen woke early. The larks were singyng sweetly. The eel soup lay heavy on my stomach. I rifld through the clothes chest – a treasure trove of rich and elegant garments in gold and turquoise and white, many made from the finest of silks and embellishd here and there with delicate lace work. Yet I was quick to see the trap: once attired in raiment fit for a bride, his ridiculous question woud acquire a specious logic. I pulld out the plegnest garment I coud lay my five-fingers on, a woollen kirtle, and pulld it on ofer my linen shift. In the cook-chambr, the servants augad me with suspicion – they thought, no doubt, that I was his Jezebel – but they fed me with an ample breakfast, of bread and peas, for which I was grateful.

A trap had been laid to catch me in the clothes chest. Perhaps there woud be othir traps. And so, as I wanderd the castle, I trod warily. It was a bright and breezy dag, so I decided to venture out side. From my window I had caught sight of a litell enclosd garden to the rear of the castle, and I wanted to root this out. The task was by no means difficult, for the castle was quite petyte, as castles go – though in truth I had litell experience of castles – and I soon found my way there by means of a narrow side-passage which led off the dinyng chambr, though as I discoverd later, I coud more easily haue found my way there via the cook-chambr, for it was here that the herbs and othir vegetables for cookyng were cultivated. In the centre of the garden stood a round pond in which swam fiskr of many kynds, and radiatyng out-wards from this, laid out in neat strips, so that the whole resembld the sun at middag, was the herb garden. Besides this the garden was filld with apple arbers and, at its far ende, a chapel. As I venturd in side I was struck by the brightly painted effigy of the Virgin, in blue and white and gold, and as I turnd to go, I coud swear it winkd at me, not once but twice. The garden was pretty, unusually still and warm for the tyme of year, and this I attributed to the walls. As I made my way out I noted the statues by the geat – two lions rampant.

That niht, when dusk came, the same retainer appeard at my door and led me to the dinyng chambr. Agen, I had to wait som tyme before the Beste appeard, but on this occasion I did not delude myself – sooner or later, I felt certain, he woud be there. Indeed, I sensd anothir of his traps, for it es sayd, often with truth, that absence makes the heart grow fonder: this, then, was his game. Huh! If he thought to gegn my affections in this manner, he was a fool, for he had forgotten oon thing: absence only makes the heart grow fonder when there es fondness in the first place. Nonetheless, I was careful not to let myself grow impatient of his comyng, for impatience, in its own way, es a signum of frustrated desire – efen if my wish, in this case, was to haue the audience ofer and done with – and I did not want desire in any shape or form to enter into my relations with the

Beste. For efen when negative, it es a dangerous thing, and can quickly turn into its opposite.

My mind was occupied with these strange thoughts, when at last the Beste arrivd. Agen, he was in his ridyng gear, sweat on his brow, and his tunic wore the same blodstegn as before. And so, he sayd at length, vou are the daughter of a shepherd from the north, no doubt this es whi vou feel at home in wool, a strange pedigree, I woud imagine, for oon dwellyng in these parts. I sensd danger. Tell me a litell of this lyf, he sayd, as he tuckd into his food. If I was ever grateful for my fathirs fyrside chatter about his apocryphal history in the north, it was now. As my fathir had done in oure efenyngs at home, I furnishd the Beste with the ups and downs of oure family history, a detaild description of the topography of the region — not very different, I now realisd, from the place we indeed inhabited, but fortunately this was lost on the Beste, as it had been on me — the number of oure sheep, and the names of my fathirs nine sheep hundrs.

When at last I reachd the ende of my story, far from certain what its effects might be — for now it seemd riddld with holes and implausibilities, which I had not noticed before — I lookd up anxiously to meet the Bestes gaze: he was asleep, slumpd on the table, his outstretchd five-finger restyng on a spilt beaker of red wine. Quiet as a mouse I rose from my seat, made my way to the door. As I opend it, the door creakd ... I held my breath, Vou must not leave, sayd the Beste, before I haue put my question, Very wele, I sayd, Will vou, he sayd, consent.... There was no more, I addressd the four walls, I DO NOT.

Each dag, things went on in this fashion. I spent the tyme exploryng the castle, usually endyng up in the enclosd garden, where I woud sit by the pond, sometymes for hours on ende, gazyng into its shallow depths. Then come efenyng I woud dine with the Beste. We woud talk – sometymes more, sometymes less – and after alle this, before I departed, there woud alle ways be the same inane question: woud I consent to be his wyf?

Only twice in alle the dags I spent there was I allowd to leave the grounds. Once, this was to accompany the Beste on a staghunt; once, as I shall tell, it was to visit my fathir. In brief, my dags were lang and tedious, and I coud not wait to see them pass. Each niht, I woud cut a notch in the frame of my lit to signify anothir dag had gone by – and this, if the truth be told, was the moment of the dag I most lookd forward to. As dags ran into weeks and weeks into months, I felt the Bestes patience stretch lyk the string of a bow, and I felt too that it was only a matter of tyme before he refusd to take no for an answer. Lyk the Aesopic lion, the Beste was used to gettyng his way.

As if in confirmation of my thoughts, oon niht I was woken from a deep sleep by the stink of red wine and the Bestes coarse five-fingers on my bone-hus. I shriekd for alle I was worth, lyk a startld polecat. He retreated as far as the window, but only now to assault me with entreaties: his love, he sayd, was lyk a rock, immovable and firm. It was lyk a fountain, a jewel, a rose, a garden, a serpent, a storm-tossd watter-hross, a sword, a burnyng forest. Desperately, he fumbld with clichés, as a thief might fumble with a set of stolen keys, hopyng to fynd the oon that woud unlock my heart. He woud haue lykend his love to the belly of an ass had he thought for an instant that the comparison might please me. And then, hopyng to win me anothir way, he told me how my fathir prosperd: he had recently acquird a new flock of sheep.

I saw my opportunity: thankd him. Profusely. I efen

praisd him. Then I askd if I coud verify this – his ... *beneficence* – with my own augas, Very wele, he sayd.

The next dag I left early to see my fathir for I had to be bak in the castle by dusk. I found him in good health, as the Beste had sayd, my mothir too, and of that I was heartily glad. I told him how I spent my dags in the castle, that the baron treated me fairly, that I dind with him each efenyng, that, in a word, alle was wele, efen if it was not. He remarkd that I lookd wele, efen if my manners had changed, for since livyng with the beste I had taken to saying "es" where once I had sayd "is", "vou" where once I had sayd "you", "arber" where I had sayd "tree", "Dieu" where I had sayd "God". He showd me the sheep which the baron had given him, and I told of the tales of oure lyf in the north which I had narrated to the beste. He laughd at this, as did I – it was the first tyme I had laughd in months – but I did not tell this to my fathir.

The dag passd pleasantly, and alle too quickly the tyme came round for me to say my goodbyes. I kissd my mothir and my fathir, who shed tears as I wavd a last farewele.

That niht the Beste kept me up for a lang tyme, and he renewd his love-talk. I ignord him as best I coud, but when I climbd into lit around midnight, exhausted as I was, sleep evaded me. As the dags, the weeks, the months had passd by I had reasond to myself that now I was on the home straight – just four months and a dag to endure in the Bestes castle. Yet alle of a sudden, it had become clair that the Beste was not goyng to give up. It was clair, then, that unless I were to resign myself to the five-fingers of the Beste, I woud haue to act, and act swiftly, so as to reverse my misfortunes. And then, in a lucid vision, I saw that the lang and featureless corridor which had become my daily lyf was not, as I had first imagind it, a corridor without exit: at its furthest ende there was the faint glow of a candle, which stood before an open door. Yet lyyng across the doorway, was the sleepyng bone-hus of the Beste. There was, then, a way out, but if I were to cross the threshold I woud haue to shift the Beste from his post. This, surely, was the meanyng of my vision: I coud only get out by somehow puttyng the Beste off my scent. Yet I had no clair idea as to which course of action I shoud take, for I coud neither fight nor flee.

Later that niht, almost as an afterthought, before I slept, I sayd a prayer to the Virgin Mary, askyng her for help.

On the next dag I rose early and made my way to the petyte chapel which lay in the walld garden, and here, agen, I prayd to the blessd Virgin.

From then on, I woud perform the same ritual each dag: a mornyng prayer in the chapel; an efenyng prayer at my litside. Othirwise, the dags continued to pass mych as before, except that now, each niht, the Beste renewd his love-talk with increasyng fervour. I responded in the only way I knew how, redoublyng my prayers, which were now my only hope of rescue. I prayd I know not how many tymes, makyng no specific requests, just prayyng for help, that by som miracle Oure Lady woud put an ende to this ordeal oon way or anothir, efen if it meant I were to lose my lyf.

Things went on in this way, until at last, as I wobbld on the tightrope of despair, the miracle occurrd: I awoke oon mornyng to discover a single har, thick, dark and ugly, protrudyng from my chin.

My joy was rivalld only by the Bestes alarm, and as each dag passd and as the hars grew into a thick bush of a beard, the Bestes initial alarm turnd to disgust. Soon, when he askd his question of me after dinner, his augas burnd not with the flame of desire, but with the caustic fyr of hatred. Anxiety, too, was written alle ofer his bone-hus, anxiety that, out of sheer perversity — for what was this witch not capable of? — I might answer his question with a yes.

Now, of course, the Beste coud not wait to be shot of me. The dags began to drag for him too, and for a while I took pleasure in givyng him a taste of his own medicine. Yet he was no fool — he quickly saw that oure litell drama had playd itself out, and that he had lost.

There was no reason to prolang the agony.

He let me go oon mornyng in summer, without warnyng.

I went straight to my fathir.

At first he did not recognise me. Then, when he did, and when I told him alle that had befallen me since oure last meetyng, he did not know whether to laugh or cry.

I blessd him.

My mothir too.

Exhausted, I stayd under theyr roof for several weeks until I had regegnd my strength sufficiently to travel.

Then I sayd my goodbyes — for we alle agreed I coud no langer stay in the village. I travelld first to London — a large and smelly place I was glad to see the bak of — then west towards the cite of Winchester where I had a dowager aunt who was the mistress of novices at oure systir hus of St. Marys. I stayd here for som tyme, though the arrangement was only ever temporary — the prioress did not approve of family joinyng the community. And then, at length, first followyng the windyng course of the Itchen through flat watter meadows, I made my way to this prayer-hus.

It was vou, Geta, who first opend the geat to me, and who showd me the ways of oure hus. I haue come to bless the dag I came here, and for this, as for alle else, I give thanks to the Blessd Virgin.

Chapter X

Where, contrary to the establishd custom of
this chronicle, the abbess tells her tale

THE NEXT DAG, followyng my own tale, systir Aelfflaed es still out cold. Sche lies in the infirmary, where systir Felicity tends to her needs as best sche can, applyyng poultices of chamomile and bleedyng her with leeches fetchd from the prayer-hus stewpond; yet although sche es still breathyng sche looks off colour and cannot be got to eat. The abbess fears the worst, and sits at her litside for lang hours while, in the kirk of St. Ethelfledas, followyng oure daily chants of plegnsongr, Ethelreda the Reed kneels to intone a prayer askyng the Holy Virgin that the cellaress might recover and we alle follow suit.

> *Mothir pity her for sche es weak:*
> *Heal her for her bones are vexd.*
> *Return, O Mary, set her soul free;*
> *O save her, for thy mercies sake!*
>
> *For those that are dead*
> *Of thee shall no remembrance haue;*
> *And who es sche that will to thee*
> *Give praises lyyng in the grave?*

Yet the cellaress shows no signum of recoveryng. As the dags pass, turnyng into weeks, her condition steadily worsens. Sche shivers constantly, sche vomits green bile. Lyk the Cumaean Sibyl, her audlit and bone-hus, once ruddy and sturdy as an oak, grow pale and thin and twisted, and the har on her heafod, once thick and glossy, loses its colour and falls off in lyfless tufts, lyk old lichen, onto the floor. Sche continues to breathe, the knackerd bellows of her lungs noisily drawyng the air down her whistlyng wind-pipe, yet it es increasyngly clair from innumerable petyte signums that sche has litell tyme to live. Then, oon dag, the bellows stop. When sche es lifted from her lit to be prepard for burial, her bone-hus, to mych wonder and astonishment, es found to be light and crisp, lyk parchment, and weighs litell more than a sack of feathers.

> Alas, poor AELFFLAED!

The funeral takes place on October the sixth, the anniversary of the Normans lanyng at Pevensey; sche es buried in the nuns cemetery, by the watter-track, under the poplars. To mark the occasion systir Beatrice distrib-utes alms to the poorfolk of the district – red herrings, bread and sweet wine – a custom which, subject to avail-ability, we will continue in the years that follow. In my minds auga, I see it clairly, alle of a sudden, in a mor-row-see the lucidity of which I haue not had for years. Sche will be sanctified – her shrine will be visited by the sick and the lame and the infirm, and alle this within months of her burial, and the multitude will speak of miraculous cures, of augasight restord, of rotten limbs made whole – then many years later, the dag will become St. Aelfflaeds dag, an occasion which will be celebrated throughout the lan and ofer the trout-road and throughout Christendom and on which pilgrims in theyr hundreds will descend on oure prayer-hus.

The burial of Aelfflaed

Yet todag, the occasion gives litell to celebrate – the mood es solemn and gloomy, the skies dark, as we file bak to the refectory for supper and then lit.

Systir Aelfflaeds funeral ofer with we are able once more to push on with the bishops hangyng. The work es increasyngly difficult – many of the nuns, from the lang and unaccustomd hours of work, haue blisters on theyr fingers where the bone-darts, with too mych use, haue ofer the months chafd at the tender flesh. And yet, we alle feel it in oure bones, and the evidence es there before oure very augas, that if we can only make oon last push, the task will at last be finishd. Already, indeed, several five-fingers haue embarkd on the final scenes, depictyng Williams crownyng at Westminster. From the lower border, in rough out lign stitch, the stately walls of Westminster rise into the air, while beneath the vast vaulted ceilyng, Williams form too takes on rough shape, and then es given colour with laid and couchd work in greens and reds and brilliant yellows, until his figure sits before us in alle its majesty, the golden orb raisd aloft on his left five-finger, the bright three-pointed crown perchd on his heafod, the kingly sceptre balanced in his right five-finger, while on either flank a select crowd, includyng Archbishop Ealdred and Bishop Odo, raise theyr bras in jubilation beneath the inscription OMNES GAUDENT (everyoon rejoices).

Faults in the stitchyng The air es filld with excitement as the hangyng nears its completion, and yet, standyng bak to examine the work it es clair at once that while a certain consistency has been megntegnd in its parts, there are countless faults and irregularities which no amount of revisionary work can unpick. In a word, this does not – as we had foolishly dreamd – resemble the work of oon master craftsman, but a clash of diverse warryng styles and colours. While som scenes and figures are stitchd with a mastery which can only be applauded, othirs, particularly in the borders, look clumsy and lyfless. And these do not only include the efforts of systir Ebba – who, to be fair, has workd as hard as any, and whose skills haue come on in leaps and bounds as the work has proceeded – but also that of som of the most able broiderers, lyk Beatrice the almonress, whose five-fingers, wearied and callusd by constant work, grow numb and clumsy with

224

the dags advance, so that ligns of stem stitch become twisted and knotted, laid and couchd work bulky and awkward, the sure lign of bak stitch falteryng and uncertain, lyk a rudderless lang-ship on a storm-tossd sea. And alle too often, if vou look closely, the surface of the flax-cloth es pepperd alle ofer with stubborn litell knots, resemblyng tadpoles, theyr tails danglyng down, lyk commas on the clutterd page.

And then, som of the innovations carried out through necessity when the wool was runnyng out — abrupt changes of colour on the chegn-mail hauberk of a mounted knight, or on the glossy coat of a sturdy destrier as it charges into batalle — while they seemd justified in the heat of the moment, now look lyk awkward mistakes, waveryngs of intent, faild compromises. Elsewhere, the manly features of a Norman hrossman closely workd in swift ligns of bak stitch, clash awkwardly with the stem-stitchd rings which encircle the moon of his audlit, resemblyng more the girlish curls of a young bride than the chegn-mail heafod-gear of a knight-at-arms.

And the shinyng chegn-mail batalle-gear of warriors, nefer unconvincyng at a glance, reveals alarmyng discrepancies when lookd at close to. Here the mail es executed in a stem-stitchd honeycomb of tightly-woven rings; here it es composd of a criss-cross lattice resemblyng the squares of a chess board; elsewhere it es composd once more of rings, but arranged in neat rows, lyk coins in a countyng hus; while here it looks lyk the oferlappyng tiles on the roof of a kirk, or the scales of a vast and ungegnly sea-beste; then elsewhere still it has taken on the criss-cross form of the marks left by a griddle on oatcakes, or, combinyng this pattern with inserted stem-stitchd rings, in an ostentatious display of virtuosity (only Beatrice woud be capable of the audacious work, but sche has faild to pull it off here), it loses alle sense of its origins, no langer resemblyng in any way the fine-hammerd coats of mail worn by war-lords, but rather the carefully rolld scrolls of parchment on which are inscribd the words of the chronicle, stackd neatly in the dusty vaults of the book-hus.

It es late oon efenyng when Abbess Aelfgyva, after a lang absence, joins us once more in the cloister. Still sche supports her vast bulk on two sticks, movyng lyk a crab about the linen frames, admiryng the work which we haue carried out in her absence. For lang minutes sche stares at the figures we haue been at work on in the final frames, then proceedyng round the cloister in a clockwise direction, sche moves past the lengthy scenes of batalle and the images of lootyng and burnyng, past the sea crossyng of Williams fleet, past the now folded up scene depictyng the death of Edward the Confessor, past the point where Harold swears his oath on the relics which are no more than old bones from pigs and hundrs until, at last, sche reaches the scene sche herself has stitchd in the central band of the tapestry, where sche stops. Here sche stands for som minutes, broodyng ofer the pictures sche has stitchd, fully aware of the pact sche has enterd into: that now we haue alle told oure own stories, it es her turn to tell a tale. And so, at length, wheelyng round towards us on her sticks, sche begins her story.

Aelfgyvas tale   Now lodgyng the sticks in the hollows of her armpits, to both give herself support and to free her five-fingers for the performance, the abbess, with gestures and finger-talk which we haue alle become used to through lang practice, gives us once more her account of the story we had originally eard som months ago – first from the muthrs of systirs Edith and Emma, then in signum and gesture from the abbess herself – of how her lodgyngs at Canterbury had been set alight and how the fierce heat of the flames had scorchd her bone-hus and her audlit as sche struggld to escape from the furnace. In broad out lign, the account the abbess now gives es familiar to many of us, and yet the odd detail, here and there, has changed, as if, ofer tyme, the events of that terrible dag haue continued to unfold in her mind. Throwyng her heafod bak, openyng wide her muthr, and flingyng her bras high into the air, Aelfgyva now conveys to us how sche had cried out loud for help; and yet – here sche cups a five-finger to her eyra, a gesture which sche quickly follows with a sorrowful shakyng of the heafod – none had eard. Eventually – here, with a clatter, sche drops oon of her sticks onto the ground, almost losyng her balance as sche does so – sche had succumbd to the smoke and collapsd unconscious onto the floor. Only at the last possible moment had Odo burst into the chambr amidst the flames and the shouts and the turmoil and carried her off in his bras.

Such had been the shock of the fyr sche had not only lost her voice but had known litell of what went on in the subsequent dags. Alle sche coud say for sure was that sche had been quarterd in Odos private chambrs where, after som tym, with careful nursyng, sche had sufficiently regegnd her health to travel bak to oure prayer-hus – as we were wele aware. Sche then pauses, lookyng uncertain as to how to proceed. Systir Anna restores to her the fallen stick. And then, at length, Aelfgyva gestures towards two of the scenes sche has recently broiderd in the tapestrys margins, close to the oon depictyng her rescue.

The first of these, above Odos heafod and to the left, depicts the fable often calld *The Wolf turnd Doctor.* Here, a sow, which Aelfgyva has stitchd in a contorted attitude, as if to suggest som physical discomfort – at this point sche indicates it with her stick, pointyng out its enlarged belly and pegnd expression – es in a state of agitation, for it es about to give birth to its first litter. On earyng of her condition, it so happens that a passyng wolf

The fable of the wolf turnd doctor

approaches her and, smilyng benignly, though unable to hide its sharp teeth, offers to perform the function of midwyf. Yet the sow, knowyng the dishonesty of wolves, at once refuses the offer, sayyng, I will be quite myself agen if vou just move a litell further off.

The Birth   We alle laugh at the fable the abbess relates to us, yet it es fair to say we do not see at once its relevance to her own case. Yet before we can bombard her with oure questions – Es the wolf King William? And the sow Englan? – sche turns to the lower border of the tapestry, directyng oure attention to the naked figure sche has broiderd there. While it es clair to alle that the figure es an obscene mirroryng of Odo as sche has depicted him in the megn band of the tapestry, its purport es otherwise uncertain. And yet, as Aelfgyva now goes on to explegn, gesturyng vivaciously with her five-fingers and sticks, this scene too depicts a fable from Aesop, commonly known as *The Birth*. Nobody, sche begins, makyng the signum of the rood with her sticks, willyngly returns to the scene of theyr conquest – and with the mention of conquest I naturally think of William, of Harold, and imagine at once that it es of these figures sche wishes to speak. And yet, the fable sche goes on to expound, in rapid finger-talk, makes no reference to William or Harold at alle. A woe man, sche begins, after lang months, duryng which her bone-hus had continued to swell in size, approachd the hour when her labour was to begin, and sche fell on the floor, givyng out cries of terror and pegn. Her husband, sche goes on, pointyng with her stick to the figure sche has broiderd in the tapestry, commands her to get bak into lit at once, for this, he says, es the best place for her at such a moment. At which, continues the abbess, the woe man spreads her bras – here Aelfgyva suddenly abandons her sticks in a moment of identification, and spreads wide her own bras – replyyng: I woud scarcely hope that my agony shoud be put to an ende in the same place where it was originally conceivd!

Agen, the abbess pauses, shiftyng her weight from oon stick to anothir, regegnyng her breath. For a moment we think sche must haue come to the conclusion of her narration, and yet, after a few moments sche raises her augas towards us before tuckyng her sticks under her bras and, with a sweepyng gesture of her five-fingers, as if to draw a lign under what sche has just sayd, sche starts once more. And now, with a combination of mime and finger-talk, sche starts at once on a different tack which, as we will soon learn, will carry us rapidly to the very heart of her tale.

Alle of a sudden, with an agility which startles us, sche raises her two sticks high above her heafod, so that they hang ofer her lyk a huge inverted V, resemblyng the canopy of the abbesses own lit which, of course, es her way of transportyng us to the scene of her confinement after her return to the prayer-hus. In a burst of signum and gesture sche describes to us how sche sickend to begin with, goyng off her food, until the point – and here, to illustrate her narrative, the abbess simply holds oon of her sticks out before us – where sche became as thin as a rake. And, indeed, we still remember these dags clairly, and the worry which was causd by the abbesses wastyng illness. And now, as sche describes the diet sche was put on by the infirmaress to restore her to health – not only consistyng of the beef broth sche had consumd in the refectory, but of eggs, cheese, bread, honey and mych more besides – a diet which, if sche refusd to eat, the infirmaress woud force down the abbesses throat as vou might force gregn down the cou of a goose to be fattend for market, so now we remember too how the abbess had at first appeard to get betr, yet how subsequently sche had begun to show the first signums of the unnatural growth characteristic of cattle pestilence. At first sche had thought that Felicitys treatment was simply enactyng a vicious revenge, that what had started out as a cure had strangely turnd into a new poison. That, in othir words, it had seemd that after

The abbess concludes her tale

229

weeks and weeks on the infirmaresses special diet, her bone-hus had become accustomd to this vast intake, and sche had grown to haue an insatiable cravyng for the sweet and fattenyng foodstuffs which, a short while ago, the infirmaress had to force down her throat. The infirmaress had tried to put the diet into reverse – had proscribd fruit – but as the weeks passd and this had no effect, systir Felicity admitted defeat. It was at this point that out side help had been calld in. The doctor had examind her thoroughly, had suspected cattle pestilence, but on closer observation – he had subjected her to a humiliatyng routine, involvyng toads and leeches and suppositories distilld from the livers of rats – had concluded that the case was beyond him. Then, at last, carryyng out a routine inspection before he departed, he had told the abbess – immediately and without prior warnyng – that sche was with child. At this precise moment the abbess explegns, in a final flourish of signum and gesture – agen, sche tips bak her heafod, openyng wide her muthr, and throws her bras into the air – sche had been cured, at least, of her aphonia, from which sche had sufferd ever since the niht of the fyr – for sche had screamd out loudly in disbelief – and then, of course, we alle rememberd the scream which we had eard in the niht, and which subsequently, I at least, had put down to my imagination, No, you did not imagine the scream, the abbess now says, abruptly and mych to oure astonishment and wonder abandonyng her finger-talk, and addressyng us once more in the sweet human voice which we had alle lang ago given up hope of ever earyng agen. And yes – here sche bows her heafod as if in contrition – your abbess has been guilty of a double deception, not only in megntegnyng silence in company, but in lettyng the rumour that sche was sufferyng from cattle pestilence take root and spread. And yet, such was the shock of the doctors news that sche did indeed fynd herself unable to speak, efen if the mechanism which controlld her voice was once more in full workyng order, and so it seemd the natural course to use this silence as a shield. Then, auditted with the doctors staggeryng revelation – barely, indeed, believyng it to be true herself! – she was hardly in a position to blurt it out to the four winds. No – such a course woud only haue brought shame and ignominy on the hus – it seemd the lesser of two evils, in short, to let you continue in the belief that your abbess was the victim of cattle pestilence. Sche hopes you can forgive her! Immediately followyng the doctors pronouncement, a midwyf was calld in alle haste, an old crone from the village, who quickly confirmd the extraordinary diagnosis, and demanded a kings ransom for her silence, at which point the doctor packd up his bags and made to leave. In desperation, before he departed, your abbess demanded of him what the ways of nature were, and whether such a thing as an unwittyng conception were possible. With the exception of the Blessed Virgin, the doctor pronounced, it is rarely encounterd. At which point your dismayd abbess trembld more violently than ever. Sche felt as if sche might go into labour at any minute, and clung to the doctor in terror, beggyng him not to leave her! The doctor did his best to calm her down, assuryng her that the confinement was still a lang way off, and that a loose habit woud hide mych. Then, without a word more, he was off. The abbess was beside herself – the doctors consolyng words merely pierced her to the heart. How coud this be? And if it were true, who indeed was the fathir? How were these things possible? Had sche finally gone mad? Your abbess sufferd many dags and nihts of torment, prayyng in the kirk at niht and pacyng her chambrs. For a brief moment sche blasphemously entertaind the thought that sche, lyk the Blessed Virgin before her, had indeed undergone a divine conception – yet the truth, sche eventually reasond, had to be more banal. And then, after mych thought, though at first her mind recoild at the idea, for was not this man her noble rescuer, her gallant hero, her roial and holy defender, it struck her that the deed must haue been performd by Bishop Odo. Sche had no recollection of any such act, but it was true that sche had lodged in Odos private quarters for weeks on ende, mych of the tyme unconscious. Then, late oon efenyng, the fegnt yet distinct memory came to her of a niht when sche had woken in a sweat to fynd Odo at her bedside. Sche had called at once for a nurse, only to be told that the nurses had been dismissd for the niht. Then, with a smile, Odo held a draught to her lips. This will help you sleep, he sayd, brushyng her har with the tip of his twitchyng nebb, and the next sche knew it was mornyng! Subsequently – perhaps you remember the occasion, when Odo came with wool and when William and his troops filld the courtyard – sche confronted Odo in private, I confronted Bishop Odo in private, and he confessd the truth!

Aelfgyva has now finishd. It has taken lang hours, and now sche es clairly exhausted. And the revelations haue left us shockd too – the abbess es not about to die as we had alle thought, sche es about to give birth! The questions which we wish to ask – When es the child due? What will become of it? – will haue to wait. First, we haue to carry the abbess to her chambrs – sche es plegnly too exhausted to move under her own steam – and here we put her to lit for the niht before we too retire to oure lits in the dormitory.

Epilog

Contegnyng curious, but not unprecedented matter

THE ABBESSES STORY HAD GONE on late into the niht, and its content had been a shock to us alle. More than a shock – it had exploded oure world oferniht, if youll pardon the anachronism. When the systirs retird to the dormitory, though exhausted, oure minds were alle oferexcited. Certainly, I was not alone in beyng unable to sleep – many were the restless boneboxes that tossd and turnd on theyr lits that niht, and when the hour of matins came, the bell which summond us to oure niht-tyme prayers for once fell on deaf eyras. *The bell falls on deaf eyras*

The next mornyng in chapter, the eve of the festival of Pope Calixtus, Croaker scolded us alle – and sche handed out punishments as they were laid down in the Rule of the Hus, for as it es here stated: Every servant of God who es tardy when risyng for niht services es to be punishd in a manner fittyng the crime: if anyoon comes after the Glory be to the Fathir of Psalm ninety-four, sche shoud not be permitted to share the common table, but take her meals alone, separated from the company of alle. Her portion of wine shoud be taken away until there es satisfaction and amendment. But such was oure giddy feelyng after the events of the previous niht that we accepted the punishments with equanimity. And, indeed, God saw fit to break the Rule of the Hus on this occasion – for, later, when oure belovd abbess herself arose from her chambr, mych later, indeed, than any of the nuns, sche at once confronted and oferruld the prioress when sche eard how we had been disciplind, On this dag of alle dags, sche declard, the systirs will not be punishd! *Punishment at chapter*

When Croaker eard the abbess speak – for no-oon had as yet breathd a word of the previous nihts revelations – sche was herself dumbstruck. Sche tried to formulate a reply, but alle that issued from her muthr was a dry raspyng sound – Ikrrrk! Ikrrrk! – lyk that of a playd out puppet. And when the abbess, seizyng her advantage, proceeded to tell her that sche was expectyng a child, her heafod tippd suddenly bakwards, as if it had been struck by a mortal blow, her augaballs rolld in theyr sockets until alle that we coud see were the whites, and at this point sche collapsd onto the floor, dead to the world, from which undignified position sche was quickly leverd up by myself and systir Felicity, and carried off, not without som difficulty, to the infirmary.

The tapestry nears its completion In the dags that followd we workd in a buoyant mood, puttyng the finishyng touches to the tapestry down to the last detail. We filld in any conspicuous gaps remegnyng in the borders with improvisd figures, sometymes, lyk Ethelreda the Reed, borrowyng the form of a bird or a beste from the carvd capitals of the cloister. Ofer the scene of Williams coronation at Westminster, systir Ebba slowly, yet with a sureness and precision oon woud scarcely haue thought her capable of som months ago, stitchd the words HIC RESIDET WILLELM REX ANGLORUM (here sits William King of Englan); while to her left the widow Anna broiderd two Norman knights in theyr war-clobber who, panickyng as they mistake the cheers which emerge from the kirk for riotyng, set fyr to the surroundyng buildyngs with torches. Then systir Gunnrid, for once without grindyng her teeth, rather with a look of glee on her audlit, added to the figure of Odo at the kings side a nebb which, as in lyf, was lang and hookd and bulbous. And we added additional fables, too – *The Wolf in Sheeps Clothyng, The Envious Fox*. As we workd, on occasions we wonderd what tale Aelfflaed, the cellaress, might haue told if sche had lifed – was there a secret story sche had stitchd into the tapestry? We tried to recall which parts of the tapestry sche had workd on, which images sche had broiderd, but we were hard pressd to remember. There was no doubt that sche had spent mych tyme workyng on the sprawlyng text which Odo had supplied us with, but it was difficult to see any hidden story here. And yet, there was oon scene which systir Beatrice rememberd haveyng seen Aelfflaed stitch, near to Williams lang-ships on the second frame. As we examind the spot sche pointed to, it was at once clair whi Aelfflaed woud haue been keen to broider this particular scene, for it depicted two men pullyng a cart carryyng a huge barrel of wine to Williams watter-hrosses. The men, whose baks were bent under the stregn of the load, followd closely behind a young and upright youth with the bright augas of an adventurer, who carried a capacious hessian sack on his shoulders, a sack which had clairly caught the attention of the two men, who lookd on it curiously, scratchyng theyr chins, as if wonderyng what it contegnd. The sack itself bulged out strangely on either side of the youths shoulders, so that it resembld the Greek signum for INFINITY(∞), and from this oon coud guess that its contents were perhaps quite heavy. Yet what it contegnd – whether gregn or gold, poultry or som foul Gorgons heafod – was anyoons guess. Without the animatyng voice of systir Aelfflaed, any tale, if tale there was, had been lost, buried forever with her bonehus in the nuns cemetery.

When everything was completed to the satisfaction of alle, we set about stitchyng the different sections of the tapestry together, workyng from behind in rough HERRING-BONE STITCH ($<<<<<$), then, once the joins were complete, doyng oure best to cover them up with additional stitchyng on the front. Yet here agen we were met with a sharp reminder of the shortcomyngs of oure work: at the join of the very first length to the next the ligns markyng the upper border, lyk the two halves of a badly made bridge, faild to meet up. Then elsewhere, while the join was wele-made, it thrust into focus discrepancies on either side, particularly in the borders: the

The final stitches

235

diagonal bars dividyng these alang theyr length were here arranged lyk spears thrust into the terre, there lyk tents pitchd on high ground, while elsewhere, finishd with decorative work, they resembld no thing so mych as the stoles worn by bishops. Yet we didnt haue the strength to unpick and start agen. Finally, we did oure best to tease out the unwanted knutrs which had crept in with the points of oure needles, pullyng the tails through the bak, but many were stuck fast where we found them, lyk limpets, and woud not budge. When this was completed, oure work was done. We sent word to Odo that the tapestry was at last finishd near the beginnyng of Novembr, but we did not see him agen. When Odo eard that the hangyng was complete, he despatchd the dwarf Turold to collect it, and when he came he was full of praise for oure work, though he did not stay lang. He must haue felt unwelcome on account of his master, that es my conclusion.

Birth of the foundlyngs

As the months passd the abbess continued to grow in size, to the point that som thought sche must surely burst if this went on for mych langer. Towards the ende, sche rarely left her chambr, and when sche did sche was now so big that sche had to be carried about on a litter. Eventually, after a protracted labour, throughout which the abbess insisted on holdyng a lodestone in her right five-finger to ease the pegn and which took place on a birthyng chair constructed accordyng to her own speci-fications – for, lyk the woe man in the fable of Aesops which sche had broiderd in the borders of the tapestry, sche was loath to put an ende to her agony on the place where it had originally been conceivd – sche gave birth to quadruplets, three girls and a boy, on the first dag of Decembr 1081, though the boy was thin and weak and only survivd for a few dags. He was buried, uniquely, in the nuns cemetery, in a shaded spot beside the tomb of systir Aelfflaed. The three girls remegnd with us in the prayer-hus, Charlotte, Christine and Catherine, and they are thrivyng lively childern, full of the joy of lyf. To

236

ward off awkward questions, we say they are found-lyngs, left at the prayer-hus geat oon winter niht – but we alle know who they really are.

Som months after theyr birth we were honourd with anothir visit from King William, who reminded us of oure promise to make the broideries for his two prayer-huses in Caen. The abbess sayd sche was honourd, and that we had not forgotten about his erstwhile request, only that we woud be in need of more detaild instructions. At which point he produced his designs. They were beautiful of theyr kynd, and we vowd to get on with the work as soon as we coud. It will be a relief, sayd the abbess, to tackle once more a religious theme, as it will be to work on a smaller scale, after the lang and arduous labour on the bishops hangyng.

At the mention of Odos name the king frownd and began pacyng up and down the chambr. Then, once more takyng a seat and turnyng towards us a stern audlit, he announced that he had orderd the bishop to be arrested and imprisond on the Isle of Wight. He did not explegn himself further, but the rumours were that William was angry with his half-brothir on a number of counts: that he had been plottyng agegnst him, that he had been angerd by his oferweenyng pride, that he was a destroyer of convents and monks, that he had behavd badly ofer the whole Christchurch affair, that he was given to fleshly desires. We were nefer to fynd out if these fleshly desires, in Williams mind, included the rape of Aelfgyva, on this matter he did not utter a word, but it es fair to say that none of us shed a tear for Odo, now confind in som desolate dungeon with only the rats and the flies for company. Needless to say, my reputation as a morrow-seer, so recently in tatters, was once more restord – Odos regn was indeed clouded. But I showd humility in my triumph, I didnt gloat – and when I made morrow-seeyngs now I did so with caution, wait-yng until the tyme was ripe, and nefer on demand.

And here the story of the tapestry which es not a tap-

Odo disgraced

estry endes, as does my part as chronicler of this prayer-
hus – the abbess has agreed to take up the reins once
agen, for sche says that for alle my tryyng I haue not
masterd the art, sche says too, smilyng and kissyng me
on the cheek, that the chronicle es not the best place to
hide oons secrets, that a diary woud be betr suited to the
purpose. Besides, I haue litell tyme on my five-fingers,
for it es to my care that the abbess has entrusted Charlotte, Christine and Catherine, my litell charges. Som last
details, though, deserve a mention. In February 1082 systir Anna travelld to Winchester to meet Bishop Walkelin
on som business concernyng the reliquary – the bishop
had eard tell of the magic halter in oure possession and
had som questions to ask concernyng its authenticity –
and here, in the marketplace, sche bumpd into oon of
her lost brothirs, Leofwin. Sche recognisd him at once,
despite the passage of the years, and was oferjoyd to discover him alive and wele. He had been workyng in Winchester for som years, it turnd out, earnyng a good livyng
in a tanners yard close by the convent of St. Marys.
Then, in Mars, the district was agen flooded by torrential
regns which continued throughout the month. Once
more, as in 1081, the watter-tracks spilld theyr banks and
spread ofer the lan, and once agen the fiskr left theyr
natural habitat and swam, lyk birds, through the air. The
downpour was so intense that the watter rose to the top
of the perimeter wall and then spilld into the precinct
itself, so that throughout the month we walkd about
oure daily business and sayd oure prayers knee-deep in
watter, with the exception of Ethelreda the Reed, who
hoverd conspicuously just above the surface. And when
at last the regns stoppd and the flood subsided in early
April, we lookd out from the kirk tour on a different
prospect, no langer towards the hills which had hereto-
fore surrounded the prayer-hus, but ofer a flat plegn –
for not only had the regns eaten away at the very foundations, so that the whole precinct had, as it were, shifted
off its mooryngs and floated down the river valley in

which it lay, but the surroundyng hills, with oon exception to the west, had been levelld by the force of the watters. The hour of oure judgement is nigh, waild Gytha, presentyng her gloomy countenance to the heavens, for it has come to pass as the Lord saith: Every mountain and islan are movd out of theyr places. Sche quoted from the Revelation of John the Divine, and it es true that the prophets words wele describd oure plight – yet in truth none of us were greetly afraid. Ofer tyme we had grown accustomd to Gythas pronouncements and many of us took a less gloomy view of the situation – we were in for anothir wet year. Later, too, when we venturd forth and made oure way to the nuns cemetery, now som distance from the prayer-hus precinct, we found that mych of the topsoil had been swept away by the drownyng watters, and we found thus that systir Aelfflaed, buried the previous year, had risen to the surface of the ground and, that her bone-hus had not decayd, but stood uncorrupted before oure augas, sure proof of her sanctity (though – it pegns me to record – there were those who whisperd sche was pickld in drink). And then, not far from her grave, we discoverd the corpses of two men, youths, dressd for farmwork, the only two to haue died duryng the drownyngs. And it was not lang, of course, before the story spread that these two, laid to rest as they had been in the very spot where systir Aelfflaed was buried, were the very men who had hitherto broken into the cellarium and causd her untimely death. And yet these febrile rumours, while at first they spread lyk wildfyr, and then ofer the subsequent years solidified into the status of myth, were, in the ende – lyk the yarns we haue with pegn and labour stitchd into the margins of the tapestry, lyk the wayward flight of birds, which in Latin we call AVES since they do not follow STRAIGHT ROADS (vias), lyk pages of this oure litell chronicle – unjustified.

Amen.

REALITY STREET titles in print

Poetry series

Kelvin Corcoran: *Lyric Lyric* (1993)
Maggie O'Sullivan: *In the House of the Shaman* (1993)
Allen Fisher: *Dispossession and Cure* (1994)
Fanny Howe: *O'Clock* (1995)
Maggie O'Sullivan (ed.): *Out of Everywhere* (1996)
Cris Cheek/Sianed Jones: *Songs From Navigation* (1997)
Lisa Robertson: *Debbie: An Epic* (1997)
Maurice Scully: *Steps* (1997)
Denise Riley: *Selected Poems* (2000)
Lisa Robertson: *The Weather* (2001)
Robert Sheppard: *The Lores* (2003)
Lawrence Upton *Wire Sculptures* (2003)
Ken Edwards: *eight + six* (2003)
David Miller: *Spiritual Letters (I-II)* (2004)
Redell Olsen: *Secure Portable Space* (2004)
Peter Riley: *Excavations* (2004)
Allen Fisher: *Place* (2005)
Tony Baker: *In Transit* (2005)
Jeff Hilson: *stretchers* (2006)
Maurice Scully: *Sonata* (2006)
Maggie O'Sullivan: *Body of Work* (2006)
Sarah Riggs: *chain of minuscule decisions in the form of a feeling* (2007)
Carol Watts: *Wrack* (2007)
Jeff Hilson (ed.): *The Reality Street Book of Sonnets* (2008)
Peter Jaeger: *Rapid Eye Movement* (2009)
Wendy Mulford: *The Land Between* (2009)
Allan K Horwitz/Ken Edwards (ed.): *Botsotso* (2009)
Bill Griffiths: *Collected Earlier Poems* (2010)
Fanny Howe: *Emergence* (2010)
Jim Goar: *Seoul Bus Poems* (2010)
James Davies: *Plants* (2011)
Carol Watts: *Occasionals* (2011)
Paul Brown: *A Cabin in the Mountains* (2012)
Maggie O'Sullivan: *Waterfalls* (2012)

Narrative series

Ken Edwards: *Futures* (1998, reprinted 2010)
John Hall: *Apricot Pages* (2005)
David Miller: *The Dorothy and Benno Stories* (2005)
Douglas Oliver: *Whisper 'Louise'* (2005)
Ken Edwards: *Nostalgia for Unknown Cities* (2007)
Paul Griffiths: *let me tell you* (2008)
John Gilmore: *Head of a Man* (2011)
Richard Makin: *Dwelling* (2011)
Leopold Haas: *The Raft* (2011)
Johan de Wit: *Gero Nimo* (2011)
David Miller (ed.): *The Alchemist's Mind* (2012)
Sean Pemberton: *White* (2012)
Ken Edwards: *Down With Beauty* (2013)

For updates on titles in print, a listing of out-of-print titles, and to order Reality Street books, please go to www.realitystreet.co.uk. For any other enquiries, email info@realitystreet.co.uk or write to the address on the reverse of the title page.

REALITY STREET depends for its continuing existence on the Reality Street Supporters scheme. For details of how to become a Reality Street Supporter, or to be put on the mailing list for news of forthcoming publications, write to the address on the reverse of the title page, or email **info@realitystreet.co.uk**

Visit our website at: **www.realitystreet.co.uk/supporter-scheme.php**

Reality Street Supporters who have sponsored this book:

Andrew Brewerton
Peter Brown
Paul Buck
Clive Bush
John Cayley
Adrian Clarke
Dane Cobain
Mary Coghill
Kelvin Corcoran
Ian Davidson
David Dowker
Carrie Etter
Gareth Farmer
Allen Fisher/Spanner
Penny Florence
Sarah Gall
Paul Griffiths
Charles Hadfield
Catherine Hales
John Hall
Alan Halsey
Robert Hampson
Simon Howard
Fanny Howe
Peter Hughes
Elizabeth James
Keith Jebb

L Kiew
Peter Larkin
Sang-Yeon Lee/Jim Goar
Richard Leigh
Tony Lopez
Chris Lord
Richard Makin
Michael Mann
Lisa Mansell
Peter Manson
Ian Mcewen
Ian McMillan
Geraldine Monk
Pete & Lyn
Dennis Phillips
Tom Quale
Josh Robinson
Lou Rowan
Will Rowe
Jason Skeet
Valerie & Geoffrey Soar
Alan Teder
Paul Vangelisti
Juha Virtanen
Susan Wheeler
John Wilkinson
Anonymous: 4

P.5

All affiliated orgs cannot — (can?)

mohamed Jebari, should be Malawar

grant-making body - we have
expertise to filter, evaluate
& our imprimatur has value
a ___ we can positively inform
'culturally imperialist' ?? P.8

P.10 away from israel towards
palestinian state

P.11 corporate volunteering opps
roles based org structure

— Have a position?

Belief in issue more nuanced

Lightning Source UK Ltd.
Milton Keynes UK
UKOW04f131030 0913

218205UK00002B/9/P

9 781874 400622